"I'm sorry, Cord. Really sorry."

"For what?"

"For everything. I'm sorry about Tom and for being so weak after the pneumonia, and I'm sorry about your wife. I'm sorry you saw my apple trees in bloom on your way to California. I'm sorry you stopped."

He sucked in a breath and held it, eyeing the daisy things he'd laid on the quilt beside her. Then he exhaled in one long, slow stream. "Eleanor, I'm sorry about Tom, and about you being sick. But I'm not sorry about your apple trees, and I'm sure as hell not sorry I stopped at your farm."

Author Note

My mother was raised on a ranch in Oregon, and she always spoke fondly of the hired men who came to help out. She remembered them as kindly, usually unmarried, men who moved from ranch to ranch in the summertime. She recalled one hired man in particular, by the name of Frank, who came every summer; he shared his cookies with her after supper and made her corncob dolls to play with.

LYNNA BANNING

The Hired Man

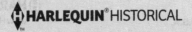

HARLEQUIN® HISTORICAL

ISBN-13: 978-0-373-29952-2

The Hired Man

Printed in U.S.A.

HARLEQUIN®
TM www.Harlequin.com

Lynna Banning combined a lifelong love of history and literature into a satisfying career as a writer. Born in Oregon, she graduated from Scripps College and embarked on a career as an editor and technical writer and later as a high school English teacher. She enjoys hearing from her readers. You may write to her directly at PO Box 324, Felton, CA 95018, USA, email her at carowoolston@att.net, or visit Lynna's website at lynnabanning.net.

Books by Lynna Banning

Harlequin Historical

Visit the Author Profile page
at Harlequin.com for more titles.

For hired men everywhere. And women.

Chapter One

Smoke River, Oregon

Cord dismounted and reached to open the iron gate, then shook his head in disbelief and patted his horse's neck. "Just take a look at that, Sally-girl. Only thing holding that gate up is rust." He laid his palm against the top and gave a little push. The decrepit gate swung partway open, hung there for a few seconds and toppled onto the ground.

He narrowed his eyes and studied it more closely. The split-rail fence looked like it was held together with spit, and there was no cattle guard. Man, this place needed more than a hired man. It needed a whole battalion of them.

A rickety-looking barn that had once been painted red stood off to one side of the dingy farmhouse, and the front yard was full of busily scratching chickens.

"Come on, Sally." He grasped the bridle and tugged his mare forward. The only thing that looked even half-alive was the apple orchard he'd seen when he rode in, the frothy white blossoms clinging to the branches like soft puffs of new snow. Even from here he could hear the buzzing of thousands of bees.

But that was the only sign of life. He tied the bay mare to a spindly lilac bush and stepped up onto the porch. His boot punched clear through the rotting middle step. The front door stood open, but he couldn't see through the dirty, spiderwebby screen. He rapped on the frame and watched flakes of rust sift onto his bare wrist.

"Just a moment," a voice called. A long minute passed, during which the only sound was the hum of bees and Sally's whicker. Finally a blurry shape appeared behind the screen.

"Yes?" The voice sounded suspicious.

"Name's Cordell Winterman, ma'am. I understand you're looking for a hired man?"

"Oh. Well, yes, I guess I am."

"You don't sound too sure about it." He dug the scrap of newsprint out of his shirt pocket. "You put this ad in the newspaper, didn't you? 'Wanted—hired man for farm and apple orchard.'" He pressed it up against the screen.

"Ah," she said after a pause. "Yes, I did advertise for a hired man. Are you interested?"

Cord swallowed hard. Hell, yes, he was interested! He hadn't eaten in three days, and he was out of money and out of sorts. "Sure, I'm interested, ma'am."

"Why?" she asked bluntly.

Cord blinked. "Why? Well, I could give you a lot of palaver about wanting to help out because I like farming, but that'd be just fancy words. The truth is I'm broke and I'm hungry."

"Oh," she said again. And then nothing more.

"Ma'am?" he prompted.

The door latch snapped and the screen swung open. "You'd better come in, Mr. Winterman."

The minute he stepped into the threadbare parlor an enticing smell hit him and his belly rumbled. Roast chicken, he guessed. Right about now it didn't matter; he'd eat roast anything. He hung his battered hat on the hook by the door and followed her to the kitchen, where he watched her shove a pan of biscuits into the oven, then turn to face him.

For a moment he forgot to breathe. A pair of wide gray eyes surveyed him from under dark brows. Soft-looking eyes, and tired. Her thick chestnut hair was caught at her nape in a scraggly-looking bun. A blue-checked apron cinched the waist of her faded green dress, and from under the hem peeked ten perfect bare toes.

But the most surprising thing wasn't those bare toes. It was her face, heart-shaped and chalk white. She'd be beautiful if she wasn't so pale. Jumping jenny, she was beautiful anyway. He couldn't take his eyes off those pale cheeks; you'd think out here on a farm in the middle of Oregon she'd at least be a bit sunburned. Or freckled. Instead, her skin looked smooth as cream.

She gestured at the round wooden table in the kitchen and pointed to a straight-backed chair, then walked to the staircase. "Daniel? Molly?"

Even her raised voice was soft somehow. Refined.

Feet thumped down the stairs and she turned back to the stove while he pulled out the chair she indicated as a shaggy-haired boy of about nine and a small blonde girl some years younger clattered into the kitchen.

"Have you washed up?" the woman asked.

"Aw, Ma," the boy whined, "do I hafta?"

She pointed to the sink, and both children groaned. "Quickly, now. We have a guest. This is Mr. Winterman."

They edged past him to pump water into the sink.

"Hullo," the boy said over his shoulder.

"H'lo," his sister echoed. "I betcha *you* haven't washed up."

Cord chuckled. "Well, no, I haven't." He rose and accepted the bar of yellow soap from Molly's small fingers and pumped water over his calloused hands.

"Set the table, children," their mother ordered. All of a sudden he realized he didn't know her name.

The boy, Daniel, slapped four blue china plates onto the

table, followed by Molly, who pushed forks and spoons into place. Then four blue gingham napkins appeared.

Cord settled into his chair and watched the children scramble into their seats, fold their hands and sit at attention while their mother brought a platter of fried chicken and a bowl of biscuits. Finally, she set a mason jar of apple blossoms in the center of the table.

Cord's stomach rumbled and Molly giggled. "You must be hungry, huh, mister?"

"Yeah, I sure am."

"Molly," her mother admonished. "That is not a polite question."

"I don't mind, Mrs....?"

"Malloy," she supplied. She perched on the edge of the empty chair and pushed the platter of chicken toward him. "Eleanor Malloy."

She didn't say another word until supper was over and Daniel and Molly had splashed through the dishwashing and racketed off upstairs. Then she set a china cup before him.

"Coffee?" she asked. He noticed that her hand was shaking.

"Thanks."

"And then we will discuss my newspaper advertisement."

They drank their coffee in complete silence, and after a while he wondered if he'd said something to offend her. He sure hoped not. He'd do almost anything for another chicken dinner. Or *any* dinner.

"Where are your people, Mr. Winterman?"

His people? "I'm da— Darned if I know, ma'am."

"But surely you have some family living? A mother? Father?"

"I don't think so, Mrs. Malloy. I was raised in the South." He cleared his throat. "When I went back after it was all over there was nothing left standing."

"So you came north?"

"Uh, yeah." He saw no need to explain everything that

had happened next. Or explain why he'd been in Kansas when the War broke out.

"I see," she said primly. "I need a hired man to help out here on the farm. I can offer meals and lodging in the barn, but I cannot offer any pay. Would that suit?"

"Yes, ma'am, it would. I can see that you need help around here. You need a new front gate for one thing, maybe a new barn roof, a new front fence, a new porch step, and..." He shot a look at the open front door. "A new screen door."

"I will also need help with the apples when they come on in the fall. I cannot... Well, I can no longer lift the heavy bushel baskets."

"Some reason?" She couldn't be expecting, could she? She looked slim as a birch rod. And, since there was no sign of a man around, he figured she was a widow.

"The doctor says I will regain my strength in time, but right now..." Her voice trailed off. She took a sip of her coffee and set the cup on its saucer with a sharp click. "I asked if the arrangement I offered would suit," she reminded him.

"Oh, sure it will, Miz Malloy. Thanks." He resisted an impulse to lean over the table and hug the heck out of her.

Eleanor studied her empty coffee cup, then flicked a glance at the man's face. He looked tanned and weather-beaten, but his eyes were kind. Very blue, she noted, but kind. He handled himself well. His body was lithe and muscular, and he had nice manners. She would not want Molly or Danny to pick up bad habits. Her instincts told her Mr. Winterman was trustworthy and well-behaved, and he was willing to work for just room and board. Until the apple harvest, that was all she could afford.

On the other hand, her instincts had been wrong before.

Mr. Winterman unfolded his tall frame from the chair and stood up, strode to the door and snagged his worn gray hat off the hook. As he went to push the screen open he caught sight of the revolver she kept above the door.

"This your gun?"

"It is, yes. I keep it for protection."

He sent her a look. "Can you fire a revolver?"

"Y-yes, if I have to."

"I mean cock it and fire it like you mean to hit something. On short notice?"

"Probably not," she admitted.

"Got any ammunition?"

"Yes, I think so. Somewhere."

He said nothing for a long moment. Then he turned to face her. "It's dangerous to keep a gun you can't fire in plain sight. Also dangerous for your boy. He might figure he wants to try it out one of these days."

"Oh, I don't think—"

"Trust me, ma'am. He's a boy, isn't he?"

She stared past him at the velvet-covered settee, then let her gaze drift to the lilac bush out the parlor front window. "I know my son, Mr. Winterman."

He snorted. "All mothers think that, Miz Malloy."

An overwhelming urge to weep swept over her and her chest tightened into a sharp ache. She did not like this man, she decided. He was too sure of himself. Too knowledgeable. She remembered his eyes when they looked into hers. Hungry.

But she needed a hired man.

Chapter Two

Cord unsaddled Sally, walked her into an empty stall in the barn and fed her a double handful of oats. Now, where should he bed down? He eyed the ladder up to the loft overhead and smiled. He liked straw, and he liked being up high; it gave him a hawk's-eye view of whatever was going on. Which wouldn't be much on a farm this run-down, he figured, but you never knew. Experience, most of it bad, had taught him that the unexpected could be damn dangerous.

He washed up at the pump in the yard. The cool water felt so good after days in the saddle he stripped off his shirt and did it again, then tossed his saddlebags and a single wool blanket up into the loft and let out a long breath. He'd always loved the smell of a barn—horses, leather, animal droppings, clean straw. This barn had two animals in roomy stalls, a sturdy gray gelding with a white star on its forehead and a milk cow contentedly chewing her cud and rolling a disinterested brown eye at him. A dusty saddle hung on one wall, and a broken-down buggy sat in one corner. It didn't look sturdy enough to get to town and back, and the cracked leather seat looked mighty uncomfortable.

He wondered how the woman, Mrs. Malloy, fetched supplies. The boy looked too young to ride into town alone, and she didn't look strong enough to make the trip. If she was a widow, as he figured, she must have had some kind of help. Then again, the place looked so run-down it was plain it hadn't been cared for in some time.

He crawled up into the loft, spread out the worn wool blanket he'd slept in ever since leaving Missouri and folded his arms under his head. This place would do until he could get his feet under him. At least he could eat regular meals and sleep with both eyes shut instead of with his Colt under his pillow and one finger on the trigger.

He wondered if he'd ever get back to feeling like a normal human being again, someone who didn't flinch at every loud noise and wonder where his next meal was coming from. Someone who could learn to trust his fellow man again. The War had shaken his faith in the human race, and his years in Missouri had taken care of the rest.

Stop thinking about it. He should count himself lucky; just about the time he was thinking about giving up, he'd come up over that hill and smelled those apple blossoms.

Breakfast the next morning made him smile. When he walked into the kitchen, little Molly was standing on a chair at the stove, poking an oversize fork into a pan full of sizzling bacon. Daniel was cracking fresh eggs into a china bowl. "Plop!" He chortled after the first one. "Plop!" he said again.

His mother laid slices of bread on the oven rack, moved the speckleware coffeepot off the heat and dumped in a cup of cold water to settle the grounds. The kitchen smelled so good it made Cord's mouth water.

She motioned him to a chair. "Coffee?"

"Please." He pushed his cup across the table toward her.

"There is no cream, I'm afraid. Bessie hasn't been milked yet."

"Black's fine."

She turned back to the stove. "Molly, lift those bacon slices onto the platter now. And no snitching!"

The girl clunked down a china platter of bacon in front of him. "No snitching," she whispered, then twirled back to the frying pan.

"Wouldn't dream of snitching," he murmured. That brought a giggle from Molly and a sharp look from Mrs. Malloy.

"Daniel, pour those eggs into Molly's pan and stir them around."

"Aw, Ma, let Molly stir them around. I'm gettin' too old for this cooking stuff. Besides, she's a girl."

"You are most certainly *not* too old for 'this cooking stuff.' In this household everyone does their share."

"Sure can't wait 'til I'm growed up," he muttered.

"Even 'growed-ups' help out!" his mother replied.

All through the meal Cord tried to catch Mrs. Malloy's eye, but she steadfastly refused to look at him. Daniel, on the other hand, gazed at him with intelligent blue eyes and peppered him with questions in between bites of scrambled eggs.

"What's your horse's name?"

"Sally."

"How old is she?"

"About three years. Got her when she was just a filly."

"Can I ride her?"

"No. She's too much horse for a boy your age."

"Do you like venison jerky?"

"Yes, I do."

"What about chocolate cake?"

"Well, sure, son, everybody likes chocolate cake. You gonna bake one?"

"Nah. But I keep hopin' my mama will bake one someday."

Mrs. Malloy said nothing at all. When the last slice of toast disappeared, Daniel and Molly scooped the dishes off the table into the dishpan in the sink, and Cord waited for orders from his employer.

Five minutes went by while Mrs. Malloy sipped her coffee. Finally he cleared his throat and she looked up. She looked paler than ever this morning.

"You want me to milk your cow, ma'am?"

"No."

"How 'bout I fix your front gate?"

"What?"

"Your gate. Yesterday I accidentally knocked it down."

"Oh. Yes, do repair it."

"And the fence? Wood looks half-rotten, and—"

"Of course."

"I'll need to get lumber from the sawmill in town. You have a wagon?"

She didn't answer.

"Then there's the barn roof and the corral and the front porch step and the rusted door screen and…" Hell, she wasn't even listening.

"Yes, fix it all, please. I have accounts with the merchants in town if you need…nails or…things."

"Kin I help him, Ma?" Daniel called from the sink.

Molly splashed soapy water at her brother. "An' me, too?"

"We'll see," said Mrs. Malloy quietly.

Cord picked up his hat from the hook near the back door. "Guess I'll be going on into town, then. You want anything from the mercantile, ma'am?"

"A newspaper. And some flour and a bag of coffee beans. Maybe one of chicken mash, too."

He studied her hands, cradling the china coffee cup. The knuckles were reddened. Daniel and Molly were making plenty of noise having a soapsuds-splashing contest, so he risked a question for her ears alone.

"Miz Malloy, how long have you been on your own out here?"

She glanced up at him, then quickly refocused on her coffee. "Seven years."

"Uh, is there a Mr. Malloy?"

Her shoulders stiffened under the faded green calico. "There is. Or rather there was."

"What happened to him? The War?"

"I assume so. He went off to fight and he never came home."

Cord's first thought blazed through his mind like a fire arrow. *What a damn fool.* "If it's not being too nosy, how have you managed all these years?"

Her laugh surprised him. "Believe it or not, until six months ago I had a hired man."

It was his turn to laugh. "Sure hope you didn't pay him much."

"No, I— Why do you ask?"

He stuffed back a snort. "I can't see that your hired man did a da— Darn thing around the place."

She set her cup down with a snick. "Most assuredly he did not," she said, not meeting his eyes. "But I trusted him around my children."

He stared at her. "Ma'am, you don't know me from Adam. How come you trust *me* around your children?"

She met his gaze with calm gray eyes. "I don't really know why, Mr. Winterman. I just do. Only once before have my instincts been wrong, and that had nothing to do with my children."

Eleanor rose and moved into the kitchen. "Children, stop that!" She rescued the suds-soaked dish towel, and when they rattled past her out the back door, she wrung it out and hung it on the rack by the stove. When she turned back, Mr. Winterman's chair was empty.

She bit her lip and watched her new hired man push carefully through the screen and walk out the front door with a slow, easy grace. She couldn't tell him everything. She just couldn't.

Chapter Three

The two kids tumbled down the porch steps after him. "Watch out for that loose board," he cautioned.

"What loose bo—?" Daniel's shoe snagged on the rotted step and just as he was about to take a tumble Cord scooped him up under one arm.

"That loose board." He set the scrawny form on the ground. "Watch where you put your feet."

Cord headed for the barn, Molly tagging at his heels. "Where ya' goin', mister?"

"Town."

"How come?"

"Need some coffee and flour and chicken mash for your mother and some lumber to repair the porch step." And the fence and the gate and the barn and…

"Kin I come?" Daniel asked.

"Maybe. If you tell me where your ma keeps your wagon and ask her permission." The boy danced off, leaped over the loose porch step and slammed the screen door.

Molly tugged his sleeve. "I'll tell you where the wagon is. It's out behind the barn. But I don't wanna go to town," she added.

"You don't? Why's that?"

"Cuz everybody there's bigger'n me and…and Mr. Ness yells at me."

"How come?"

The girl gazed up at him with huge blue eyes and he went down on one knee in front of her. "How come?" he repeated.

"Cuz I knocked over his candy jar once. But I didn't mean to, honest. It just fell over when I reached in to get my lemon drop."

Daniel came flying off the porch. "Ma says I can go!"

The wagon was behind the barn, all right. It should have been chucked onto the trash heap. Cord had never seen a more rickety pile of boards and rusted wheels. Probably wouldn't hold even a light load of lumber.

In the barn he led out the gray gelding and lifted a saddle off the wall peg. When he blew off the dust he groaned. The leather was so dry it practically creaked.

"Got any saddle soap, son?"

Daniel sent him a blank look. "What's that?"

"Stuff you rub on leather things like saddles to keep them soft."

"How come?"

"Because…" Oh, the hell with it. "Come on, son, let's go to town."

The trip into Smoke River was one Cord wouldn't soon forget. Daniel asked so many questions Cord's throat got dry answering them. And one of them brought him up short.

"You ever been in jail, mister?"

Cord hesitated. "Yeah. A long time ago."

"What for?"

"For…" He swallowed. "For being on the wrong side." For getting shot in the leg in the field and then captured because he couldn't run. It wasn't something a young boy needed to know.

And the rest of it, spending eight years in a Missouri prison, he didn't want *anyone* to know, especially Eleanor Malloy. He was trying like hell to put that behind him, to stop drifting and find some purpose in life, but it was rough. Everywhere he went people wanted to know things about him. That was one reason he decided to go to California, so he could start over.

He clenched his jaw. If he had his life to live over, he wouldn't even carry a gun.

Smoke River's main street looked like a hundred small towns in the West except that it was clean and the stores looked spruced up and well-painted. Ness's mercantile, between the barber shop and the feed store, stood out like a sore thumb with a shiny coat of pink paint. *Pink?* What next?

Inside, the proprietor lounged behind the counter, bent over a newspaper. Cord read the upside-down headline.

MONTANA GOLD RUSH!

Suddenly the man looked up and scowled at him. "Need some help, mister?"

Daniel disappeared down an aisle lined with men's hats on one side and boots on the other. "Yeah," Cord said. "I need coffee, flour, salt and a bag of chicken mash. And some lemon drops," he added quietly.

"You new in town? I'm the owner here. Name's Carl Ness."

"Cordell Winterman. I'm working for Mrs. Malloy a couple of miles out of town."

The man's shaggy eyebrows shot up. "*Eleanor* Malloy?"

"Something surprising about that?"

"Heck yes. Miss Eleanor, she, uh, she usually has her supplies delivered by one of the young men around town. Matter of fact, they have fistfights over who gets to do it. Leastways they did 'til Sheriff Rivera put a stop to it. You puttin' these purchases on Miss Eleanor's account?"

Cord nodded. When Carl Ness studied him a mite too long, he couldn't resist.

"Pretty shade of pink on your storefront."

Ness's face turned the same shade. "Blame my daughter Edith for that." He gestured one aisle over, where two young women stood examining bolts of cloth. "Wants to be an artist, she says. Didn't know what she'd done to the store 'til one morning all my customers came in laughing."

"Women can be unpredictable, all right," Cord allowed.

One of the young women looked up from a bolt of gingham and studied Cord for a moment. Quickly she detached herself from her companion and scooted up the aisle toward him. She was extremely pretty, with blond ringlets that bounced at every step and a yellow ruffle-encrusted dress.

"Ooh, Mr. Ness," she cooed. "Edith's been telling me all about…" She gave Cord a flirty look. "Um…all about… Well, aren't y'all going to introduce me to this handsome stranger?"

The proprietor rolled his eyes. "Fanny Moreland, Cordell Winterman. There, now you're introduced!" He went back to his newspaper.

Miss Moreland giggled and sent Cord a dazzling smile. "Well, *hello* there! Fanny is short for Euphemia. Ah'm so very happy to meet you!" She slid her hand into his in a handshake of sorts. "Ah find this county is woefully short of good-looking gentlemen."

Cord resisted an impulse to roll his eyes back at the proprietor. "Pleased to meet you, Miss Moreland." He disengaged his imprisoned hand. "Now I—"

"Oh, please, you must call me Fanny."

"Okay."

"And ah may call you—?"

"Like the man said, my name's Cordell Winterman. Now, I—"

"Oh, surely you're not leavin' already?"

The mercantile owner made a choking sound.

"Yep," Cord said. "I sure am." He stuffed a bag of lemon drops and one of caramels in his shirt pocket, hoisted the flour sack onto one shoulder and called out to Daniel. "Think you can wrestle that bag of coffee out to the wagon?"

"Yessir." The boy grinned, waved goodbye to the girl at Cord's elbow and bolted out the door. Cord followed him.

The owner came out with the bag of chicken mash over his shoulder, plopped it into the wagon bed and gave Cord a grin. "Kinda entertaining morning, I guess."

"Not too much, no," Cord replied.

Carl Ness chuckled all the way back into the mercantile.

The next stop was the feed store, and then the sawmill, where once again Cord managed to raise the owner's eyebrows. "*Eleanor* Malloy? Say, mister, you know I could have all this delivered."

"Nope. I brought a wagon."

"Miss Eleanor know about this?"

"Yeah, she does. It's her wagon."

On the way back to the farm, he fed Daniel caramels and plied him with questions. "How come your mama has all her deliveries made by somebody else? Didn't your previous hired man bring the wagon into town?"

"Nah. Isaiah was too old to drive it. Besides, people like helpin' Ma out."

"Men, you mean?"

"Yeah. Lots of 'em, ever since I was little. Even Sandy, the sheriff's deputy. The only one who doesn't bring her stuff is Doc."

"Doc?"

"Doc Dougherty."

That brought Cord's own eyebrows up a notch. "Your ma's been real ill, huh?"

"Yeah. She had pneumonia for a long time. She was real sick. I had to learn how to milk Bessie, and Molly and I cooked all the meals and took supper up to Ma every night."

"Is she well now? She looks kinda pale."

"Doc says she'll be fine, but she's gonna be weak an'

tired for a real long time. I'm sure glad you're here, Mr. Winterman. I can't hardly chop enough wood by myself."

"How old are you, Daniel?"

"Nine. Molly's just seven, and Ma won't let her touch the ax, so I have to do it all by myself."

The oddest sensation crawled into Cord's chest. Here he was, out here on the Oregon frontier with no home and no money, trying to stay alive on an apple farm with not one thing that was working right. God had some sense of humor.

"You gonna stay with us, mister?"

"Yeah, I think so. For a while, anyway." The warm feeling in his chest got bigger. Somebody needed him. Or at least needed his help. It made him feel…wanted. Worthwhile.

Eleanor glanced up as the wagon rumbled into the yard, a new screen door riding on top of a load of lumber. Oh, my heavens, she couldn't afford all this, not even after the fall apple harvest came in and she had money in the bank. Her hired hand must have intimidated Ike Bruhn at the sawmill. Which wasn't surprising, she thought as she watched him set the brake and climb down from the bench. Her hired man was tall and muscular; Ike Bruhn had been overplump for years.

Mr. Winterman headed for the house with a bag of something—flour? Coffee beans?—over one shoulder. Daniel struggled to keep up with those long legs.

Her heart gave a queer little thump. Maybe if her hired man was around she would no longer have to make conversation with those too-eager young men from town, not until she was completely well and could fetch her own supplies.

Danny burst through the screen door. "Ma, guess what? Mr. Ness painted the mercantile pink!"

"Pink? Why on earth would he do that?"

"Actually, Miz Malloy," said Mr. Winterman at Danny's

heels, "Ness claims his daughter Edith painted it. You want these coffee beans in the pantry?"

"Yes, thank you."

Danny stopped short in front of her. "You all right, Ma? You look kinda funny."

"Yes, I— Well, I tried to milk Bessie and I guess I overdid it."

Cord stopped short. "I milked her before I went into town this morning, ma'am, even though you said not to. Didn't you see the milk pail? I set it inside the back door."

"I… Well, I…" How could she ever confess what she'd done?

He waited, a frown creasing his tan forehead.

"I, um, I accidentally kicked over the bucket. I had to mop it all up, and then I decided to milk her again, but first I had to catch her and…" She closed her eyes in embarrassment. Only an ignorant city girl would try to milk a cow twice in one morning, and she was certainly not a city girl. Ignorant, maybe, but not a city girl. And only a clumsy idiot would kick over a pail of milk.

Molly came to her rescue by stomping her little feet down the stairs. "Mama made me go to my room!" she announced in an aggrieved tone.

"How come?" her brother asked.

She stared at the floor. "Dunno."

The hired man and the burlap bag of coffee beans disappeared into the pantry, and then he tramped back out through the screen door. When he returned he had a big white sack of flour over his shoulder. But this time the screen door twisted off its one remaining hinge and hung sideways. Without breaking his stride, he yanked it all the way off and sailed it off the front porch.

Molly and Danny watched, wide-eyed. "Wow," her son breathed.

Suddenly Eleanor was bone-tired. She made an effort to breathe normally, in and out, like Doc said. In and out, slowly. She couldn't manage all of this, the milk pail, the mop, the cow, Molly's incessant questions, the screen door… she couldn't manage any of it. She closed her eyes. She wanted to scream, but she didn't have the energy.

She felt a hand on her shoulder and she snapped her lids open.

Cord stood beside her, dusting flour off his jeans. "Got any whiskey?"

"In the pantry," she said wearily. "Top shelf." She shut her eyes again and concentrated on her breathing.

"Ma'am?" He stood in front of her, holding out a cup of coffee. She hesitated, then lifted it out of his hand and downed a big swallow. Her throat convulsed as something hot burned its way down her throat. Tears came to her eyes.

"Guess you don't drink much liquor," he observed.

"I don't drink liquor at all," she rasped. She risked a dainty sip of the brew this time. "It tastes awful, like varnish."

He chuckled. "You drink a lot of varnish?"

She laughed in spite of herself—in spite of her exhaustion, in spite of everything. She breathed in the scent of sweat and sunshine and caramel. "Mr. Wint—"

"Name's Cordell."

"Cordell—"

"Cord," he corrected. At that moment Danny streaked out through the front door, stopping to inspect the space where the ruined screen had been. Molly tagged at his heels.

Cord pulled his attention back to Eleanor Malloy. "Guess you've had a tough morning, huh?"

At her nod, he continued. "Me, too. First there was that pink-painted storefront. Then what's-his-name at the sawmill gave me some grief about putting the lumber on your account. And then," he said with an exaggerated sigh, "Daniel ate all the caramels and wanted Molly's lemon drops, too."

"You bought lemon drops for Molly?"

"Sure. I knew Daniel'd brag about his caramels when we got home, so I figured—"

Without warning she started to cry.

"Well, now, maybe Molly doesn't like lemon—"

"She l-loves lemon drops. Th-thank you." She handed her coffee cup to him. "Mr. Winterman, I am feeling a bit tired. I think I will lie down for a few minutes."

She managed to stand up without swaying and reached the settee in the parlor before her knees gave out. Cord thunked his cup onto the kitchen table, walked over to her and lifted her into his arms. She sure didn't weigh much.

He started up the stairs. "Where's your bedroom?"

"Last door," she murmured.

Cord tramped down the hallway, swung open the door of her room and strode across the rag rug beside the bed. Then he bent and carefully laid her on the quilt. At once she curled up like a little girl and before he straightened up she was asleep.

The room was Spartan, just the bed and a battered armoire and a chest of drawers with a basin and china pitcher on top. No mirror. Ruffled white muslin curtains fluttered at the double window. Which, he noted in passing, looked out on the front yard where the discarded screen door lay between two maple trees. Daniel and Molly were squatting on their haunches with their chins propped in their hands, contemplating the rusty mess. He hated to think what project they'd come up with for the old screen—a safe one, he hoped. Mrs. Malloy, Eleanor, didn't need any more worry.

He noted the intent look on both children's faces and how they kept poking each other with their elbows. Guess he should be prepared for anything. Eleanor's children were turning out to be fun to watch.

With a chuckle he went back down the stairs, climbed up onto the wagon bench and drove the load of lumber around behind the barn.

Chapter Four

Eleanor stretched luxuriously and opened her eyes. Doc Dougherty had ordered her to take afternoon naps, but really, this was ridiculous! From the angle of the sun through the bedroom window, she guessed she had slept for hours.

The sound of hammering came through the open window, and she dragged her aching body off the bed and peeked out. Danny was perched at Mr. Winterman's elbow, handing him nails, which he pounded into the new porch step. Molly was playing with something in the porch swing. She wondered what it was until a tiny ball of orange fur tumbled off onto the floor.

A kitten! Where had she found a kitten? As she watched, another orange ball dropped off the swing, and then another! She groaned aloud. Surely Cord wouldn't have brought kittens from town without asking her first?

Molly gave a squeak and scrambled out of the swing to corral the animals, and Eleanor turned away from the window. She splashed lukewarm water over her flushed cheeks and patted some on her neck. Imagine, sleeping away the afternoon when she should be baking bread and starting the beans for supper. It was probably because of that whiskey Cord had slipped into her coffee. The man was a bad influence.

Well, maybe not so bad, considering that he'd apparently worked all afternoon and watched over Daniel and Molly while he repaired whatever he was working on. She looked out the window again.

The front porch step was fixed. Oh, yes, she surely did need a hired man! She was glad she had hired Cordell Winterman. She thought about the tall, sun-browned man all the way down the stairs and into the kitchen to start supper.

An hour later the children tumbled in through the new screen door, dusty and happy. And hungry. "Wash up," she ordered.

"We already did," Molly answered.

"Oh? Where?"

"At the pump out front," Danny volunteered. "With Cord. I mean Mr. Winterman."

She propped both hands on her hips. "With soap?"

"With soap," Cord said as he came through the door. He took the chair she indicated, tipping it back until the two front feet lifted off the floor.

"You're gonna fall over backward," Molly observed.

"You want to bet on that?"

"Yes!" the girl shouted.

"Okay. I bet three lemon drops that I won't tip this chair over."

"Please," Eleanor interjected, setting a platter of fried potatoes on the table. "Do not teach my children to gamble!"

He stared up at her. "You mean I can't bet even one lemon drop?"

"I mean exactly that," she said, keeping her voice extra-crisp. "And kindly tell me where those kittens came from? Not from town, I hope?"

Molly went rigid. Cord returned all four chair legs to the floor. "Well, ma'am, to tell you the truth—"

"Don't tell her anything!" Danny yelled. "She'll make us get rid of 'em."

"Would you do that, Mrs. Malloy?" Cord inquired, his voice quiet. "Make your children get rid of some kittens?"

"Well…"

"Because," he continued, "actually they're *your* kittens. They were born in your barn, up in the hayloft."

"Are you absolutely sure about that?" She couldn't soften the suspicion that tinged her voice.

"Oh, I'm sure, all right," he said with a laugh. "Mama Cat and the little ones snuggled right up to my belly last night. They're yours, all right."

She sat down suddenly, completely out of steam. "What? Oh. Well, then, I suppose…"

"Yaaay!" Molly cried. "Tomorrow I'm gonna give them all names."

Cord studied the white-faced woman sitting across from him. "Daniel," he said quietly, "why don't you check on whatever's in the oven."

"Oh, yessir, Cord."

"And, Molly," he continued, "get your mother's napkin and wet it under the pump at the sink."

The children bustled about their tasks while Eleanor sat limp as a cooked noodle. When Molly handed her the wet napkin, she took it without a word and laid it against the back of her neck.

Cord kept his eye on her while he pointed to the oven. "Dan?"

Danny opened the oven door and sniffed. "Beans, I guess. A big pot."

Cord stood, grabbed two potholders and lifted the pot of bubbling beans to the table. Danny handed him the big serving spoon, and Cord ladled out a dollop onto a plate and pushed it over to Eleanor.

She pushed it back across the table to Cord. "I'm not hungry."

Cord added a square of corn bread and slid the plate back to her.

"I said I wasn't hungry," she murmured.

"Yeah, I heard you. Eat some anyway. You've got two kids who need their mother, so don't argue."

"Well!" She ruffled herself up like an angry banty chicken. "Mr. Winterman, just who do you think you are, giving me orders?"

He drew in a tired breath. "I'm your hired man, Eleanor. I'm trying to help you here, so do what I say, all right?"

Molly and Danny exchanged wide-eyed looks and picked up their forks without a word. Cord ladled some beans onto their plates and then some onto his own. After a long moment their mother picked up her fork, and the kids exchanged another, even longer, look.

Cord caught Danny's eye and gave him an imperceptible shake of his head. *Don't say anything, son. Nobody likes to give in when they've made a speech about refusing something.* To Molly he sent a smile and a wink.

After that, supper was dead quiet except for the clink of utensils against the china plates. Finally Danny broke the spell. "We got any dessert, Ma?"

"No, I'm afraid not," she said. "I meant to bake an apple pie, but…"

"I make a humdinger of an apple pie," Cord announced.

Three startled pairs of eyes stared at him. "Aw, you can't neither," Danny said.

"Don't bet on it, son."

Eleanor pinned him with a disapproving look but he paid no attention, just grinned.

"You all get ready for apple pie tomorrow night, all right?" He held her gaze just long enough to make her a little nervous.

Eleanor stared at him. *Apple pie?* Surely he was joking. After an announcement like that, she found she couldn't *stop* looking at him. Well, maybe it was more than his apple pie promise. Maybe it was his way of taking over, of making her feel…cared for somehow.

She gave herself a mental shake. The man left her with an uneasy, fluttery feeling in her stomach. She watched Danny and Molly gobble down their beans, butter extra squares of corn bread and gulp down their milk. Then, without a word from her, they gathered up the plates and pumped water into the teakettle to heat for washing up the dishes.

Things were certainly different since Cord Winterman had appeared at her door. She wasn't sure she liked it. She wasn't sure she even liked *him*. Could a man like that really deliver on a challenge to bake a pie? She didn't think so for one minute. Not for one single minute!

That night, Cord lay awake in the loft until long past moonrise, not because he wasn't tired from fixing the screen or the porch step or the front gate, but because Mama Cat brought her wriggly kittens to curl up against his back and he was afraid to roll over for fear of crushing them. He could move them, he supposed. But after a few hours he kinda liked hearing them purr next to him.

You know what, Winterman? You are a damn fool.

Maybe. He didn't know exactly what he'd landed in here at Eleanor Malloy's apple farm, but he was grateful for the roof over his head, even if the barn was drafty, and three meals a day with no one prodding him to hurry up or move on or…anything else.

God, it was good to be here! It felt good to buy lumber at the sawmill, buy lemon drops for Molly and caramels for Danny. It felt especially good to talk to a pretty girl at the mercantile. What was her name? Fanny something. Even if she did giggle and flutter her eyelashes at him, it was good to know he still looked like a normal man on the outside, even if the inside was pretty much broken.

He drifted off to sleep with Mama Cat warming his backside and a woman's face floating in his mind. But it wasn't Fanny What's-her-name's face. It was Eleanor Malloy's.

In the morning he milked Bessie, saved a saucerful for

Mama Cat and the kittens, laid out the lumber to repair the rotten corral fence and ate the best breakfast he could remember in the last seven years. Molly fried up a mess of bacon, Daniel mixed up thick sourdough pancake batter and Eleanor made coffee with one hand and flipped pancakes with the other.

She looked better this morning, more rested. The dark circles under her eyes seemed less pronounced. Maybe that nap yesterday afternoon had done her some good. Or maybe he should slip whiskey into her coffee more often.

It took all day to repair the fence. Halfway through the afternoon he remembered his promise to bake an apple pie for tonight's dessert. He was sure ending up doing some strange things on this farm, cuddling kittens and plying kids with lemon drops and caramels. And now he'd gotten himself into baking a pie. Still, any single hour of life here on this farm was better than sixty seconds of where he'd been before.

After midday dinner he shooed the kids outside and watched Eleanor nod off on the parlor settee. After a while he tiptoed out onto the porch, where Molly and Danny were arguing about what to do with the old rusted-out door screen.

"Let's build a bird cage."

"No! Let's make a chicken coop."

"We've already got a chicken coop," Molly pointed out.

"Yeah," Danny conceded. "But it's pretty rickety. How about making a dirt-strainer."

"A dirt-strainer!" Molly's blue eyes went wide. "That's a dumb idea. What's a dirt-strainer, anyway?"

"You know. When Ma plants tomatoes 'n' carrots she hoes the dirt real fine. A dirt-strainer would make it easier."

They argued and discussed until their mother woke from her nap, and Cord strode into the kitchen to bake his apple pie.

Eleanor shook her head at the sight of the rangy man in

her kitchen and when he tied her blue-checked gingham apron around his waist she had to smile. Danny disappeared into the pantry and emerged with a big bowl of last season's red Jonathan apples. Cord sat him down at the kitchen table with a paring knife and showed him how to cut them in half, remove the core and peel them. He showed Molly how to slice them up fine, and while the children labored away, he started his piecrust.

She watched with misgivings. Piecrust was hard to get just right. Adding too much water made it tough; adding too little made the crust crumble into nothing when you tried to roll it out.

Cord scooped two cups of flour out of the barrel and dropped in a palm-size lump of her just-churned butter. She didn't really believe he knew what he was doing, but his motions were decisive. He was even humming! Well, maybe he did know and maybe he didn't, she sniffed. The proof would be in the pudding. Or the pie, she amended.

Part of her hoped he would fail, that his crust would turn out tough and the apples mushy. Another part of her admired him, a rugged-looking man too tall for her low-ceilinged kitchen, for even attempting to bake a pie. And, she thought, studying her two children absorbed in their apple peeling and slicing, Molly and Daniel were certainly learning something new! Not only that, she acknowledged, they weren't squirming or whining to go play outside.

Cord must have threatened them with something. In just two days, this man who'd ridden in from God knows where, and about whom she knew absolutely nothing, had tamed her over-curious son and her lively daughter, and *that* was a miracle if there ever was one.

She trusted Cord Winterman, and she had to wonder why. She was no green girl, one who was easily bowled over by a handsome face and skill with a hammer. In all the years she'd been alone, she had never hungered for male company. She knew this was a source of gossip and speculation on

the part of the townspeople, and it was definitely cause for
frustration on the part of the parade of men who brought
supplies and mail and news from town and dropped broad
hints about staying for supper. None of them had ever set
foot in her kitchen, or sat at her supper table, or anywhere
else inside the house. She wasn't interested, and until this
moment she had never wondered why.

Isaiah, the old hired man she'd had for years, had rarely
even spoken to her children, let alone taught them anything. Isaiah had been lazy and inept and dull-witted, but
she'd been desperate for help and for all his shortcomings,
she had trusted him around Danny and Molly. When the
crotchety old man had moved on, she wasn't sorry, but then
she'd fallen ill.

But *this* man, Cord Winterman, was a different kind of
fish. He made her children sit up and take notice. He made
her sit up and take notice. He made her wonder about things.
Why, for instance, was he content to work as just a hired
man when it was plain he was capable of so much more?
Where had he come from? Where was he going? She should
have demanded answers to these questions, but somehow
when he had appeared at her front door, all the questions
had flown out of her head.

She watched him sprinkle flour over the breadboard, di-
vide his pie dough into four equal parts and search for her
rolling pin. So he was making not just one but *two* pies!

The man knew his way around a kitchen, and she couldn't
help but wonder whose kitchen it had been in his past.

He let Danny and then Molly try their hand at rolling out
the crust. Then he took over, rolled it thin and expertly laid
it in the tin pie pan. He showed Danny again how to roll out
the next bottom crust, and then they all heaped in handfuls
of sliced apples and brown sugar. *Brown* sugar? She never
used brown sugar in apple pie! And then he added bits of
butter and…cheese? *Cheese!* Whatever was he thinking?

When he slashed the top crusts and slid the filled tins

into the oven, the children clapped their hands and Cord
half turned toward her. A flour smudge marked one cheek
and his apron was spotted with something, but he sent her a
grin that curled her toes. Even from here she could see the
triumphant light in those unnervingly blue eyes.

Suddenly she wished she had some whiskey in her coffee cup.

into the oven, she smiled, slipped the handle of Cord half-turned around to... the spindle... and his arm... as... but he... grip that could... Even from here she could see the tremulous light in those unnervingly blue eyes.

Suddenly she realized she had started to move to her end her ford.

Chapter Five

Cord knew she was watching his every move, assessing him, judging him. Eleanor resented his presence in her kitchen, rooting around in her pantry and in the cutlery drawers. But she wanted an apple pie, didn't she? If there was one thing he'd learned in this life, it was that you don't get something for nothing. No rooting around in a pantry, no apple pie.

He worked on, trying to ignore her, and trying to ignore the undercurrent of pleasure he felt knowing that her eyes were following every move he made. It made his chest feel as hot inside as he felt outside in the stifling kitchen with the roaring fire in the stove heating up the oven.

While the pies baked, the children drifted out the back door to play in the yard and Cord warmed up the coffee, poured two cups and carried them into the parlor, where Eleanor sat.

She looked up at him with a strange expression on her pale face. He sucked in his breath and waited.

"You're not just a hired man, are you?" she said. "I mean, that's not what you did before I hired you, is it?"

"I'm a hired man *here*," he said carefully. "I'm not sure what I'd be somewhere else."

She reached for his offered cup of coffee, then glanced up again. "Do you have plans for 'somewhere else'?"

He gave her such a long look that she lowered her eyes. "I was planning to go to California, to the gold fields."

"What stopped you?"

He didn't answer for a long time, just focused his gaze out the window on the apple orchard. "To be honest, I wouldn't have stopped here if I hadn't been so hungry, even though I'd seen your advert in town. But then I came up on that little hill and saw all those apple trees covered with lacy white blossoms. Kinda made my heart feel funny, so I stopped and...well, you know the rest."

She paused with her cup halfway to her mouth. "How long will you stay?"

"It's April now," he said slowly. "I thought I'd give it five months, say 'til August, before I move on."

"Very good. Doc Dougherty tells me I should be completely well and strong long before August."

"Yeah? You gonna chop wood and hitch up the horse and drive that wagon to town and muck out your barn by yourself? You need some help out here, ma'am. Even if I'm not going to be here, you should have a hired man to help out."

She gave him a half smile and sipped her coffee for a full minute before she spoke. "I chopped wood and mucked out the barn before I fell ill, Mr. Winterman. I have been on my own here for almost seven years, ever since Molly was born."

Cord studied her. Her cheeks were getting pink. "It's too hard for a woman alone. That's most likely why you got sick."

"That is pure nonsense. I got sick because I fell in the creek while I was chasing the cow and took a chill. A week later it turned into pneumonia."

He stood up suddenly. Dammit, he didn't want to concern himself with her well-being. He didn't want to like her kids, and he didn't want to like *her*. But he did. And he had to admit it scared the hell out of him.

"Think I'll check on the pies," he growled. He moved into the kitchen and bent over the oven door, and when he returned he brought the coffeepot and filled her cup. He didn't look at her. But he did ask the question that had been niggling in the back of his mind.

"Do you and your husband own this place free and clear?"

"I own it. I removed Tom's name from the deed when he…when he left home to go off to war. It's been seven years now, and he is considered legally dead."

"You said you had a hired man before you hired me."

"Yes. Isaiah. As I told you, he didn't do much."

"Why'd you keep him, then?"

"He needed a place to stay and I needed someone to help about the farm. Molly was just a baby then, and Danny was too little to be much help."

"How'd you manage after this hired man, Isaiah, left?"

"I managed," she said in a quiet voice.

"And then you got sick," he observed dryly.

She took a swallow of her coffee. "Well, yes I did. Doc Dougherty came, and he sent a woman out from town, Helen, I think her name was, to nurse me and take care of Molly and Daniel. She stayed until I was strong enough to get out of bed. I am growing stronger with every day that passes."

"Mrs. Malloy. Eleanor," he amended. "Seems to me you're just hangin' on by a thread. You've got two kids. You owe it to them to take better care of yourself. That means no more milking and no chopping wood."

She pressed her lips into a thin line but said nothing.

Cord studied the rigid set of her shoulders and the white-knuckled grip she had on the handle of her china cup. "I get the feeling you don't take orders too well."

She gave him a wobbly smile. "You are most likely correct. I was a great trial to my parents."

That made him laugh out loud. "I bet you're still plenty stubborn when it comes to doing things your own way."

"Oh, maybe just a little." Her cheeks turned an even deeper shade of rose.

"Maybe you're more than a *little* stubborn," he said. "Maybe a *lot* stubborn."

"Oh, all right, maybe I'm a lot stubborn." By now her cheeks were flushed scarlet. "Now that you're here, I will take better care of myself. Especially," she said with a little bubble of laughter, "since you can bake an apple pie. Which," she added with an impish grin, "you have quite forgotten is still in the oven."

Instantly he wheeled away from her and strode into the kitchen. The pies were not burned, as he had feared, just nicely baked. He grabbed potholders and lifted them out of the oven. Oh, man, they looked just right, golden brown on top with rich juice bubbling out the vents he'd slashed in the crust. They smelled wonderful! He was damn proud of them.

Eleanor followed him into the kitchen, cup and saucer still in her hand. "Who taught you to make a pie? Your mother?"

"No," he said shortly.

She looked at him with another question in her eyes, but he ignored it. Best not to dig around in those long-past years. No good ever came from opening a wound that had healed over.

He set both pies on the open windowsill to cool and stacked the mixing bowl and the paring knives in the sink for the kids to wash up after supper. Eleanor returned to the parlor, where she curled up on the settee and gazed out the front window.

"You don't like talking to me, do you?" she asked suddenly.

Whoa, Nelly. How'd she figure that?

"Why is that?" she pursued, her eyes on his face.

"Guess I haven't been around many ladies lately."

"Silence is perfectly all right with me," she went on. "I spent years and years not being talked to."

She closed her eyes against the late-afternoon sun's glare, and that gave him a chance to really look at her. Her lids were purplish with blue-black smudges shadowing her eyes. She might not be sick anymore, but she was obviously exhausted.

So even if she was as stubborn as three ornery mules, now she had a hired man to help her. He drew in a long, quiet breath. For the first time in longer than he could remember he felt needed.

And that, he thought with a silent groan, made him nervous.

The kids raced through their supper of biscuits and something Eleanor called bean stew, which as near as he could figure out was last night's baked beans with cut-up carrots and potatoes added. Tasted good, though.

His apple pie was received with oohs and aahs. Even Eleanor wanted a second piece.

"Ma, Miz Panovsky says we're gonna have Student Night at school on Saturday."

Eleanor looked up from the table. "Oh?"

"You gonna come? You were too sick the last time."

"Well, yes," she said quickly. "Of course I'm going to come, Danny. I'm much stronger now."

Cord thought the boy looked somewhat unsettled at that.

"What about me?" Molly wailed. "When do I get to go to school?"

"As soon as you're big enough, honey."

"But I'm big now!"

"Molly, you're still too young to walk three miles to town and then three miles back home, and you're too little to ride a horse."

Her face scrunched up. "When will I be big enough?"

Cord stood up suddenly. "How 'bout I measure you, see how tall you are? We can make a mark on the back door frame." He sent Eleanor an inquiring look, and she nodded.

"Then later I'll measure you again, and you can see how much you've grown. How about it?"

Molly's eyes sparkled. "Can we do it right now?"

"Sure." He caught Eleanor's eye. "You got a tape measure handy?"

"It's upstairs in my bedroom. But—"

"I'll get it," Cord said. Eleanor had looked peaked all afternoon and during supper she'd seemed short of breath. "Where is it, exactly?"

"It's in my top dresser drawer. Molly can show you, but she's too short to reach it."

Cord followed the girl as she scampered up the stairs. He'd been in Eleanor's bedroom only once, the day she'd almost fainted and he'd carried her upstairs.

Molly banged the door open and streaked toward the walnut chest standing against the far wall. "Up there." She pointed to the top drawer.

Something about being here made him nervous. Too private, maybe? Too…female?

Carefully he pulled the drawer open. Her possessions were all neatly arranged, lacy handkerchiefs, a red knit hat and two blue silky-looking scarves. No jewelry, he noted. He wanted in the worst way to open the second drawer. Maybe he'd find some of her smallclothes, drawers or chemises, or a sheer nightgown. Nah. Eleanor wouldn't wear a sheer nightgown.

Or would she?

Concentrate on the tape measure, man.

He gingerly laid one finger on the tumble of scarves and pushed one aside, looking for the tape. But what he uncovered instead was a framed daguerreotype. A man and a woman, apparently on their wedding day. A long veil fell below her slim shoulders. She was not smiling.

His gut clenched. What made a woman not smile on her wedding day? He wished he hadn't seen it.

Molly danced at his side. "Didja find it?"

He pushed the photograph to one side and there underneath it lay a neatly coiled measuring tape. "Got it." Reluctantly he pushed the drawer shut.

Molly darted out the door and down the stairs. "Measure me! Measure me!"

While Eleanor and Danny washed up the supper dishes, Cord lined Molly up against the door frame and made a pencil mark for her height. "You're thirty-two inches tall," he announced.

"Now do me," Danny insisted. He dried his hands on the dish towel, marched to the back door and stood at attention. Cord dutifully marked his height and turned to Eleanor.

"How tall are you, Miz Malloy?"

"Why, I have no idea."

"Shall I measure you?"

"Oh, I don't think—"

"Aw, come on, Ma, do it!" Danny ordered.

Obediently Eleanor moved to the back door and straightened her spine against the frame. She sent him a self-conscious look and closed her eyes.

Closed her eyes? Why in hell would she close her eyes?

He snapped the length of measuring tape in his two hands, moved toward her and stopped. He couldn't lay the tape against Eleanor's body. He didn't trust his hands anywhere near her. They were already shaking and he wasn't anywhere close to her.

"You'd better hurry up, Cord," she said. "You and Molly have to dry the dishes."

He swallowed. "Right. Open your eyes and turn around, Eleanor. Face the door and put your nose right up against the wood."

She obeyed, and he ran the tape from the back of her work boot, over the curve of her hip and along her upper spine to the top of her head. "Okay, now step away."

She ducked under his hand and moved back a step while he made a pencil mark on the door frame. Next to it he inscribed her initials. E.M.

"Now you!" Danny insisted.

Before he could refuse, Eleanor snatched the tape measure out of his hand. "Stand up against the door," she ordered.

"Front or back?" he asked. Wait a minute. The thought of her touching him anywhere near his groin was unnerving. He turned toward the door and put his back to her.

He felt her touch his ankle, felt the tape slide along the back of his jeans and then over his butt. He stopped breathing.

Then her hand skimmed up his spine to his neck, and he couldn't help the shiver that shook him.

Suddenly she stopped. "The tape measure's not long enough," she announced.

Cord said a silent prayer of thanks. Her every touch was arousing. Actually, he didn't dare turn around just yet because his groin was engorged and…well…active.

"How tall is Cord?" Molly asked.

"Over six feet," Eleanor said.

"Golly," Danny breathed. "Do you think I'll be that tall when I'm all growed up?"

Eleanor wound the tape into a tight coil and slipped it into her apron pocket. "I don't think so, Danny. Your father was…" She stopped abruptly. "Shorter than Cord," she continued. "So chances are you will be—"

"Tall enough," Cord interrupted. "Tall enough to be a really good rider."

The boy's gray-blue eyes widened. "Really honest?"

"Yeah, really honest." He caught Eleanor's gaze. She was shaking her head no.

"I don't want Danny riding a horse yet. There's been no one to teach him, and besides, he's too young."

Cord stepped away from the doorway and surreptitiously adjusted his jeans. "He's not too young, Eleanor. I've been riding since I was five years old."

She bit her lip. "I still don't think—"

"Please, Ma?" Danny yelped. "I'll do all the dishes every night for a month, I promise."

Cord laid his hand on the boy's shoulder and squeezed lightly. Then he turned to Molly.

"Come on, Molly. I guess it's up to us to dry the supper dishes."

Chapter Six

"You ever think you'd like to eat pie for breakfast?" Cord asked the next morning.

"Yes!" Molly and Daniel shouted in unison.

"No," Eleanor said decisively.

Cord shrugged and watched her crack eggs into the skillet. "Apple pie is not a proper breakfast for growing children," she pronounced in a no-nonsense tone.

"Aw, Ma," Danny moaned. "I'm sick of eggs."

"Eggs," their mother said with an edge in her voice, "are what civilized people eat for breakfast."

Both children dawdled through the meal of fried eggs and bacon, and suddenly Cord realized why they were eating so slowly. It was Monday, a school day for Danny.

An hour later the grumbling boy hoisted his satchel over his shoulder and plodded out the front door. Molly moped around the yard petting the chickens until her brother trudged back through the gate late that afternoon.

"Danny, you know maybe you could ride my bay mare to school," Cord remarked casually. "I could teach you to ride."

"Nah. Ma won't let me. You heard her. She says a horse is dangerous. Besides, you said it was too much horse for me."

"It is dangerous if you don't know how to handle a horse. You ever been on a horse?"

Danny shook his head.

"How long does it take you to walk to school?"

"Most of an hour. It's over three miles."

Cord nodded. He'd like to see the boy get to and from school faster, if only because Molly was always underfoot when her brother was gone. An extra hour morning and evening could be well spent if Danny was around to entertain the girl.

After supper that night Cord again raised the subject with Eleanor.

"Absolutely not," she said shortly. "He's too young to manage a big animal like that."

"He's not too young, Eleanor. I told you I learned to ride when I was younger than Molly."

"Then your mother was a fool."

"My mother was dead. My father was the fool, but he taught me to ride anyway. And hunt and read and write. He even taught me to dance a Virginia reel."

Eleanor's face changed. "Did he really? How extraordinary!"

"He also taught me how to repair a barn roof, which is what I'm going to do tomorrow. Unless," he added, "you have something else that needs doing."

"Does the barn roof really need fixing?"

"It does. The holes are so big, at night I can look up and see the stars. Come winter it'll leak like a sieve."

"I take it that you are sleeping up in the loft?"

"Yeah." He sighed. "Along with Mama Cat and her kittens."

"I think Isaiah slept in one of the horse stalls. He wouldn't climb the ladder up to the loft. He said it made him lightheaded."

Cord chuckled. "Then he never knew about the holes in the roof, did he? Or about Mama Cat?"

"Oh, very well," she said with a laugh. "Fix the barn

roof. I certainly wouldn't want a wet cat and kittens when the winter rains come."

She stood up, untied her apron and hung it on the hook by the stove. "Thank you for making those pies, Cord." She hesitated. "A man who can not only bake a pie and dance a Virginia reel but repair barn roofs is certainly rare in my book."

Cord thought about her remark all the rest of that day. Rare, huh? He'd been called a lot of things in his life, but "rare" wasn't one of them. Still, he thought with a smile, a man liked a compliment now and then, didn't he?

It was Saturday, Danny's School Night. All day the boy moped around the yard with such a long face Eleanor wondered if he was sick. Finally she couldn't stand it any longer and set aside the basket of green peas she was shelling and stood up on the back porch step. "Danny, are you feeling all right?"

"Sure, Ma. I guess so. Got something flutterin' around in my belly is all."

Cord looked up from the chicken house, where he was nailing a new roost in place. "Butterflies, huh?"

"Guess so," the boy muttered.

"You have to give a speech or something? That can make a man plenty nervous."

Danny perked up at the word *man* and sent her hired man a pained look. "Yeah. I gotta recite the Bill of Rights from memory and give a speech about it."

"Hey, just yesterday you wanted to be 'all growed up' so your ma would let you ride a horse," Cord reminded him. "Part of gettin' there—" he shot Eleanor a look "—is, uh, standing up to those things that are hard."

"Like giving a speech?" Danny muttered.

"Yeah, like giving a speech."

Eleanor sat back down on the step and again started shelling peas. Cord made a good deal of sense at times.

And then her hired man opened his mouth and spoiled it. "Believe me," Cord called from the chicken house, "you're gonna find ridin' a horse easy after makin' a speech in public."

Her son's eyes lit up. "Oh, yeah?"

"Yeah," Cord said.

"No," Eleanor countered. "No horse-riding. Not yet."

Cord pounded another nail into the chicken roost, tossed the hammer to Danny and strode across the yard toward her. But instead of starting an argument with her, he asked about her daughter. "Where's Molly?"

"She's in the barn, playing with those kittens."

"She's not near the horse stalls, is she? Or up in the loft?"

"She is not allowed up in the loft, Cord. I don't want her falling off that narrow little ladder. And she's scared to death of horses."

"But you trust her, right? She's sensible enough not to get hurt."

"Well, yes. But…"

"Ma," Danny called, his voice plaintive. "Do I really have to go to School Night?"

"Yes," both she and Cord said together. "You really do. Now, go find Molly and both of you wash up for supper."

Thankfully, Cord kept his mouth shut about horses and riding all through her supper of creamed peas on biscuits. When she shooed the children upstairs to put on clean clothes, Cord went out to the barn to hitch up the wagon.

Upstairs in her bedroom, Eleanor quickly sponged off her face and neck and donned her blue gingham day dress. She was the last to descend the front porch steps.

She felt as nervous as Danny. All her life she had disliked public gatherings. Her mother had criticized her for being shy, but Eleanor knew better. She was not just shy; she was frightened of people, especially crowds of people. Somehow she felt she never "measured up," in her mother's words.

Cord took one look at her, jumped down from the driver's seat and lifted her onto the wagon bench beside him. Before he picked up the reins he leaned sideways and spoke near her ear.

"You all right, Eleanor? You look white as milk."

"I'm fine," she said shortly. "Just a little scared."

"Scared about what?"

She twisted her hands in her lap and looked everywhere but at him, but she didn't answer. Finally he laid down the reins and turned to face her. "Scared about what?"

"About all those people," she admitted. "About... I guess I'm worried about Danny. It's so hard to be on display."

"Yeah." He raised his eyebrows but said nothing. Instead he picked up the traces and they started off.

Danny clambered down to shut the gate behind them, then climbed back into the back. He looked so preoccupied Cord had to chuckle. Probably rehearsing his speech in his head.

The schoolhouse was lit up like a Christmas tree with kerosene lamps and candle sconces along the walls. Children milled about in the schoolyard, and as Cord maneuvered the wagon into an available space he heard Danny let out a groan.

"I don't wanna do this!" he moaned.

"I don't want to do this, either!" Eleanor murmured.

Molly stood up in the wagon, propped her hands at the waist of her starched pinafore, and at the top of her voice screeched, "Well, I do! I *do* wanna do this!"

All the way into the schoolhouse Cord chuckled about Fearless Molly in a family of Nervous Nellies. Danny disappeared into the cloakroom, and he followed Eleanor to an uncomfortable-looking wooden bench near the back. He lifted Molly onto his lap, careful not to squash the ruffles on her clean pinafore, and then looked around.

He recognized Carl Ness, the mercantile owner, with a thin-faced woman he took to be Carl's wife, flanked by two young girls. He recognized Edith, the girl who had painted the mercantile front pink; the other girl looked exactly like her so that must be Edith's twin sister.

Ike Bruhn, the owner of the sawmill, sat with two women, one with a baby in her arms and the other tying a bow on a young girl's braids. Then a very beautiful young woman with a bun of dark hair caught at her neck with a ribbon stepped to the front of the room and clapped her hands.

That must be Danny's teacher. At the clapped signal, a humming sound began at the door behind him, and all at once he heard singing.

Twenty or so students, ranging in age from about six or seven to a strapping blond boy of maybe fourteen, marched in two by two, singing "My Country 'tis of Thee." A chill went up Cord's spine.

Danny was the seventh in the line, walking next to a small blonde girl in a pink gingham dress. The boy looked like he wanted to sink through the floor.

The teacher, Mrs. Christina Panovsky, arranged them in rows against the front wall and turned to the audience. "Welcome, everyone. This is an extraordinary class of extraordinary young people—your sons and daughters. We want to share with you what we have been learning this school year."

What followed was impressive. Four students acted out a scene from a play about Robin Hood they had written themselves. Then a small choir sang "Comin' Through the Rye" in three-part harmony and a larger choir presented a "spoken word" song, a clever recitation of geographical names chanted in complicated rhythms. "Ar-gen-*tin*-a. Smoke *Riv*-er. *Clacka*-mas *Coun*-ty. *Mex*-i-co *Ci*-ty."

Molly loved it; she bounced up and down on his lap in time with the words.

Finally Danny stepped forward to deliver his speech.

Molly sat up straight and craned her neck to see. Eleanor clutched Cord's arm. He felt a tightening in his chest.

"Ladies and gentlemen…" The boy's voice shook slightly,

but as he progressed through his speech it grew stronger, and when he finished with, "We are one people, one nation… We are Americans," his words rang with assurance. He stepped back to spirited applause.

Eleanor still clutched his arm, and now she was crying. Cord pried her fingers off his bicep and pressed his handkerchief into her hand.

"Th-thank you," she wept.

It made him chuckle deep down inside. Molly twisted around and flung her small arms about his neck. "Wasn't Danny wunnerful? I wanna go to school, too!"

Following Danny's speech there were more songs and recitations, ending with the little blonde girl in the pink dress, who sang a haunting folk song, first in French and then in English. Something about yellow daisies in a meadow.

"That's Manette Nicolet," Eleanor whispered. "Her mother is French, from New Orleans. Her father is Colonel Wash Halliday, over there." She tipped her head to the right, where a small, very attractive woman sat holding the hand of a well-muscled gent with a bushy gray-peppered mustache. His eyes were so shiny Cord could see the moisture from here.

"Colonel, huh?" he murmured. "Blue or gray?"

"Blue, I think. Union. His full name is George Washington Halliday. It's her second marriage. Her first husband was killed in the War."

"The daughter, Manette, doesn't look much older than Molly. Looks like she does well in, uh, school."

Eleanor let the remark lie.

When the presentations and recitations drew to a close, Mrs. Panovsky invited them all to stay for cookies and lemonade.

"Oh, boy, lemonade!" Molly sang. She scooted off Cord's lap and bobbed excitedly at her mother's side until Eleanor rose and moved toward the refreshment table in the far corner. Cord was about to follow when a feminine voice called his name.

"Why, Cordell Winterman, is that really you?" A ruffle-bedecked Fanny Moreland made a beeline across the room toward him. "Y'all remember me, don't you? Carl Ness introduced us at the mercantile? You were buying coffee and lemon drops and—"

"Chicken mash," Eleanor said from beside him.

"Oh, hello, Mrs. Malloy. I haven't seen you in town for such a long time I thought you might be…well…you know, expecting. Are you?"

"Expecting what?" Eleanor inquired with a perfectly straight face.

"Um…well, you know," Fanny said, lowering her voice. "Expecting a…baby." She whispered the last word.

"I am not, thank you," Eleanor replied, her voice cool. "My husband, you may recall, has been away for some years."

Fanny looked nonplussed for just an instant. "Oh, that's right, I remember now. Why, you're practically a widow!"

Molly reached up and gave Fanny's flounced skirt a sharp tug. "That's not very nice! My mama is not a widow."

Cord lifted Molly into his arms and started to move away, but Fanny wasn't finished yet.

"Oh, Cordell, I am so terribly thirsty. Would you be so kind as to fetch me some lemonade?"

Cord gave her a level look. "Sorry, Miss Moreland. As you can see, I have my hands full." He shifted Molly's weight to emphasize his point.

"Why, who is this darling little girl?" Fanny gushed. "Surely you are not the father? You're not married, are you, Cordell?"

"No, he's not!" Molly blurted out. "I'm Molly, and he's not married. He lives with us!"

Fanny's expression changed. "Oh, you mean with Mrs. Malloy?"

Molly nodded. "Yes, with my mama."

Cord cleared his throat. "I work for Mrs. Malloy. I'm her hired man."

"Well, isn't that interesting! I was just about to pay a call on Mrs.—"

"No, you weren't," Cord interjected.

"Well, why ever not? I only want to extend a friendly gesture."

"You want a helluva lot more than that, Miss Moreland. And I'm not interested."

The smile on the young woman's face never wavered. "Oh, come now. I'm sure you don't really mean that, do you, Cordell?"

Molly squirmed. "Oh, yes he does!" she shouted.

Cord could have kissed her. He spotted Danny across the room. "Excuse us, Miss Moreland."

He met the boy halfway across the room. "Didja see me, Cord? Was I all right?"

Cord dipped to extend his hand to Danny without dislodging Molly. "You were very all right, Dan. Congratulations."

He took the boy's small hand in his and gave him a firm, manly handshake. Danny grinned up at him and Cord thought the boy was going to float up off the floor.

After cups of watery lemonade and too many chocolate cookies, Cord herded his little entourage out the door and across the schoolyard to their waiting wagon. He tightened the cinch on the gray horse, lifted Molly into the back and watched Danny climb in beside her. Then he walked around to the other side, where Eleanor stood.

He didn't even ask, just slipped both hands around her waist and lifted her onto the wooden seat. She said nothing until he drove out of the schoolyard and started on the road out of town.

Chapter Seven

"It must be wonderful to be young and pretty," Eleanor said at last. She kept her voice down so Molly and Danny in the back of the wagon couldn't hear.

"It's wonderful to be young, for sure," Cord said. "Don't know about being 'pretty.'"

"Men don't worry about 'pretty.' Women do."

"Are you jealous of Fanny Moreland?"

Eleanor jerked. Oh, Cord could be so maddeningly blunt! No, she wasn't jealous of Fanny. She did envy her boldness, though. She was jealous of Fanny's *youth*. She acknowledged that she had squandered her own, trying to be a good mother to Danny and Molly and struggling to keep her farm going through winter storms and scorching summers that left vegetable seedlings dried up as soon as they sprouted. Now she was thin and tired and…not young anymore.

And she envied Fanny Moreland's *health*.

"Cord, do you ever wish you could be young again?"

He surprised her with a harsh laugh. "Young and what, handsome? Rich? Smart?" He thought for a moment. "Yeah, I wish I was young enough to live some parts of my life over again."

"What parts?"

He didn't answer. She regretted her question the instant

she uttered it; it was none of her business. Then after a tense minute or two of silence he surprised her by answering.

"Maybe getting married. Getting shot during the War." He let out a long breath. "Killing a man."

She gasped. "You killed a man?"

"I killed more than one in the War, Eleanor."

The tone of his voice made her wish she had never asked.

Cord glanced quickly into the back of the wagon, where both Eleanor's children were asleep. "Tell me about Fanny Moreland," he said. He held his breath. It was obvious Eleanor didn't like her. But he didn't want to talk about his wife.

"Oh, Fanny." Eleanor shifted on the bench next to him. "I guess it's sad, really. Fanny is from the South. New Orleans, I think. She lives with her aunt, Ike Bruhn's wife, Ernestine. And Ike, of course."

"Why is that sad?"

"Well, Fanny has pots of money she inherited from her father. About three years ago she was jilted, left at the altar by a man Ernestine said was just after her fortune. Her father sent her out West to get her away from the city."

Cord laughed. "Smoke River's about as far from 'a city' as one can get."

"Fanny has no use for small towns, and she is desperately looking for some man to spirit her away from here to a big city. *Any* big city."

Cord made a noncommittal noise in his throat.

"Why?" Eleanor asked. "Are you interested in Fanny?"

"Not much. She doesn't look like the type who'd be too interested in panning for gold in a California mining camp."

"How do you know?"

He chuckled. "Too many expensive ruffles."

Eleanor laughed out loud, and Cord shot her a look.

"You feeling better now that this school shindig is over?"

She nodded, but he noticed she was still twisting her hands together in her lap. He flapped the reins over the gray's back and picked up the pace. After a moment he slowed the horse down again. Something had been crawling at the back of his mind for the last few days.

"You said that Mrs. Halliday's first husband was killed in the War. Are you sure that's what happened to Mr. Malloy?"

She didn't answer for a long time, and before she did she checked to make sure Molly and Danny were asleep. "I—I don't honestly know what happened to Tom. If he had been killed, you would think they would notify the next of kin."

"Maybe. Maybe they didn't know where to find you."

"How could they *not* know? I've lived on this farm since before the War."

"Or maybe," he said with studied calm, "he's not dead." He shot a look at her. Her face changed, but not in the way he expected. Her mouth thinned into a straight line, and she stared down at her clenched hands.

He couldn't blame her. "I guess you don't want to talk about your husband."

"And you don't want to talk about your wife," she replied.

"Ex-wife. She divorced me after I—did something I lived to regret."

He sucked in a breath and let it out in an uneven sigh.

"Oh, Cord," she breathed. "I am so sorry. I didn't mean to pry."

"Don't be sorry, Eleanor. I'm not."

In silence he drove up to the gate, climbed down to unlatch it, then guided the rattling wooden wagon up to the front porch. Molly popped up behind them. "Are we home?"

"Yes, we're home," Eleanor said. "Wake up Danny."

Cord lifted both sleepy children out of the wagon bed and carried them up the front steps. Then he returned and reached up for Eleanor. He half expected her to stiffen up and brush past him and climb down by herself, but she let him circle her waist with his hands and swing her down to the ground.

"I'll drive the wagon around in back of the barn, so I'll say good-night now. It's been an…interesting evening."

Again he glimpsed that half-amused expression on her pale face. "Good night, Cord. I'm making French toast for breakfast tomorrow, so don't be late."

French toast? What in blazes is that?

She herded the kids through the front door screen and he heard them clatter up the staircase. He waited, but he didn't hear the click of the lock on the front door. Was she crazy? Way out here with two kids and a revolver she didn't know how to fire and she didn't lock her front door at night?

He shook his head and climbed back onto the wagon bench. He'd argue it over with her tomorrow morning while eating her "French toast."

Somehow Eleanor guessed Cord wouldn't know what to make of French toast. It didn't seem like the kind of thing a man like Cordell Winterman would eat, and she was certain sure it would never have been served on trail drives in Kansas. If, she thought with a dart of unease, that's how he'd spent his time after the War. He'd never really said.

Molly and Danny waited patiently while she dipped the slices of day-old bread in the milk-and-egg mixture and plopped them onto the hot iron griddle. Before the first slice was ready to turn, she heard Cord tramp up the front steps.

But when he stepped into the kitchen she could tell something was wrong.

Chapter Eight

"Good morning," Eleanor said.

"Morning," Cord grumbled.

Well! That wasn't like Cord at all! Usually he grinned at Molly and ruffled Danny's shaggy hair.

"Morning, Cord," her children sang in unison. "Hurry up," Danny added. "We're about to starve."

He sat down heavily and tilted the chair back. "Eleanor?"

Her stomach turned over. He sounded angry about something, but what? She flipped the French toast slices onto a platter and set it down before him. "Yes, Cord? What is it?"

"Your front door," he said tersely.

Danny pounced on the platter, speared a slice with his fork and flopped it onto his plate.

"What about the front door?" she inquired as she laid three more slices onto the griddle.

"Ma, we got any syrup or honey?"

"What? Oh, yes. In the pantry, Danny. Why don't you fetch it? It's on the middle shelf." Maybe Cord would forget about the front door. She watched him stab his fork into a slice of nicely browned French toast.

Or maybe not.

"Your front door..." He paused to dribble the honey Danny had found over his plate.

"Yes? What about my front door?" Her appetite was fast fading. The expression on his face was… *Thunderous* was the only way she could use to describe it. Like clouds before a storm. A bad storm.

She couldn't stand this suspense one more minute. "Just what is wrong with my front door, Cord?" It came out sounding more strident than she'd intended, but it certainly got his attention. She sat down across from him, folded her hands on the table and waited.

"The door…" he said between bites of honey-slathered French toast "…should be…" He chewed and swallowed and cut another bite.

"Should be what?" she said, her voice tight.

He looked up from his plate with narrowed blue eyes. "Should be *locked* at night."

"Locked! Why, I've never locked the door in all my years on this farm! Nobody locks their door out here in Smoke River."

"Eleanor," he grated. "I'm asking you to lock the door at night."

"Why? Give me one good reason and maybe, *maybe*, I will consider it."

Cord sent her a hard look. "Molly and Daniel," he said. "That's two good reasons. And you. That's three reasons."

Eleanor stared at him like he had green cabbages for ears. "That's ridiculous," she shot out.

"No, it isn't," he shot right back. "We'll continue this discussion after the kids finish breakfast."

Danny straightened up in his chair. "But we gotta stay and do the dishes!"

"I'll do the damn dishes!" Cord shouted. Danny and Molly gaped at him, their eyes widening. Eleanor's eyes narrowed. He reached out his fork for another slice of French toast and found his hand was shaking. Yeah, he was het up about her front door, but maybe he was madder than he thought. Very rarely did he allow any anger he might feel to show on the outside. It was one of the hard lessons he'd learned in prison.

Maybe that was why he'd just drifted when he got out. He hadn't wanted to get involved with anything that made him feel anger or desperation or…anything much at all. There was safety in being numb.

"Very well," she said primly. She pointedly removed his empty coffee cup from the table.

He pushed back his chair, stood up and grabbed the speckleware coffeepot off the stove. Then he grabbed his cup out of her hand, sloshed it full and sat down again.

Eleanor's frown etched deep lines into her forehead. "Cord, what is *wrong* with you this morning?"

Cord caught Danny's eye. "Kids?" He tipped his head toward the back door. "Outside."

"C'mon, Molly. Let's go find the kittens."

"No! I wanna see what's gonna happen."

Danny blinked at his sister. "Molly," he whispered. "What do you think's gonna happen?"

"I think he's gonna spank Mama!"

Eleanor made an involuntary jerk, shooed both children out the back door and moved toward the sink. When the door slammed shut, she sat back down and stared at her folded hands, waiting until Cord looked at her.

"It's not the door, is it? It's something else."

He clamped his jaw shut. "Well," he said after a long minute, "it is and it isn't."

"All right," she said as patiently as she could manage. "What *is* and *isn't* it?"

Cord swallowed a double gulp of coffee and pushed the cup around and around in a circle on the table. "I think…"

He made an effort to keep his voice calm. *Stay rational. Don't let too much show.* "I don't care what people in Smoke River do. I think you should lock your front door at night."

She just stared at him, her eyes looking more like hard agates every second.

"And the back door," he added. "You've got no way of knowing who might come snooping around, Eleanor. You've lived a very protected life."

"This is something you learned at some point from people who weren't exactly honest."

"That's partly true. The rest I learned just living somewhere that's not a little town like Smoke River. This place is…well, it's like a little bit of heaven. Peaceful and quiet. Nothing much goes wrong here unless it's some mercantile store getting painted pink. Most places aren't like this."

She sat without moving for so long he thought maybe she hadn't heard him. Then she absentmindedly reached for his coffee cup and downed a big swallow. "All this upset is about locking my doors?" An unexpected little spurt of laughter escaped her. "The children think you're going to spank me!"

He chuckled at that. "Maybe I would if I thought I could catch you."

He rescued his cup from her fingers and stood up to pour some coffee for her. Before he set it down in front of her he reached for the brandy bottle she kept on the top shelf of the china cabinet and dolloped some of the liquor into her cup.

Monday morning Cord decided he needed to go into town for another pound of nails and some hinges, and he timed his trip so he'd be riding back when Danny would be walking home from school. He had an idea. He knew Eleanor wouldn't like it, but it was a good idea anyway.

Sure enough, half a mile after he left the mercantile he spied the boy trudging along the dusty road, his satchel slung over one drooping shoulder.

"Hold up, Danny." Cord reined up his bay mare and waited. The boy looked up and his dusty, heat-flushed face broke into a tired smile.

"Didn't know you was comin' to town today, Cord. You see that Miss Fanny lady at the mercantile?"

"Nope. Wasn't looking for Miss Fanny. Bought some nails and some sugar for your ma. Glad I ran into you, though."

"Oh, yeah? Why's that?"

Cord leaned down and spoke quietly. "Thought you might fancy a ride on Sally here."

Danny's eyes lit up. "Oh, boy, would I? You mean it?"

"I never say things I don't mean, son. Now just hold on a minute, all right?" Before the boy could say another word he slipped out of the saddle and was unbuckling the cinch.

"You ready to ride her?"

"Can't. Ma won't let me."

"Maybe your ma won't know about it."

Danny frowned up at him. "You're kidding, right?"

"Like I said, Dan, I never say things I don't mean." He lifted his saddle off and hefted it onto his shoulder.

"Golly, Cord, I don't know."

"Thought you wanted to learn to ride," Cord said.

"Oh, I sure do, but—"

"No buts."

Danny bit his lower lip in exactly the same way Eleanor bit hers. "How come you took the saddle off?"

"Because first you're gonna learn to ride bareback. The saddle comes later."

The boy dropped his book satchel in the dust and reached up to touch the mare's nose. "H'lo, Sally. Gosh, you're real handsome, and…" All at once he looked doubtful. "How am I gonna get up there without a stirrup?"

"Indian boys don't use saddles or stirrups. How do you think *they* do it?"

"They… I bet they stand on something so's they can reach."

Cord shifted the saddle so he could make a foothold with his hands. "Step here," he ordered. "Now, grab some of the mane and haul yourself up." He watched the boy hold tight to a fistful of mane and clamber onto Sally's broad back.

When he was sitting upright, he sent Cord a triumphant smile. "What do I do now?"

"Squeeze your knees right around her belly and let go of her mane. Then pick up the reins. You won't fall off if you keep your knees tight."

"O-okay. My knees are squeezin' like anything and I'm gonna let go of all this hair." He lifted one hand a scant inch from Sally's thick mane, then gingerly freed the other and grabbed the leather lines.

"Now," Cord said, "give her a little nudge with your heel."

"Can't," Danny announced.

"Why not?"

"I'm scared she'll move!"

Cord chuckled. "That's what you want her to do, Dan. Try it."

The horse moved ahead a single step and Danny yelped. "Hell, Cord, she's moving!"

"Watch your mouth, son. There are some things I *will* tell your ma about."

"S-sorry." He patted the mare's neck. "Sorry, Sally."

Cord bit back a grin, turned away and headed down the road. "You know how to make her go," he called over his shoulder. "If you want her to stop just pull back on the reins and say 'whoa.'"

"Hell— Golly, Cord, I don't know…"

But after a moment Cord heard the unmistakable *clop-clop* of Sally's hooves on the road behind him. He dropped back to walk alongside the mounted boy and tried to remember how he'd felt the first time he'd ever felt a horse move under him. Scared. Proud. All "growed-up," as Danny put it.

Well before they reached the turnoff to the farm, Cord raised his hand and the boy brought the mare to a halt and slipped off. "You gonna mount up like you just rode in from town?"

"Nope." He grasped the reins and walked alongside

Danny until they reached the farm. He motioned the boy to open the gate and walked the horse through.

"Won't Ma think it's strange, you walkin' and carryin' your saddle like that?"

"Probably. But your ma thinks a lot of the things I do are strange, like wanting her to lock the doors at night."

Danny chortled. "And baking pies."

They both laughed all the way into the barn.

Chapter Nine

The sound of insistent hammering stopped conversation on the porch, for which Eleanor was extremely grateful. Red Wilkins looked up from the glass of lemonade she had just poured. "Whazzat?"

She always made sure Red had a full glass; he talked less when he was guzzling his lemonade. "My hired man is repairing the barn roof."

Silas Maginnis nudged his spectacles down and peered over the thick lenses at the barn. "Hope he knows what he's doing, Miss Eleanor. Can't be too careful about hired help these days."

She gritted her teeth. "More lemonade, Silas?" Silently she prayed the hammering would resume and the conversation with her two unwanted callers would stop. She could hardly wait.

"He's workin' on the Sabbath, too," Red observed. Mighty un-Christian-like."

Silas nodded his shiny bald head. "Mighty unhelpful, too, makin' all that clatter while we're out here on your porch tryin' to be sociable."

At that, Eleanor almost laughed aloud. *Please*, she silently begged Cord. *Make some more clatter. Lots more.*

She settled back into the porch swing and pushed it into motion with her foot. She hated being sociable.

For the hundredth time this spring she wondered why Silas and Red and the half dozen other young men from town bothered to bring her supplies or her mail or the town gossip or come calling, since for all they knew she was a married woman. Since she had never received word of Tom's death, in many ways she considered that she was *still* married, even though Judge Silver in town said that technically she wasn't.

She had never given even one hint of encouragement to the stream of male visitors from town, and she often wondered why they didn't give up and stop coming. They couldn't possibly be interested in her. Or maybe, she thought with sudden misgiving, it was not her they were interested in, but her farm?

She checked the lemonade level in their glasses and tried to close her ears to the debate about whether goats were easier to raise than sheep. Reciting the multiplication table would be more interesting than this conversation!

Her gaze drifted up to the barn roof, where Cord was pounding nails into a long piece of wood. It was hot this afternoon, the sun relentless and the breeze absent. Bees hummed in the lilac bush, and somewhere a mockingbird trilled and twittered an ever-changing song.

Eleanor is bored, it seemed to sing. *Bored, bored, bored!*

From his vantage point on the barn roof Cord had a bird's-eye view of the activity on the front porch. He flipped the new board over and paused to study the two visitors Eleanor was entertaining. Town types. Pressed creases in their trousers, boots polished to a shine, shirts starched so stiff they could stand up by themselves. The fellow with the spectacles had brought the mail out from town; the other gent had brought a tin of fancy chocolates, which he was devouring along with his lemonade.

Molly had fled to the barn to play with the kittens. Danny

had groomed Cord's bay mare and was now lounging around the yard playing marbles with himself. Cord positioned another two-by-six to replace a rotted plank and set a nail in place. He had just raised his hammer when Eleanor's suddenly upturned face made him check his motion.

She picked up the lemonade pitcher, pointed her forefinger at it and raised her eyebrows at him. Did he want some lemonade?

Sure he did. But she was down there on the porch and he was up here on the roof, so he shook his head. A look of resignation crossed her face, and she turned her attention back to her visitors.

He had to laugh. It was plain she wasn't enjoying this social call, but he had to wonder why the men lounging on her porch didn't take the hint.

In the next minute he figured it out. They wanted something. Cold lemonade on a hot day? Female attention? The goodwill earned by bringing offerings of mail or chocolates or spools of thread from town?

His hammer slowed. Or maybe they wanted *her*?

He drove the waiting nail home in a single blow. When he positioned the next one, he purposely shifted his body around so his back was facing the front porch and he couldn't see her. But he could still hear the continuous drone of the two male voices. Made him clench his jaw.

Eleanor didn't seem to be saying much, and that was kinda odd. Wasn't an afternoon social call an occasion for give-and-take conversation? As far as he could tell, this afternoon was all "take" by the two gents but no "give" from Eleanor.

He stopped pounding in nails and strained his ears to hear her voice. Nothing. Either he was going deaf or she wasn't saying anything. What, exactly, was going on down there?

It's none of your business, Winterman.

True. But that didn't mean he wasn't *interested*. He

thought that over for a full minute, then corralled his thoughts and addressed himself once more to the barn roof.

By the time he finished the repairs and climbed down the ladder, the two gentlemen visitors were gone. Eleanor had disappeared into the house and Molly and Daniel were squatting in the front yard playing marbles.

Cord spent the rest of the afternoon mucking out the horse stalls and oiling the cracked leather saddle he'd found in the barn. If Danny was going to ride the three miles to school instead of walking in all kinds of weather, he'd eventually need a saddle of his own and some instruction on how to take care of it.

That night at supper an oddly quiet Danny ate his beans and corn bread in silence, and when it came time to wash up the dishes he stomped over to the sink and carelessly dropped all four plates into the dishpan at once. Soapy water splashed out onto the wooden counter.

Eleanor jerked upright and spilled half her coffee. "Daniel! Whatever is the matter with you tonight?"

Danny said nothing, but his rigid back told Cord something was definitely wrong. He rose, snagged the dish towel out of Molly's grasp and mopped up the spilled coffee. Then he used the same towel to mop up the dishwater on the counter. As he did so, he leaned in close to the boy.

"Something on your mind, son?"

Danny lifted his chin but said nothing.

"Okay, have it your way," he intoned. "Just thought you might like to have a man-to-man chat."

At the words *man-to-man*, the boy's stiff shoulders drooped. "I don't like that guy."

"Who?"

"The one with the glasses. He's always bragging about…" He closed his lips tight and shook his head.

"About what?" Cord pressed.

After a long silence, Danny twisted his neck and shot a

glance at his mother. "About Ma," he murmured. "About how he's gonna marry her and…"

Eleanor sent him an inquiring look from where she sat at the table, and Cord picked up the coffeepot from the stove and refilled her cup. "Your boy's got a thistle up his— Uh, got something bothering him," he said quietly.

"Shouldn't he be confiding in his mother?" she whispered. She started to rise from her chair, but Cord laid a hand on her shoulder.

"Not this time. It's, um, man talk."

"Oh." She studied Danny's back for a minute and then shrugged. "I suspect I wouldn't be much help with 'man talk.'" She took her coffee into the parlor and settled on the settee. She could still see into the kitchen, but she couldn't hear what was said.

Cord dug a clean dish towel out of the linen drawer and ambled back to the sink. "Okay, the one with the glasses says he's gonna marry your ma and…what?" he reminded Danny. "Marry her and what?"

"Be my pa."

"Nope. He won't do that. First of all, nothing any man does will ever make him your pa. And secondly, he'll never marry your mother."

Danny eyed him with doubt written all over his face. "How come?"

"She doesn't like him."

The boy's eyes widened. "Huh? How do you know that? She feeds him cookies an' lemonade every Sunday afternoon."

"Cookies and lemonade don't mean diddly, son. That's just a woman's way of being polite."

"If she doesn't like him, how come she has to be polite?"

Cord rolled his eyes. "Darned if I know. Sometimes there's no comprehending why a woman does what she does."

A relieved-looking Danny turned toward him. "Yeah?"

"Yeah. Look at it from her point of view, Dan. Let's say she gets all frosty and the gent with the glasses doesn't come around again. There's gonna be five more guys lined up right behind him, wanting cookies and lemonade and female attention, so then she gets rid of another one."

"Good riddance," the boy muttered.

"You're missing the point, son. Your ma's real pretty. There's always gonna be some man mooning around her, drinking up her lemonade and taking up her time."

"*You* don't moon, Cord."

"No," he said carefully, "I don't." Mooning wasn't exactly what he was doing around Eleanor, but he guessed it might come close. He liked Eleanor Malloy. He didn't *want* to like her, but he sure as hell did.

Daniel listlessly pushed the dishrag over a dirty plate. "Don't you like Ma?"

Cord almost laughed out loud. *Like her?* Eleanor Malloy was getting stuck so deep in his thoughts he couldn't sleep nights.

"Sure, I like her. But a man doesn't have to 'moon,' as you put it, over a woman to show his…uh…regard."

"You think Ma likes any of those guys that come around here?"

Cord swished the clean plate through the rinse water, automatically dried it off and set it on the counter. "I don't know, Dan. A woman is real good at keeping her feelings to herself. But if you watch close, you might be able to figure it out."

"Gosh, thanks, Cord. And," he added, eyeing the growing stack of plates Cord had run his dish towel over, "thanks for drying the supper dishes. Molly ran off to the barn to feed the kittens 'stead of helping me."

At that moment Eleanor appeared in the kitchen, the empty coffee cup and saucer in her hand. "What about the kittens?" She plunked the cup into the dishwater.

"Molly's feedin' them," Danny said quickly. "Again. Pretty soon they're gonna be bigger than Mama Cat."

"No, they won't," Eleanor said. "Mama Cat's pretty small."

"What about the papa cat?" Danny pursued.

Eleanor frowned. "What about him?"

"Well, he's real big."

"How do you know that? How do you know who the father cat is?"

"Aw, I heard that old tomcat Isaiah used to feed yowlin' real loud one night, and I figured…well, that's how they do it, isn't it? The papa cat makes a bunch of noise, and after that…"

Eleanor turned scarlet. Cord wanted to laugh so bad his jaw ached. "Yeah," he said, his voice tight, "that's how they do it, all right. But it takes more than—"

"Cord!" Eleanor sent him a look that could freeze ice cream and pressed her lips together.

"Yeah?" Danny said with sudden interest. "They yowl real loud and then what?"

"Cord…" Eleanor said in a warning tone. She busied herself stacking the clean plates on the china cabinet shelf.

Cord cleared his throat. He thought about escaping into the pantry or out the back door, but that would be a coward's way out. "Well," he said after thinking a moment, "Mama Cat and Papa Cat…uh…kinda lie down together and…" He cleared his throat again.

"Yeah? Then what?"

"Daniel!" Eleanor interjected. "It's time for bed."

"What? No, it ain't, Ma. It's still light outside."

Cord busied himself hanging the damp dish towel on the hook near the stove. He couldn't see avoiding the boy's question. Danny had a normal boy's curiosity and a right to ask about such things. He touched his shoulder.

"Mama Cat," he said quietly, "and Papa Cat touch each other in a special way."

"Gee," the boy breathed. "That's nice. That's real nice. I'm real glad you told me about it, Cord."

Eleanor's face was a study, part embarrassment, part relief and part…he hadn't the faintest idea what.

Whistling, Danny folded the dishrag, laid it on the counter and wrestled the dishpan out of the sink. "You want the dishwater poured on your roses, Ma?"

At her nod, he tramped out the kitchen door and Cord heard his boots clomp down the back steps. After a moment there was a splashing sound.

A silence thicker than valley fog descended over the kitchen. Cord racked his brain for what to say and finally decided to change the subject. "What kind of roses do you have, Eleanor?"

"Pink ones," she said tightly. "Cecile Brunner."

"Pretty," he said. He lifted his hat off the hook by the back door. "'Night, Eleanor. Sleep well."

"Surely you're not leaving! Why, it's still light out!"

He couldn't help grinning at her. "I've dried all the supper dishes so there's nothing left for me to do tonight. Unless," he added with a chuckle, "you want to talk about Mama and Papa Cat?"

She turned an enticing shade of raspberry and he found himself staring at her lips. A wave of heat flooded his groin.

Oh, no, Winterman. No! Not interested.

Well, heck yes, he was interested. He just wasn't going to do anything about it. He'd had enough Mama Cat, Papa Cat experience in the past to know that he didn't want to follow where thinking about a woman's lips might lead. *Never again.*

He tore his gaze away from Eleanor's mouth and moved toward the back door. "Think I'll, uh, check on Molly and the kittens out in the barn."

Chapter Ten

Eleanor flopped over on the double bed and tried to keep her eyelids from popping back open again. Cordell Winterman had to be the most puzzling, annoying, know-it-all man she'd ever had the misfortune to meet. Not only could he bake apple pies that tasted better than hers, he could talk to her son about the facts of life—at least some of them. He could fix gates and fences and chicken houses and...whatever needed fixing.

He'd even worked the squeak out of the porch swing and oiled the hinges on her oven door so it opened more easily.

She turned over again. Nothing was more annoying than being mad about something when she couldn't say what it was, exactly. But it concerned her hired man, that much she knew. All six-foot-something of him, with those incredibly clear blue eyes that laughed at her and winked at her children when he thought she wasn't looking. Maddening man! His piecrust was flakier than hers and...and...well, he was just maddening.

Daniel worshipped him, which made her grit her teeth. She supposed a boy needed a man in his life, someone to look up to. Molly followed Cord around like one of the kittens, firing endless questions at him and giggling at his wacky answers.

Why do cats have four legs when chickens only have two? Molly wanted to know.

Cord had answered, *Because cats can't fly and they need four legs to escape their enemies.*

Hah! Eleanor snorted. Chickens couldn't fly, either. But Molly had just grinned and nodded and asked another question.

What does Bessie the cow dream about at night?

Cows have cow dreams, Cord had told her. *They dream about green grass and shady trees to lie under, and soft hands squeezing their teats for milk.*

Cow dreams! What utter nonsense. And then he'd shown her daughter how to squeeze Bessie's udder to squirt milk out for the kittens, and Eleanor'd had to smile. Perhaps someday milking would be a pleasure for Molly instead of the twice-daily drudgery it was for her and every other farm wife in Oregon. Even when she'd been woozy with fatigue, she still had to milk that darn cow!

She rolled over onto her other side and suddenly heard a noise in the yard. Quietly she slipped out of bed and tiptoed to the window. Was that a shadow moving behind the maple tree? The skin prickled up and down her arms.

Very quietly she raised the sash and leaned out. The shadow moved again, slow and low to the ground. With a shudder, she glided to her bedroom door and down the stairs to the front door and carefully lifted the loaded revolver from its leather holster. She rested her finger over the trigger and waited, peering into the darkened yard and holding her breath.

The gunshot brought Cord upright in an instant. What the—? He grabbed his Colt and was down the ladder and out the barn door before the horses even stirred.

Good God, would you look at that? A figure swathed in something white was sitting on the porch swing, clutching a revolver none too steadily in both hands. He ducked behind the open barn door just in case she turned it on him.

"Eleanor?" he called cautiously. "What happened?"

"I—I don't know, exactly."

He stepped into the moonlit yard. "What *do* you know, exactly?"

"I heard a noise, so I came downstairs and shot it."

He chuckled. "No, you didn't."

"I most certainly did. You just look behind that tree."

Instead, he tramped over to the porch. "Not with you sitting there with a loaded revolver. Put the gun down on the porch."

"What if it's still there, behind the tree?"

"I'm armed, Eleanor. Put the gun down. I don't want you shooting me while I'm looking for your noise."

She leaned forward and plunked the revolver at her feet, then watched him walk silently toward the maple tree. Good heavens, the man was half-naked, wearing only his jeans and no shirt! In the moonlight his bare back looked smooth and well-muscled. His longish dark hair was mussed, and, she noted, he was barefoot. She flinched. Her feet were bare, too.

He moved quietly to the tree, looked behind it and then disappeared into the dark. After a long minute he stepped out from behind the companion maple tree, a few yards to the right.

"Nothing here but tracks," he called.

"What kind of tracks? A man's?"

"Nah. Some kind of animal, a raccoon, maybe. Or a skunk."

"Skunk!"

"Could be after your chickens. Tomorrow I'll check the henhouse. After—" he came up the porch steps toward her "—we have a shooting lesson."

"I don't need a shooting lesson. I already know how to fire a revolver."

"Anyone can *fire* a revolver, Eleanor. It's hitting your target that's important."

"Pooh! I can hit—"

"No, you can't. Otherwise, there'd be a dead raccoon in the yard. We'll have a lesson tomorrow morning after breakfast, all right?"

"No, it is *not* all right. First you want Daniel to learn to ride the horse. Then you tell him how cats mate, and now you want to teach me how to shoot my own gun. No, no, *no*!"

He said nothing, just calmly began removing bullets from his weapon and slipping them into his jeans pocket. Then he stuffed the Colt in his waistband, unloaded her revolver and settled on the porch swing beside her. "After breakfast," he repeated, his voice quiet.

"I said no, Cord. Tomorrow is my wash day. I will be busy after breakfast."

"Wash day, huh?"

"Yes. I always do the laundry on Mondays, so tomorrow I will have no time to spare for a shooting lesson."

All at once she realized she was sitting here in the dark clad in her nightgown with a half-naked man. What on earth was she thinking?

The truth was she was *not* thinking.

"How about I help you do the wash tomorrow?" he said.

"That's ridiculous! I've never heard of a man who could do laundry."

He gave her a sharp look. "So? You think a man *can't* do laundry?"

"I most certainly do."

"Wanna make a bet?"

Eleanor stared at him. She wished he wasn't sitting so close to her. She could hear him breathing. She could even smell him; he smelled like sweat and horses and…mint? It was not altogether unpleasant, just…unsettling.

What was he saying? Oh, yes, a bet. Very well, she would

make a bet with him, and when she won she would never let him forget it.

"All right, Mr. Smarty-Pants, I will bet that you don't know the first thing about doing laundry. I bet you don't know a washtub from a butter churn."

He laughed. "Eleanor, you'd make a really lousy poker player."

She stiffened. "And just why is that, may I ask? As if I would ever lower myself to playing poker."

He laughed again and she clenched her fists.

"You make bets before you calculate the odds," he said. "Now, I admit that the odds in this case are that I don't know a thing about washtubs. But you might be surprised, right?"

"I might be," she retorted. "But I am betting that I won't be."

"Okay, what'll we bet? Not money, because I don't have any."

"Um… I'll bet you an apple pie."

"Nope. It's gotta be something I really want."

"You wouldn't want an apple pie?"

"Not particularly. I can get an apple pie anytime I want just by making one." He gave her a thoughtful look. "How about this. If you win, you can name your prize. If I win…"

A squad of butterflies zoomed into his belly.

"…I want what all those men buzzing around you are hankering for."

"Oh? And what is that?"

"A kiss."

Cord watched her face as his challenge registered. First she blinked and her eyes went real wide. Then her fingers fluttered around on her lap, and finally her tongue darted out and she bit her lip. He wished she hadn't done that.

He forced his gaze away from her mouth. "Well? Do we have a bet?"

Her fingers flew around her lap some more. "Oh, all right, we have a bet. Now, I really must go inside."

She stood up and the swing jolted. Oh, God, her night-dress didn't cover her tiny little bare toes. He caught his breath.

Not only that, but with the moonlight behind her, her gown was transparent. She was so beautiful his mouth went dry.

She spun away toward the front door. "Good night, Cord," she said, her voice icy. She disappeared through the screen door.

"Eleanor," he called after her with a laugh. "Don't forget your revolver." He picked it up from the floor and moved toward the door, but before he could step inside a feminine hand emerged and snatched the weapon.

He chuckled all the way back to the loft, where he found Mama Cat and her kittens curled up in the warm spot he'd left. He tried hard to get back to sleep, but he couldn't stop thinking about the sight of her almost naked body under that sheer nightgown. Even more, he couldn't stop thinking about winning that kiss from her.

"After breakfast this morning, I am doing the wash," Eleanor announced the following morning.

"You do the wash every Monday," Danny said. "How come you're telling us like it's something new?"

"And Cord will be helping me," she added.

"Really?" The boy's voice rose. "Oh, boy, can I watch?"

"You have school today, Daniel."

"Aw, Ma, let me stay home, please?"

"Absolutely not. Education is important."

Molly grinned at her crestfallen brother. "I'll watch, Danny. And I'll tell you all about it when you get home from school."

Eleanor glared at both her children. Cord walked out onto the back porch and lifted the big tin washtub off the hook, then pumped a bucket of water and strode back into the kitchen to set it on the stove.

A glum Danny dragged himself off to school with his book satchel over his shoulder, and Molly danced excitedly around the kitchen while the water pail heated up. Eleanor went up to strip the sheets off the beds and gather up the children's dirty clothes.

When she started downstairs, Cord met her halfway and lifted the wicker laundry basket out of her arms. She waited to see what he would do next.

To her surprise, he piled the sheets and all the underwear—hers, the children's, and even his own drawers—in the washtub. "Got any sal soda?"

She shook her head. With a shrug he dumped two buckets of cold water into the tub, shaved in some soap and walked away.

"Huh," she scoffed. "You don't wash clothes in cold water."

"Huh yourself," he said calmly. "I let 'em soak while the water heats up."

Well! Her hired man was telling *her* how to do her own wash? She'd just see about that!

When the first bucket of water came to a boil she lifted it off the stove and staggered toward the back door. Cord intercepted her and reached to take it out of her hand.

"I do not need your help!" she said sharply. He stepped back with both hands raised, and she lugged the bucket over and dumped it into the washtub, then refilled it at the pump.

"Eleanor, that's too heavy for you."

"Leave me alone, Cord. I have been lifting buckets like this every Monday for the last nine years."

He grabbed the pail from her hand anyway and strode into the house, and Eleanor took the opportunity to sink onto the back porch step and catch her breath. She stayed there, breathing heavily, until he dumped the second bucket of boiling water into the tub.

"Filling up the tub isn't 'doing laundry,'" she called.

"I'm not done yet."

She settled back to watch him. She knew the washboard hung on the back porch hook, but she made no move to tell him where it was. And he didn't ask. Ha! He knew *nothing* about doing laundry.

He shaved more soap into the tub and swirled the clothes around in the hot water. "Got a plunger?" he called.

A plunger? She had no idea what he meant. She waited until she knew the water was beginning to cool, brought out the washboard and propped it in the tub. Then she started scrubbing the small undergarments up and down across the metal ridges. It was hard work, and she had to take frequent rests. Just as she reached for a pair of her laciest drawers, Cord knelt beside her and pushed her hands away.

"You're tired," he said.

"I am *not* tired. I do laundry every single week."

He bent over the washboard and started scrubbing. "Maybe that's why you're not getting well, Eleanor. You work too hard."

"I do *not* work too hard!" She had to stop for breath. "I...am...not the least bit...tired." She reached to snatch her drawers away from him, but he batted her hand away.

"On second thought," he said, "you'd make a pretty good poker player. You're getting to be an expert at lying."

She plunged her hand into the tub and scooped hot soapy water out onto his shirt. "Hey," he yelped. "Cut that out!"

"I couldn't resist," she admitted.

He grinned and splashed a double handful of suds down the front of her skirt. She gasped and her mouth stayed open to shout at him. "You cheater!"

"Truce!" he said with a laugh. "We're even."

Molly was giggling from the back steps.

Cord propped both fists at his waist. "You have to admit I know my way around a washtub," he announced. "Don't I, Molly?"

"Yeah!" the girl yelled.

Eleanor made a face. "Well, maybe."

"Maybe, nothing. I've won the bet."

She took a deep breath. "Maybe," she said again.

"After supper," he said quietly. "Right now, my hands are all wet."

Chapter Eleven

Cord tossed Eleanor's lacy drawers back into the soapy wash water and to her intense relief began scrubbing one of Danny's shirts. Eleanor busied herself uncoiling the clothesline from the corner of the back porch and attaching it to the ash tree near the chicken house.

When she had pegged the last of the clean laundry to the line, she retreated to the kitchen, and Cord went off to the henhouse to see how raccoon-proof it was. Big holes gaped in the chicken wire, large enough for any animal smaller than a coyote to squeeze its way in.

He hitched up the wagon and drove into town for lumber and more chicken wire. On the way back he picked up Danny, walking home from school at foot-dragging pace. The first thing out of the boy's mouth was a question. "Did you prove you could do the wash, Cord?"

"Sure did. Your ma's madder than a wet hen about it."

"Women always wanna be right about everything, huh? I guess they're partic'lar about a lot of things like washin' clothes. It makes no sense."

"It makes sense to *them*, Dan, something we men ought to keep in mind. Women take pride in their work, just like we do."

When they rattled into the yard, Eleanor was gathering

in the dry clothes and Molly was folding them none too neatly into the wicker basket and chattering away as usual. Cord unloaded the wagon, then noticed Danny and Molly were holding a whispered conference on the back porch. He caught the words "wet hen" from Danny and heard delighted giggles from Molly.

Eleanor had made chicken stew for their supper that evening. When she served it up, along with a pan of biscuits and fresh-churned butter, she seemed unusually short-tempered and out of breath.

They ate in uneasy silence. After his second cup of coffee, Cord pushed back from the table and stood up. "I'm gonna repair the holes in the chicken house. Danny, you want to help me?"

"And me, too," Molly sang.

Eleanor's face looked pasty. "Let's wash up the dishes first," Cord suggested.

"*I* will wash the dishes," Eleanor announced, her tone crisp. "I am not helpless, just a little tired."

Danny caught Cord's gaze and raised his eyebrows. *What's going on with Ma?* Cord tipped his head toward the brimming laundry basket in the corner, and the boy nodded. When he started for the back door, both children scooted out ahead of him. Before he could follow them, Eleanor gathered up the plates and stomped over to the sink.

"I suppose you can *iron* as well as do laundry?" she shot at him.

"You want me to answer that?"

"Yes. No! I suppose you want to make a bet about that, too?"

He chuckled. "I've never been within a yard of a sad-iron," he responded. "I wear my shirts wrinkled."

A glimmer of a smile touched her mouth. Before he reached the back door, she swooped over and brushed her lips against his cheek. "There. Now you've been paid!"

"Oh, no," he said. "Not by a long shot."

"But I just kissed you! Now we're even."

"No," he said again. "We're not. A bet is a bet. I want a real kiss."

"But…"

"And," he continued, "I get to say when."

He didn't think her eyes could get any bigger or look more steely. She opened her mouth, then shut it, then opened it again. "Now just one min—"

"I won that bet fair and square, Eleanor, and I've been thinking about that kiss all day. You'll just have to wait to pay up because I have to admit that I damn well like thinking about it."

She hurled the biscuit pan at him. He managed to escape out the back door, but he heard it bounce off the wood and clatter to the floor.

"What was that noise?" Molly and Danny said in unison.

"Just your mama letting off a bit of steam. Come on, kids, let's go fix up the henhouse."

Eleanor sank onto the kitchen chair and gulped down the last of her cold coffee. Why, *why* did Cord make her so mad? For just an instant she considered adding a splash of whiskey to her cup, then thought better of it. She had bread dough to mix and set to rise. And Doc Dougherty had ordered her to take a nap every afternoon, so after she finished the dishes she guessed she should follow his advice.

She was most definitely feeling uneasy. Maybe it was because she was extra-tired from being on her feet all day. Or maybe it was thinking about Cord kissing her.

The last kiss she could remember was the morning seven years ago when Tom had gone off to war, and that was just one of his hasty pecks. Tom had never been demonstrative that way. Sometimes she wondered why she had married him. True, he had rescued her from her parents' miserable household, where her preacher father lectured her every day at the top of his voice about sin and the devil and her schoolteacher mother constantly criticized her lack of refined manners and social graces.

As a girl, Eleanor had preferred fishing and swimming and playing kickball with the neighboring children. But because her playmates had been immigrants from Poland, her mother had loudly disapproved.

When Tom proposed, she knew she would never again have to spend Sundays on her knees in prayer or serving tea to dour, starched Portland ladies who were prejudiced against almost everyone. She couldn't wait to leave Portland and come to Smoke River and the farm, where Tom planned to grow apples.

But as the years passed, she'd grown increasingly unhappy. Tom had struck her just once, but once had been enough. After that she'd taken care never to annoy or displease him, and it had been just like living with her critical, disapproving mother and her rigid, unsmiling father. Later, when Danny was born, she'd resolved she would never raise her own children without the love and understanding she had missed when she was young.

Tom had always been more interested in the farm than in her, and she had to admit she had only the most elementary understanding of what was between a man and a woman. After he left for the War, all the responsibility of running the farm had terrified her at first, but as the years passed she grew increasingly confident. She was capable and hardworking, and she liked being independent. Her mother had always lectured her about a woman's place, but Eleanor had observed such subservience in her mother's marriage that deep down she knew it wasn't fair. It wasn't loving. It wasn't even kind.

A woman on her own could certainly prosper, even on an apple farm with two young children. Her long bout with pneumonia this spring hadn't dimmed her zeal, though it had certainly decimated her stamina. She simply had to get her strength back because this year's apple harvest promised to be ever better than last year's, and she needed the money. She would be ready. She would be able to handle that or anything else that came up.

But now Cord wanted to kiss her! The mere thought sent butterflies careening around in her stomach. It would be over in two seconds, but that thought didn't help much. Still, she reasoned, after the dreaded two seconds, things on the farm would go on as they had before. A kiss was a small thing, really.

She wondered why she couldn't stop thinking about it.

Chapter Twelve

Cord knew it was Sunday because once again the front porch was crowded with young men, all pressed and shiny, guzzling lemonade and gobbling up Eleanor's molasses cookies. Molly was in the barn, trying to stuff a kitten into one of her doll dresses; Danny skulked near the honeysuckle-covered trellis, spying on his mother's visitors.

Eleanor reclined as usual in the porch swing, her legs tucked up under her blue gingham skirt, rocking listlessly back and forth and saying nothing.

Cord jammed his boot down onto the shovel for the fortieth time in the last half hour, spading up the ground behind the two maple trees in the front yard where Eleanor wanted a flower bed. As he worked he kept half his attention focused on the porch. He wasn't exactly sure why, since Danny's sharp ears would hear anything troubling, but he kept his eyes on the porch.

Today there were three gents perched on the front steps below where Eleanor sat rocking in the swing. Two of them must be brothers, since they were dressed almost alike, one in a green-striped shirt and one in red stripes, buttoned tight at the wrist even though the afternoon was scorching. The third male was the red-haired blusterer from last Sunday.

Cord liked seeing two or three men on the porch with

Eleanor. Just one man might sweet-talk his way onto the swing next to her and then slip an arm around her and… who knew what. He figured there was safety in numbers.

Sometimes young Sammy Greywolf drove his mother, Rosie, out from town with a basket of tomatoes or some flower seeds, and occasionally old Mrs. Hinckley and her sister paid a short call. But usually the Sunday-afternoon visitors were male.

Masculine laughter drifted from the porch and he clenched his jaw. Why did those men keep coming out here? As far as he could tell, Eleanor gave them no encouragement, and besides, she was a married woman. Today they'd brought no mail and no bags of dried beans or coffee from the mercantile had been unloaded. It was plain they'd come out to the farm only to see Eleanor.

He turned over another shovelful of rich dark earth, chopped up the clods and tried to keep his mind on Eleanor's garden plot instead of her pale cheeks and gray eyes.

Molly appeared, clutching a wriggling kitten dressed in a bright pink doll dress. "Whatcha doing, Cord?"

"Digging a garden for your mama."

"How come those other men aren't helping?"

Cord rested one hand on the spade handle and looked down at the girl. "I'd guess they don't want to get dirt on their fancy duds."

"You don't got dirt on you," Molly pointed out.

"My duds aren't fancy, honey. My duds are just plain old duds."

"How come?"

"Because I'm working, not visiting with your mama."

"Do you ever wear fancy duds?"

He chuckled. "Not often, no. Last time I wore anything fancy was the day I got marr—" He bit off the rest.

Molly patted the kitten's pink dress. "Do you think Roscoe's dress is fancy duds?"

"Roscoe! Is that your kitty's name? Seems kinda funny to put a pink dress on a boy cat, doesn't it?"

She turned wide blue eyes up to his. "I din't know how to tell if it was a boy cat or a girl cat, so I decided Roscoe was a boy."

Cord chuckled and poised his boot over the spade again, but her next question stopped him cold.

"Cord, how do you tell a boy cat from a girl cat?"

He worked hard to keep from laughing out loud. He sure wasn't going to get into another explanation about sex with one of Eleanor's kids. "You ask your mama to show you, all right?"

Before he could stop her, she was racing for the porch, the kitten clutched in her arms. "Mama! Mama!"

He stomped down hard on the shovel. After a minute he heard guffaws of laughter coming from the front porch, and he risked a peek. Eleanor was cradling both Molly and the kitten on her lap. Her face was a study, her cheeks bright red and her mouth pressed into a line straight as a fence post. The men at her feet were slapping their knees and laughing.

All at once he wanted to toss a shovelful of dirt all over their shiny Sunday shoes.

Eleanor set Molly on her feet and watched her scamper away to the barn. Roscoe. Well, why not? It was easier to misname the kitten than explain why "Roscette" would be more appropriate. She gazed down on the Mankewicz brothers, and suddenly she wanted to be anywhere but sitting on her porch swing discussing the price of winter wheat with two—no, three—of the dullest men in the county. She wanted to be in her kitchen rolling out piecrust, or at the dressmaker's in town, selecting calico for a new dress for Molly, or…working alongside Cord spading up the soil for her new flower bed.

Well, why not? She brought the swing to an abrupt halt.

"Gentlemen," she announced, "I am afraid I must draw your visit to a close. There is something I must attend to."

The men goggled at her, then rose, stammered polite goodbyes and edged off the porch to the buggy hitched outside the front gate. The minute they were out of sight, she raced up the stairs to her bedroom, threw on her blue denim work skirt and an old chambray shirt of Tom's and jammed her worn work boots on her feet.

Cord looked up when she walked out past the maple tree. "What happened to your gentlemen callers?"

"Urgent business," she said blandly. She needn't tell him it was *her* business that was urgent.

"All three of 'em gone?"

She didn't answer. He glanced down at her partially spaded garden plot. "I'm only half done, Eleanor. It's too soon to plant anything."

"There's another shovel somewhere in the barn, isn't there?"

"Yeah, I think so. What do you want a shovel for?" he asked suspiciously.

"So I can spade up some dirt," she said pointedly.

"What for?" he repeated.

"Oh, for heaven's sake, Cord. So I can plant the flower seeds Rosie Greywolf gave me before I have to start supper."

He leveled a long, penetrating look at her. "Shovel's in the barn. Might be you left your good sense in the house."

She found a small-size spade with the other tools hanging from sturdy hooks on one wall. Funny, she didn't remember hanging up any tools. She'd always just leaned the hoes and rakes and shovels in one dusty corner.

When she returned, Cord studied the spade in her hand, gave her a look of disbelief and exasperation, and bent over his shovel. He had outlined the plot with wooden stakes and string; she decided she would start digging at the opposite end from where he was working.

Her first shovel stroke clanked into a rock. She repositioned it and drove it into the earth again. Another rock. She tried to dig around it, but the spade kept hitting nothing but a big stone of some kind. Cord stopped digging, walked over and lifted the spade out of her hands. "Whatever it is, it's bigger than a rock." He made short, shallow strokes in widening circles until the cuts outlined an oblong shape, and then he started to dig in earnest. At last he stopped, one foot resting on his shovel.

"It's a marker of some sort," he said.

"What kind of marker?"

"I think it's a gravestone."

She dropped her spade and clapped her hand over her mouth.

"You want me to uncover it?"

She nodded. Ten minutes later he smoothed the dirt off a slab of stone with some faint words chiseled on it.

"'Amanda Martin,'" he read aloud. "'Eighteen thirty-three to eighteen thirty-six.'"

"Oh!" Tears flooded into Eleanor's eyes. "Oh, she was only three years old!" She turned away and clutched her belly. She heard Cord's shovel hit the ground and then his arms were around her.

"I... Oh, the p-poor little th-thing." His hand moved to the back of her head, pressing her face into his shoulder, but her tears kept coming. She couldn't seem to stop them, even though she was wetting his shirt.

"Do—do you think there are more graves here?"

"Don't know. I'll have to dig around some to find out." His voice sounded rumbly inside his chest and so somber it started her crying all over again.

"I'm s-sorry, Cord. It's so sad, only three y-years old. I wonder why—"

"Might be best not to ask, Eleanor. Knowing how she died won't make it any easier."

She lifted her head and swiped tears off her cheeks. "D-don't let Molly or Danny see it."

"I won't. You want to wait on the porch while I—?"

"No. I want to know. I can't plant zinnias and delphiniums on somebody's grave."

He released her and picked up his spade.

She waited off to one side, afraid to look, afraid not to look, while he ran the blade into the earth up and down the area he'd marked off. After a quarter of an hour, he stopped and walked toward her.

"There are no more graves, just that one."

More tears came stinging into her eyes and she covered her face with her hands. Again Cord moved to her side and folded his arms around her. But this time when she stopped crying he didn't let her go.

Chapter Thirteen

He rested his lips against her forehead, and the next thing she knew he bent his head and his mouth found hers. At that moment everything seemed to stop. She grew intensely aware of the twittering of sparrows in the maple trees, the breeze sighing through the branches, even Molly and Daniel's laughter from somewhere behind the porch.

How far away things seemed. And how beautiful.

His lips moved slowly over hers, telling her something, asking something. It was like being a little tipsy, as if a warm velvet cloak were enveloping her. A sweet, insistent ache started below her belly and spread through her entire body. This was heaven. This was fire. And she never wanted it to end.

When he lifted his mouth from hers she was weeping. "Oh," she breathed. She kept her eyes closed to prolong the delicious, languid feeling inside her. "Oh, my. What a lot I have missed in life."

Cord said nothing for so long she wondered if she had dreamed these last few moments. He still held her, and finally he cleared his throat. "That wasn't because of our bet."

"Oh? What was it, then?"

"Damned if I know. Maybe because we uncovered a gravestone and that reminded us of something."

"Reminded us of what?"

He hesitated. "That life is short. That life can be hell or it can be sweet. That we're all gonna die someday. It'd be nice if everybody could have a moment like..." He cleared his throat again. "Like what we just had."

All she could do was look into his eyes and nod.

"How about we make your flower bed a bit shorter?" he said after a moment. "I'm sure Amanda won't mind."

Fresh tears flooded into her eyes. "Maybe she would like some flowers on her grave."

They finished preparing her flower bed at dusk, and during all that time Eleanor hadn't said a single word. She just worked steadily alongside him, turning over the earth and pounding out the clods with her shovel.

When they had done all they could in one afternoon, he washed up at the pump in the yard and she disappeared upstairs for a long time. When she came back down to cook supper, she looked fresh and clean in a green print skirt and white shirtwaist, though her face looked like paste and her voice shook when she spoke. She had exhausted herself.

He thought about offering to cook supper, but he figured that would just get her dander up. She might be tired, but Eleanor never let you forget she had a mind of her own.

"Ma, how come your eyes are all red?"

"Eat your potatoes, Daniel."

"But Ma—"

"Your mother and I spaded up her new garden plot today," Cord said smoothly. "I think something made her sneeze."

"Yeah?" he said, his voice full of disbelief. "Like what?"

"Dust," Eleanor said quickly.

"Dust never bothered you before," Danny pursued.

Cord reached for his coffee cup. "Things have a way of creeping up on a person, Dan. Sometimes you don't notice something until it's too late."

"And then you get all sneezy," Molly interjected. "The barn makes me sneezy."

Eleanor looked everywhere but at him—the coffeepot, the back door, even the whiskey bottle on the top shelf of the china cabinet. He'd give a silver dollar to know what was going on in her head.

The silence grew thicker, and her one-word comments got sharper right up until she served the chocolate cake she'd baked that morning. He noticed her hand shaking when she cut the slices. Jehoshaphat, she was worrying her children and driving him crazy. He didn't want to just kiss her; he wanted to shake her. He'd never mistreated a woman in his life, not even...

You don't want to think about that, Winterman.

The kids gobbled down their dessert and pelted out the back door. Eleanor started to clear the dishes, and then abruptly she slammed one plate down on the table.

That did it. He was on his feet in a heartbeat and, reaching for her, he closed his hands around her upper arms. "You know something, Eleanor? Not only do you have a stubborn, I-can-do-it-myself streak, but at times you can be downright maddening."

"*I'm* maddening! *You're* the one who's maddening, Cord."

"Really?"

"Yes, really."

"Well, maybe we just don't like each other!" Hell's bells, he knew that wasn't true, but she could sure get under his skin.

"Maybe we don't," she retorted. Then she burst into tears.

Cord sat her down, poured two fingers of whiskey in her coffee and pushed the cup across the table toward her. For the next half hour she sipped and coughed and cried, while he washed and dried the supper dishes and stacked them in the china cabinet. Finally he hung the damp dish towel on the hook by the stove and sat down across from her.

"Feeling better?"

She gave him a hesitant nod.

"Well, *I* don't feel better," he said shortly. "Maybe you *don't* like me, Eleanor, but you do like your children. You're not the only farmwife with two rambunctious kids and too much work to do. When you get overtired you scare Molly and Danny."

And me.

She shook her head, but she wouldn't look at him, just stared down into her coffee cup.

"I don't know what's going on with you," he went on, "but I don't think it's because you're bothered by your gentlemen callers or by digging up a gravestone in your garden. I think it's something else."

She said nothing, so he splashed some whiskey in his own cup and downed it in one gulp.

After another long, agonizing minute she looked up at him. "It isn't that I don't like you, Cord. It's just that sometimes you and the children get under my skin and I...well, I say things I don't mean."

"You get under my skin, too, Eleanor. But I'm saying *exactly* what *I* mean. I think you're working too hard and that's keeping you from getting your strength back. And I think that makes you mad because it scares you half to death." He waited three long, tense breaths. "Am I right?"

She drained her whiskey-laced coffee and stood up on unsteady legs. "You are exactly right, Cord. And I'll thank you not to remind me of it ever again!"

He rose and stuck out his hand. "Deal."

She shook his hand like an old ranch hand would, a swift, hard grip and a fast getaway. Made him smile. In fact, touching her made him warm all over.

Eleanor tucked Molly and Daniel into their beds, heard their prayers and read them a chapter of *Uncle Fox's Railroad*. Then she tiptoed down the hall to her own bedroom with an unsettled feeling in her bones. If there was one thing she really hated about Cord Winterman it was his uncanny ability to put his thumb on the truth and grind it in until it hurt.

She pulled her white lawn nightgown over her head and blew out the lantern. She wasn't the least bit sleepy, so she lay awake, puzzling over why Cord nettled her so much. He didn't waste time or treat her unfairly or speak sharply. Well, not *too* sharply. He was helpful with the chores. He did whatever she asked of him and more. And both Molly and Daniel liked him.

So why didn't *she* like him?

With a cry she sat bolt upright in bed. She *did* like him.

And that was the problem. Liking Cord Winterman was the last thing, the very last thing, she wanted to do.

Cord made her nervous. He made her angry. He made her aware of how lonely she'd been all these years. He made her…hungry. The memory of his mouth on hers, hot and inviting, haunted her every waking moment.

Well, she would simply not think about it anymore. Not ever.

She flopped back onto her pillow and stared up into the dark until her eyes burned. *Don't think about it. That kiss. Him.*

Oh, dear God in heaven, what was she going to do about the rest of her life?

Chapter Fourteen

"Would anyone like another flapjack?" Eleanor asked.

Danny's fork clanked onto his empty plate. "I do, Ma."

"Eat it quickly, Danny. You'll be late for school."

The boy slathered syrup over his plate. "Whatcha gonna do while I'm at school today, Cord?"

"I'm giving your mother a shooting lesson right after breakfast."

Eleanor dropped the pancake spatula onto the griddle.

"Golly, Cord," Danny blurted out. "I sure wish I could watch!"

"*No one* is going to watch," Eleanor said firmly.

Molly's lower lip pushed out. "Not even me?"

"Not even you," Cord said. "It'll be real noisy, and your mama's probably gonna get upset and say a lot of words she won't want you to hear."

"I will not!" Eleanor rapped his knuckles with the spatula, but he could see she was smiling. Sort of.

"And after that," Cord added, "I'm going to help her plant some flower seeds."

Molly heaved a theatrical sigh. "What am *I* gonna do?"

"You mean after you dress Roscoe up in your dolly's pink dress?"

"Roscoe is a boy!" she announced.

Cord lifted one eyebrow. "Well, now. How did you figure that out?"

"Mama told me."

He shot a look at Eleanor, but she was intent on buttering the pancake on her plate and wouldn't look up. Just as well, he figured. Talking about sex with her, even cat sex, would be just plain foolhardy.

After breakfast he took her revolver and his Colt and walked Eleanor out behind the apple orchard, where he set an empty tomato can on a stump.

"I can't hit that," she protested. "It's too far away."

"Maybe. Maybe not." He positioned the revolver in her two hands and instructed her to raise the barrel slowly. "Now, fix your sight on the target."

"I can't hold it steady, Cord."

"You waited too long and your arm got tired. Lower the gun, wait a moment and raise it again."

Her first shot made her jump. "Oh, it happened so fast! Now I'm scared the gun will go off on its own!"

"It won't. Just take it real slow, like I showed you." He moved behind her and lifted both her hands in his. "Don't rush. Now, breathe in and then let your breath out partway."

Her back brushed his shirt buttons and he felt her relax against him. Her hair smelled of roses. This time *he* was the one who jerked at the shot. He guessed he was startled because he wasn't paying close enough attention.

She tried another shot and again the bullet whined past the tin can. She groaned. "I missed again. What am I doing wrong?"

"You're rushing it. Try to slow your breathing down."

After numerous corrections to her stance and the speed at which she raised the revolver, she managed to clip the tin can with a bullet and surprised him with a triumphant yelp. He reloaded for her and stepped away.

She fired, *snap-snap-snap*, and the can just sat there.

"You always do things in such a hurry?" he asked.

"Yes, I suppose I do."

"Well, don't."

Again he positioned himself at her back and talked her through *slowly* sighting down the barrel and *slowly* squeezing the trigger. He bent forward to guide her hands, and her hair, caught in a bun at her neck, tickled his chin. He sucked in a rose-scented breath and closed his eyes.

Winterman, you'd better get this woman out of your arms or you'll end up kissing her all to hell and back.

When she finally sent the tin can spinning off the stump, she gave an unladylike squeal and he had to laugh. It was plain as sunshine on Sundays that Eleanor Malloy liked to succeed. And he was learning that success made her reckless.

She waved the revolver around until he caught her arm and knocked it out of her hand. "Eleanor, no matter how good you're feeling, waving a weapon around isn't safe."

She listened intently, nodded and then did the very same thing after her next shot.

Cord shook his head in frustration and explained it all over again. Then for the next hour he did more laughing than lecturing, and finally—*finally*—she got the message. Her aim improved and at last he began to relax.

"Are you a good shot?" she inquired as he reset the tin can on the stump.

"Fair," he said.

"Show me."

A big dose of male pride made him rattle off five shots that had the tomato can dancing over the ground. She studied the target, then pinned him with penetrating gray eyes.

"Why are you such a good shot? Were you once a lawman?"

He laughed it off, but her question sobered him like a bath in a cold creek. Once he'd been on the wrong side of the law, and after he served his time in prison in Missouri, he'd just drifted aimlessly, cowboyed some in Idaho, drove a

herd of cattle to Abilene, joined a posse or two. Just drifted.
He sure as hell wasn't going to tell Eleanor any of that, especially the part about prison.

They walked back to the house through the blossoming
apple orchard. Cord inhaled deeply of the sweet-scented
trees, and was just thinking that the morning had gone well
when she shattered his calm.

"Cord," she said suddenly. "Who taught you to do laundry?"

He stopped short. "My wife."

She spun to face him, her eyes wide. "Your *wife*? You
are still married? I thought she divorced you."

"She did."

"What happened to her?"

Cord clenched his jaw. He knew he'd have to tell someone one of these days; he just didn't want it to be Eleanor.

"She's dead."

"Oh, Cord, I am so sorry. That must have been terrible
for you."

He said nothing. Yes, it had been terrible, but not in the
way she thought. What came afterward was much worse.

"However," he said in an effort to lighten the moment,
"my wife didn't teach me to iron."

Eleanor sensed he didn't want to be drawn further into
talking about his wife.

"It's bad enough having a hired man who can bake pies
and scrub dungarees. If you could do any more things, I
would have nothing to do all day but rock in the porch
swing, drink lemonade and read books."

Eleanor spent the afternoon bent over the ironing
board, running the sadiron over Danny's school shirts
and Molly's ruffled pinafores. It was dreadfully hot. She
swiped the perspiration off her forehead and attacked two
of her white long-sleeved shirtwaists. All those ruffles!
Why did she even bother? She never dressed up to im-

press anyone; when she was working around the farm she wore an old shirt of Tom's.

By the time she finished the ironing it was time to start supper, cold chicken left over from supper the night before and potato salad from the eggs and potatoes she'd boiled before breakfast. She chopped up an onion and a few dill pickles and was mixing it all up with a dollop of fresh mayonnaise when Danny burst in.

"Gosh, Ma, I just about melted walking home from school! I sure wish you'd let me ride to school. How 'bout it, huh?"

At that moment Cord came through the back door.

"Cord has other things to do besides teach you to ride," she said loudly.

Cord stopped short and he and Danny exchanged a long, private look.

"I'll be mucking out the stable after supper," he said. "You want to help, Dan?"

"Uh, well…"

Cord laughed and squeezed the boy's shoulder. Eleanor noticed water droplets clinging to her hired man's longish dark hair. She also noted how he kept brushing it out of his eyes.

"You need a haircut," she blurted out without thinking.

"You think so?"

"Oh, I—"

"Yeah, you do, Cord!" Danny chortled. "You need a haircut. You look like old man Ness's sheepdog."

"And you need one, as well, young man," Eleanor announced. "After supper."

"Aw, Ma, have a heart."

"I do have a heart, Danny. I also have eyes. Your hair is so long you're starting to look like a girl."

"I don't neither! Do I, Cord?" The boy sent him a pleading look.

"Well, son, if *you* look like a girl, *I* must look like Sadie Sunday."

"Who's Sadie Sunday?"

"A woman in a book with a shady reputation."

"Never you mind about Sadie Sunday, young man," she said firmly. "Go find Molly and both of you wash your hands."

When he clattered out the back door and down the steps, Eleanor began laying out plates and forks, then set down the platter of cold chicken and the big ceramic bowl of potato salad.

"When does your barbershop open?" Cord asked.

"After we finish supper."

"What do you charge for a haircut?" he asked with a grin.

"An hour's worth of work watering my seeds."

"Deal."

All through the meal Cord thought about how it would be to feel Eleanor's hands in his hair, and he couldn't eat fast enough. Danny, however, dawdled over his chicken drumstick and took only the smallest sips from his glass of milk. Halfway through washing up the dishes, Eleanor started to hum "Down in the Valley" under her breath.

"Ma always gets real happy when she cuts our hair," Danny confided.

She scrubbed off the last dinner plate and splashed it into the pan of hot rinse water.

"Yeah," Molly whispered. "But when she cuts my hair I always cry, and then Mama cries, too."

Cord tried not to smile. "Well, kids, I'll tell you what. *I'm* not gonna cry!"

Eleanor's humming changed to "Sweet Betsy from Pike," and she disappeared upstairs to retrieve her scissors.

"Gosh, Cord," Danny breathed. "Can we watch when Ma cuts your hair?"

"Sure, I guess so."

"No!" Eleanor reappeared in the kitchen, clicking the blades of her scissor together.

"Yes!" Molly sang. "I wanna watch!"

Eleanor sighed. "It's up to Cord."

"You can watch on one condition," he said. "Danny gets his hair cut first."

Eleanor snapped her scissor blades together. "All right, everybody out on the front porch. Quickly, now, before it gets too dark to see what I'm doing."

Danny's haircut went so smoothly his mother stepped back and studied him. "Not one squawk or even a moan. What," she murmured, "have I been doing wrong all these years?"

"Nuthin', Ma. Guess I just growed up and stopped moanin' when you cut my hair."

When the last shock of his sun-bleached brown hair tumbled onto the floor, Danny scooted off the kitchen chair Cord had dragged out, pushed him into his place and tossed him the dish towel Eleanor had draped around his shoulders.

"I'm not gonna cry," Cord teased.

Eleanor rapped the scissor handles against his skull. "Hush. This is serious business." She tentatively drew her fingers through his hair, then followed with the comb. After a long, speculative silence, she started to snip.

Cord sat as motionless as he could manage with the scratchy towel draped around his shoulders and Eleanor running her fingers through his hair. Shivers prickled his spine. She touched the back of his head, tipping it forward, then moved it to one side, her hand gentle, almost caressing. He bit his lower lip and closed his eyes.

The scissors crunched through his hair, then snip-snipped some more. He kept his eyes shut and heard her satisfied little "Mmm-hmm."

"Tip your head to the left," she directed. More snips, and then more crunches. Her humming changed to "Bonnie Blue Flag." Sure was an odd choice for a Yankee.

She slid her forefinger under his chin and tilted his face up. "Keep your eyes closed," she instructed. The scissors crunched across his forehead, then around the tops of both ears.

"Your hair is difficult to cut, Cord. It's wavy, and you have a definite cowlick." She stepped in closer and her breast brushed his cheek.

He stopped breathing. Quickly she moved away and continued wielding her scissors. Maybe she hadn't noticed.

"How much do you want taken off the back?" she asked.

"Dunno. How much is there?"

"It's touching your collar."

"That's too long, huh?"

She stopped combing. "Well…"

"Just don't let it tickle my neck, okay?"

She laughed and her warm breath gusted against his forehead. Suddenly he wanted to knock her busy scissors away and pull her down onto his lap. He kept himself under control by gritting his teeth and thinking about flower seeds.

And then she made a major mistake by nudging his knees apart and moving in between them to reach something in front.

"Look up," she ordered.

He obeyed, then wished he hadn't. There was nowhere to look but into her face, and what he saw there made his body so hot it felt like torture.

She gazed into his eyes without blinking, looked away and then looked back. Her cheeks had turned rosy. And her mouth… Lord save him, just then her tongue came out to slide over her lips.

He groaned silently. At least he hoped it was silently. She refocused on the hair straggling into his eyes, and he clenched his fists. Every muscle in his body wanted her to look at him again, and when she did he wanted to crush her mouth under his.

God help him he wanted more than that. He concentrated

on pushing air in and out of his lungs, taking it slow and counting his breaths. In...two...out...three...

Didn't help. He was still aching to kiss her.

"Cord? *Cord?*"

He jerked to attention. "Yeah?"

She touched his shoulder. "You're finished."

Not hardly, lady. I'm just getting started.

She slipped the comb and scissors into her apron pocket. "I'm feeling a bit faint, so I'm going upstairs to lie down for a while."

"You all right?"

"Of course I'm all right. Just tired. When I get up I'm going to sow my black-eyed Susan seeds. And don't tell me I shouldn't."

"Okay, I won't tell you."

"And don't look at me like that!"

"Like what?"

"Like you do when you disapprove of what I'm doing."

He raised his arms, then let them drop. "I would if I thought it'd do any good, but..."

"Correct." She marched through the screen door and disappeared into the house.

Danny paced all the way around him, eyeing his hair. "She didn't cut your hair half as short as mine," he pronounced.

Cord grinned. "There's always next time, Dan."

"Yeah? Whaddya gonna do next time?"

He shrugged. "Don't know. Maybe next time I'll volunteer to cut *her* hair."

That brought giggles from both Danny and Molly, and they scampered off the porch toward the barn. Cord stood for a long moment, studying the screen door. He felt himself splitting into two parts. He definitely did not want to get involved with a woman. He knew what it cost a man to love someone, and long ago he had resolved never to risk it again.

But boy did he want Eleanor Malloy.

Chapter Fifteen

⟨∽≈⟩

Cord paused while rubbing saddle soap into the leather saddle he'd found hanging in the barn and stepped closer to the two children playing in the open doorway. They weren't arguing about a game of marbles or which kittens were girls and which were boys. This was about something else.

"*You* ask her," Danny ordered.

"No," Molly insisted. "*You* ask her. Mama won't like a picnic."

Picnic? What picnic? Guess he'd have to wait until supper to find out, but he knew instinctively that Eleanor wouldn't want to attend a picnic, especially if it involved a crowd of Smoke River townspeople. She didn't like dealing with people in bunches. He smoothed his hand over the softened leather and started counting the hours until Eleanor called that supper was ready.

The meal was Eleanor's special creamed something over biscuits. The biscuits were light and fluffy as usual, but the creamed whatever it was tasted suspiciously like corn and carrots from the vegetable garden out back. Didn't matter, though. Dessert was strawberry shortcake, and Cord could put up with a lot of carrots for a few strawberries.

He kept waiting for Danny to bring up the picnic, but the boy circled around and around the subject, talking about his teacher, Mrs. Panovsky. About his classmate Adam Lynford and his sister, Sally. About the A he'd gotten on his geography test. Last he brought up the subject of the Fourth of July picnic.

"It's just a few weeks away, Ma. I hope you got lots of vacation chores saved up for me to do."

Eleanor's hand stopped over the bowl of crushed strawberries. "What did you say, Danny?"

"Chores," he said with unusual enthusiasm. "You know, Ma, stuff you want me to do this summer."

His mother stared at him, then at Molly, then at Cord. "I feel I am missing something here. What is going on?"

"Danny wants us to go to the Fourth of July picnic!" Molly blurted out.

"Oh. I see." She went on slicing up strawberries as if she hadn't heard the word *picnic*.

"Well, Ma? Whaddya say? We can go, can't we?"

"No," she said calmly. "We cannot."

"But, Ma," Danny wailed. "It'll be the Fourth of July picnic! You know, down by the river. You didn't let us go last year, so I thought maybe…"

Eleanor's face tightened, but she kept on slicing up the berries. "Molly, peek in the oven and see if the shortcakes are getting brown. Use the potholder!"

Cord tilted his chair back onto two legs. "Who all is invited to this picnic, Danny?"

"Everybody! All the students and their parents and their brothers and sisters."

"Well, that sounds interesting," his mother remarked in an offhand manner.

"Just about everybody in Smoke River'll be there!" Danny added.

Cord could see her interest deflate.

"The shortcakes are done," Molly called. "Can I have two?"

"One will be plenty, Molly."

"But I hafta grow bigger so I can go to school next year!"

Eleanor sniffed. "You can grow bigger on creamed vegetables."

Danny caught hold of Eleanor's blue-checked apron and gave it a tug. "Can we go, Ma? Huh? Can we, huh? There'll be fireworks and everything, even a band."

Cord thought the boy would jump out of his seat before he got an answer from his mother.

"I could take a couple of my apple pies," Cord offered.

Danny grinned. "And I could pick some more strawberries and maybe some blackberries, too."

"No," Eleanor said again.

"Aw, Ma. Why not? It's only a picnic."

Cord rose, grabbed Molly's potholder and removed the pan of shortcakes from the oven. "Yeah, Eleanor, why not?"

She shot him a look. "We will discuss it later. Now, who's ready for shortcakes, and who wants whipped cream on top?"

Molly and Danny remained uncharacteristically silent. Their mother frowned. "You two don't want any dessert?"

Both children shook their heads. She turned to Cord. "What about you, Cord?"

He gritted his teeth, folded his arms across his midriff and shook his head. Sure was hard to smell the enticing scent of that bowl of ripe berries and refuse dessert. But he did.

All at once Eleanor sank back onto her chair and lowered her head in her hands. "Oh, very well, we might as well go to the picnic."

An hour later, Cord folded his hands across his belly and sent Danny a wink. "Strawberry shortcake never tasted so good, did it?"

The river, bordered with frothy cottonwoods and groves of birch trees, rippled lazily through a grassy meadow of yellow goldenweed and purple lupine, interspersed with sprangly clumps of wild roses. Eleanor wore a blue gingham dress with lace at the neck; her dark hair, loosely gathered with a blue ribbon, shone like polished mahogany.

Cord tried not to look at her too much, but no matter what he did to distract himself, his gaze eventually returned to her. From the moment he lifted her down from the wagon bench, he sensed her unease. It took only ten minutes to see why.

No sooner had he spread a blanket near the riverbank and settled the wicker picnic basket on it than a slicked-up blond fellow appeared, followed by the red-bearded one with the horsey laugh. Cord had seen them both before, draped over Eleanor's porch steps, drinking her lemonade on Sunday afternoons.

Molly and Danny raced off to join a game of Run Sheep Run. Eleanor smoothed out her skirt, laid aside her straw sun hat and paid no apparent attention to the men. Instead, she began unpacking the picnic basket. She sent Cord off to the river to chill the two mason jars of lemonade. He immersed them between two large rocks, surreptitiously keeping one eye on Eleanor.

A band was playing somewhere, and the strains of "She'll Be Comin' 'Round the Mountain" floated on the warm afternoon air. Townspeople spread blankets and opened picnic baskets while children waded in the river or played catch with their pet dogs or each other. A low hum of contentment spread along the riverbanks and over the meadow.

Now another man joined the growing circle gathered around Eleanor, someone Cord hadn't seen before. She shared the molasses and burnt sugar cookies she'd brought, but he heard her explain that the lemonade was chilling in the river.

Cord decided to ignore the company, and he stretched out and pulled his hat down over his eyes. He could still hear, though.

"Miss Eleanor, you never did answer the question Red asked last Sunday."

"Oh? What question was that, George?"

George! Who's George?

"You know," a baritone voice said, "whether you're going to join the church choir."

"That would mean coming into town every single Sunday, would it not?"

"Well, yes, it would. And we rehearse every Wednesday evening. How about it?"

Eleanor's answer was indistinct, but from the flurry of protests, Cord guessed she had declined the invitation. That made him smile for two reasons—first because the fellow was pushy and second, while he was sure she was perfectly capable of driving the wagon, he didn't want her going into town without him.

So, she didn't want to sing in church, did she? And from the next conversations he overheard he gathered she didn't want to attend square dances or taffy-pulls or anything else.

"Gentlemen, I am a wife and a mother. I am far too busy keeping up my farm to do any of the things you are proposing."

Then another voice joined the circle. "Are you gonna stay for the fireworks tonight, Miss Eleanor? I'd be pleased to keep you company."

Cord swiped his hat off his chest and sat up. The speaker was one of the workers at the sawmill, Sam something. Cord didn't want *anyone* to keep her company, especially not during fireworks after dark. He couldn't stand this one more minute.

Eleanor was facing him, still seated on the blanket next to the picnic basket. She caught his eye and shrugged.

"I'm going down to the river," he announced. "I'll bring you some cold lemonade, Eleanor."

He thought the attentive males looked hopeful, but he'd be damned if they guzzled any of her lemonade. She had sliced up the lemons and he had squeezed them for her; that lemonade was for Molly and Danny and Eleanor and him and no one else.

Guess he was a little hot under the collar today. Maybe he was just a tad jealous. He tramped off to the river, grabbed a jar of lemonade and went in search of the kids. He found them playing hopscotch.

He pointed at the lemonade jars and they scampered over to his side. Cord unscrewed the top and Danny slurped down three big gulps. "Gosh, thanks, Cord, I was really thirsty!" The boy handed the jar to Molly, but Molly handed it right up to Cord.

"You have some, Cord. You look really hot."

His chest got real tight and he went down on one knee before the girl. "There's plenty here, Molly. You have some."

When she'd drunk her fill, he swallowed a mouthful or two and had just taken half a dozen steps back toward Eleanor when a feminine voice hailed him.

"Oh, Cordell, is that you?" Fanny Moreland appeared at his elbow. "And lemonade! Oh, my."

"Yeah. I was just taking it over to—"

"Why, aren't you sweet!" She reached for the jar and tipped it into her mouth. Cord reached for it, but he was too late. He watched her swallow in silence.

"Are y'all staying for the fireworks tonight?"

"Uh… I don't know whether Mrs. Malloy—"

Fanny laid a possessive hand on his forearm. "Oh, ah wouldn't worry about her, Cordell. She won't be alone. She'll have just scads of company."

"Might be she doesn't want company."

"Don't be silly. Every woman wants company."

"Mrs. Malloy isn't exactly 'every woman,' Miss Moreland."

Fanny laughed. "Why, of course she is. Goodness, you men don't see what's right smack in front of you sometimes."

Cord resisted the impulse to roll his eyes. "Yeah? What don't we men see?"

Fanny gave his arm a squeeze. "Oh, you know. A woman's smile says a great deal about what she wants. And a man's, too. All a woman has to do is look."

Cord took care not to look at her for fear she would imagine an interest he didn't feel. At least not in Fanny Moreland. Across the meadow he spied Eleanor, still perched demurely on the picnic blanket and still surrounded by her bevy of admirers.

That did it. Eleanor was *not* hungry for male attention. Eleanor was *thirsty*!

"Excuse me, Miss Moreland. Mrs. Malloy's waiting for this lemonade."

"What? Oh." She laid one hand on his forearm. "Perhaps we could meet later on to watch the fireworks?"

"Sorry. I promised Molly and Danny I'd watch with them." He detached her fingers from his arm and started to move away.

"But…but… Well, ah'll be just over there with mah aunt and uncle—" she waved a hand in the general direction of the riverbank "—in case y'all change your mind."

Eleanor watched Cord across the meadow, where he stood talking to Fanny Moreland. She edged away from Todd Mankewicz, who was blocking her view, and narrowed her eyes against the sun's glare. Molly and Danny were plodding across the meadow toward her. She straightened and made it very obvious to the men gathered around that she was ready for lunch when she pulled the wicker picnic basket toward her.

Now Fanny had attached herself to Cord's arm. That poor girl was so obviously desperate for attention Eleanor felt sorry for her in a way. She couldn't bring herself to be too critical since she herself had once felt just as desperate to escape from an unhappy situation. In many ways she felt that women—all women—were sisters under the skin.

She pressed her lips together. However, she did not want Cord to be the one to assuage Fanny Moreland's loneliness. When the young woman reattached herself to Cord's arm, Eleanor found herself on her feet.

Chapter Sixteen

"Miss Eleanor, where are ya going?"

She didn't know which of the men gathered around had spoken and she didn't much care. What she did care about was rescuing Cord. She grabbed up her sun hat and headed across the meadow. "Gentlemen, you must excuse me. I see my children over there."

Halfway to where Cord stood talking with Fanny, she met Molly and Danny coming toward her. "Cord gave us some lemonade, Mama, and now we're hungry. Can we eat our picnic now?"

"Yes. You two start unpacking our lunch. I'll just go tell Cord."

"Aw, he's being 'costed by that pretty Fanny lady."

"'Costed? Daniel, what does that mean?"

"Aw, you know, Ma. Cord says it's when something jumps on you and you didn't see it coming."

She tried not to smile. "Molly, you help Danny unpack our picnic, all right? I'll be there in a minute."

"And Cord, too?" Danny inquired.

"I...think so. Unless he has other plans."

"Aw, Ma, he doesn't want to be with that lady. He wants to eat with us."

"And just how do you know that?"

Her son dug the toe of his shoe into the ground. "Cuz he's sweatin'. I saw him sweatin' when I passed by him talkin' to that Fanny lady."

"Maybe he was just hot," Eleanor suggested. "After all, it is a very warm afternoon."

"Nah," her son insisted. "He's sweatin' an awful lot."

He streaked off toward the picnic blanket, followed by Molly, who flopped down and opened the wicker basket.

Eleanor moved on across the grass toward Cord.

"Oh, Mrs. Malloy," Fanny called out. "How nice that y'all could bring your children to the Fourth of July picnic!"

Eleanor smiled and nodded.

"Ah do hope the fireworks won't be too late for them," Fanny continued. "Ah have no idea how late children are allowed to stay up in the evening since ah have never had any of my own…" She sent Cord a look Eleanor could only describe as simpering.

"…though ah have often longed to have a child."

"I understand," Eleanor said quietly. "However, before such a blessed event befalls one, one might want to get married first."

Fanny's smile slipped. She seemed suddenly at a loss, and Eleanor recognized the naked expression of pain and longing on the woman's face. Immediately she regretted her barbed comment. But when Fanny possessively slipped her hand into Cord's, Eleanor regretted that she had not been even more pointed.

She rescued the jar of lemonade from Cord's other hand and he purposefully disengaged himself from Fanny's grip. "I hate to drag you away," she murmured, "but Molly and Danny are getting hungry." She then turned to Fanny.

"It was nice to see you again, Fanny. Be sure to remember me to your aunt and uncle."

"Oh, ah will. Uncle Ike talks about you all the time. Aunt Ernestine, too," she added. With a melodramatic sigh,

Fanny moved off toward the riverbank, and Cord fell into step beside Eleanor.

"I saw you start off," he said. "I thought you'd never get here."

Eleanor laughed. "You looked like you were enjoying yourself," she teased. "I hated to interrupt."

He shot her a sidelong look. "Are you joking?"

"Well…yes. Actually I was dying to interrupt."

"Why?"

"I told you," she said with another laugh, "Molly and Danny are getting hungry."

They walked on in silence for a few yards and then Cord stopped, unscrewed the top of the mason jar and held it out to her. "Thirsty?"

She accepted it without a word, tipped it up and swallowed three good gulps. "Yes, I was thirsty. And hungry, too. It's time for our picnic."

"Thank God. I thought you'd never ask." They moved on a few more steps and then Cord halted again. This time he moved to face her.

"Eleanor, I…uh…have a confession to make."

"Oh?" His tanned face looked so serious she experienced a sudden misgiving. "What is it, Cord?"

"Well, I— Oh, jumpin' jennies, there's no easy way to say it." He looked at the ground, then up into the sky, then his gaze moved back to her. "I've been teaching Danny to ride."

She laughed aloud. "I know."

"Huh? How could you know? We're always at least two miles from the farm."

"I know," Eleanor said again, "because Danny's jeans and shirts have smelled like horse for weeks."

"We thought for sure we'd fooled you," he confessed. "You're pretty sneaky."

"Oh, no, Cord. I am merely observant. *You* are the sneaky one."

He downed a big swallow of lemonade and studied her with raised eyebrows. "Hot damn."

"Don't tell Danny that I know just yet, Cord. He's been on such good behavior that I'd hate for it to end. He's been watering my garden without my asking, and yesterday he hung the parlor rug out in the yard and beat the dust out with my broom."

"Okay, that's a deal. I won't tell him. Now, let's go eat. Confession makes me hungry."

They feasted on fried chicken and potato salad and lazed the afternoon away while the sun dropped toward the smoke-colored hills in the distance and guitar music drifted on the air. Cord taught Molly to play Mumblety-Peg with his pearl-handled pocket knife, and then he began to wonder why none of Eleanor's admirers were hanging around any longer. Eleanor apparently didn't care. She laid her sun hat on the blanket beside her and stretched out, keeping the children between them.

After a while she sat up. "Cord, wouldn't you like to go over and visit with Ike and Ernestine Bruhn? And Fanny?"

"Why would I want to do that?"

"Don't go, Cord!" Molly begged. "I wanna play more Mumblety-Peg."

"Because," Eleanor said slowly, "I was rude to Fanny earlier. I would like to make amends."

He gave her a long look. "Then why don't *you* go visit with Ike and Ernestine. And Fanny. I'm happy playing Mumblety-Peg with Molly."

"And besides," Danny pointed out, "it's gettin' dark. The fireworks are gonna start any minute."

"Oh," Eleanor said with a quiet smile. "I'd forgotten about the fireworks."

When it was full dark, the fireworks started with a spectacular red-white-and-blue starburst that brought gasps and cheers from the crowd sitting along the riverbank. Molly flopped onto her back beside her mother, and Danny craned his neck to peer upward.

As the showers of colored stars floated down from the blue-black sky, Cord watched Eleanor out of the corner of his eye.

The exploding fireworks overhead reminded him of something. After a full minute of trying to recall what it was, he groaned and bit the inside of his cheek. It was like the burst of light at the moment of climax when one made love to a woman.

He shut his eyes, wishing he hadn't made that particular connection. He wanted to touch Eleanor so bad he had to bend his knees as his groin swelled. He gritted his teeth, trying to keep his gaze from straying to where Eleanor lay prone beside him.

The little flowery bursts overhead went on and on until Cord couldn't stand it one more minute. He stood up.

"Are you gonna visit that pretty lady?" Danny asked.

"No. Just…getting some air."

"That don't make sense, Cord. We're outside. There's plenty of air right here."

"That *doesn't* make sense," Eleanor corrected.

"Maybe not," Cord said in a hoarse voice. "But I'm goin' for a walk anyway." Anything to keep him from watching more of those firework climaxes.

He made a circuit of the entire picnic area, from the maple trees at one end of the meadow to the tangle of vines and cottonwoods near the riverbank. Then he made another circuit, his hands jammed in the pockets of his suddenly too-tight jeans. On his third trip around the picnic grounds, a shadow slipped to his side. Eleanor. Oh, God.

"Cord, is something wrong?"

"No." *Yes, dammit. Something is eating my gut and burning up my privates.*

"Was it something I said? Or did?"

"No." *Yes. You've got to stop looking like you're glad to see me every morning.*

"Do you want to talk about it?"

"No." That was the God's honest truth. He didn't want to talk to Eleanor. He wanted to kiss her.

She tipped her head back and gazed up at the sky. "The fireworks are beautiful, aren't they?"

"Yeah. Beautiful." If she only knew *how* beautiful. And why.

"Cord—"

"Sorry, Eleanor. Guess I don't feel much like talking."

A long, pregnant silence followed. Just when he'd gotten himself under control she opened her lips and blew it all to hell. "I feel like that, too, sometimes," she said softly. "Like not talking. Like I just want to be quiet and stop thinking about things."

Cord mumbled some sort of response.

"Do you know what I do when I feel that way?" she pursued.

"What?" He didn't mean it to come out so gruff. Then again, he was feeling gruff, so why not?

"I go for a long walk, like you're doing. And I talk to my apple trees. I tell them all about… I tell them what's on my mind."

"Yeah? Do your apple trees give you any advice?"

"Oh, of course not. They just listen. And pretty soon I'm feeling calmer inside and I can go back to sleep."

He shook his head. "You want to be my apple tree tonight?"

"Yes, I'll be your apple tree, Cord. What's wrong? Is it Fanny Moreland?"

He laughed out loud. "Why do women think a man's troubles are always about a woman?"

"Because we're women. We have a great deal of intuition and understanding and—"

"Eleanor?"

"Yes, Cord?"

He took three long, deep breaths. "Eleanor, stop talking."

"What? But I thought—"

"Eleanor, for God's sake, shut up."

"Molly, stop fidgeting!"

"I'm not fidgeting, Mama. I'm dancing."

"Dancing! Here? At the dressmaker's?"

Verena Forester leaned over the Butterick pattern book spread open on the counter. "It don't bother me none, Miz Malloy. These new dresses you want, they for the dance out at Jensen's Saturday night?"

"Oh, no, Verena. I had in mind just an everyday dress for…every day."

"I wanna go to the dance!" Molly cried. "And I wanna wear my pretty new dress."

Eleanor fingered the bolt of red-and-yellow calico Verena had laid across the thick pattern book.

"This'd be real nice made up with a deep square neck and a double ruffle at the hem," the dressmaker observed.

"Oh, I think not a deep square neckline, Verena. Just a shallow neckline and only one ruffle at the bottom."

"And what about yer daughter, Miz Malloy? You want just the one ruffle on the skirt?"

"I—"

Molly tugged on her sleeve. "Mama, can I please have two ruffles? Please? And make them twirl out," she added in an aside to the dressmaker.

"Twirl out? Child, whatever do you mean, 'twirl out'?"

"You know." Molly spun in place and lifted her skirt so it belled out.

Verena caught Eleanor's eye and grinned. "How 'bout I make both yours and your daughter's a full six gores? Oughta be real fetching in this here red calico. Oughta 'twirl out' just fine."

"Well…"

"You can pick 'em up on Friday, Miss Eleanor. The dance isn't 'til Saturday," Verena said with a smile.

"We are not attending the dance."

"Oh. I thought your girl here—"

"No," Eleanor said decisively.

Molly tucked her small hand in Eleanor's as they left the dressmaker's shop. "Can we get some ice cream, Mama?"

Eleanor mentally calculated how much money she had left to last until the apple harvest in the fall. "Maybe a small dish."

"Where'd Cord go?"

"He stopped at the mercantile to get some more flour and ten pounds of sugar."

"And some lemon drops?"

Eleanor laughed. "I don't know about any lemon drops." They crossed the dusty street and stepped into the restaurant next to the Smoke River Hotel, where the waitress showed them to a table.

"Expectin' anybody else?" she asked.

"Why, no, Rita. Just us."

"Oh. Saw yer hired man go into the mercantile a while back. Thought he might be joining you."

"He's buying some lemon drops!" Molly announced.

"I see. That means you won't be wanting any strawberry ice cream, then, does it?"

"No, it doesn't," Molly protested. "And Cord might want some."

Eleanor caught Rita's eye and shrugged.

"Maybe he's talkin' to that pretty lady," Molly whispered.

Eleanor shrugged again. It was quite possible that Cord was, in fact, talking to the "pretty lady," Fanny Moreland. It was no concern of hers. Lately he hadn't even mentioned her, but he'd seemed tense and preoccupied, and that was a sure sign that something, or someone, was on his mind.

A little stab of something poked into her belly. A hunger pang, maybe. She had skimped on her breakfast to come into town with Cord, and she knew that while she and Molly had visited the dressmaker, Cord had intended to go to the mercantile. Maybe Fanny would be there. She knew that Fanny and Edith Ness, the owner's daughter, were good friends.

Another niggle of something wormed its way into her brain. Fanny. Fanny was everything she wasn't—young, pretty and available. Had Cord ever kissed Fanny? Did he *want* to? She thought about that day when Cord had dug up that gravestone in her new flower bed and he had ended up kissing her. Was that kiss in payment of the bet he'd won about the laundry?

Or was it something that had just happened, and he was still expecting the kiss he'd won? And if he was still expecting it, when would he ask for it?

"Ma'am?" The waitress tapped her pencil on her order pad.

"You two want something to eat?"

"What? Oh, yes. We'll have—"

"Strawberry ice cream!" Molly cried.

Rita hid a smile. "Two dishes?"

"Make it three," a voice called from the doorway.

"Cord!" Molly screeched.

Eleanor glared at her daughter. "Hush, Molly. It isn't polite to shout."

The girl turned wide blue eyes up to her. "Why not, Mama? You do it all the time."

The waitress gave a strangled laugh and coughed.

"Three dishes of strawberry ice cream," Cord said as he slid onto the chair across from Eleanor. "And some coffee for me."

"Sure thing," Rita said. She slapped her order pad into her apron pocket and bustled away toward the kitchen.

Cord sent a smile across the table. "You ladies get your shopping all done?"

Molly grinned at him. "I'm gonna have a beautiful new dress, just like Mama's."

"Really?"

"An' we're goin' to a dance!"

His face changed. "Really? Eleanor, I thought you didn't—"

"Molly," Eleanor said in a low voice, "we are not going to the dance."

"What dance?" he asked. A cup of coffee appeared at his elbow and he nodded his thanks at the waitress.

"There's a big dance out at Peter Jensen's place on Saturday," Rita volunteered. "Everybody in town will be there, and most of the ranchers and their wives will come, too."

"And Mama doesn't want to go," Molly added.

"Oh, yeah? Why not?"

"Well," Eleanor began, "because…" She stopped when Rita returned to set down three big bowls of ice cream and three spoons.

"Is that strawberry?" Cord asked, picking up a spoon.

"That it is, sir."

"Oh, boy!"

"Oh, boy!" Molly echoed.

Cord pinned Eleanor with an inquiring look. "You were saying about the dance?"

"I was saying that we are not going."

"Some reason?"

She closed her lips over a spoonful of ice cream. "Well, you know how I feel about gatherings with lots of people—"

"Yeah, I know. But—" he cut his gaze sideways toward Molly "—have you considered that it might be good for… your children to learn to dance?" Again he glanced toward Molly, who was busily shoveling ice cream into her mouth and paying them no attention.

"She's too young."

"She's not too young," he countered. "Girls are girls the minute they're born."

Eleanor frowned. "What does that mean?"

"Might be good for her older brother, too."

Eleanor just looked at him, a bite of ice cream halfway to her mouth.

Then he looked straight at her. "Might be good for their mother, too."

She choked on her ice cream. "I," she said when she could talk, "already know how to dance."

Cord waited until she looked up. "So? Molly and Danny don't."

"I don't need to go, Cord. Molly and Danny could go in the wagon with you, couldn't they? And I could stay home."

"That won't work, Eleanor. Leaving Danny on his own at a dance wouldn't be a problem, but I'd have to stick pretty close to Molly, and I'd, um, want to do my share of dancing."

She sent him an exasperated look. "Oh, for heaven's sake, Cord."

"The least you could do is come just to keep an eye on your daughter," he said quietly.

"Oh…oh, all right," she said sharply.

"Good," he said mildly. He glanced at her half-empty bowl. "Want some more ice cream?"

"No, thank you." Her voice was so crisp it could cut paper. Then she changed the subject. "Was there any interesting news in town?"

Cord laughed. "Well, the mercantile's pink storefront is now purple."

Her eyebrows went up. "Purple? Not really!"

"Yeah, really. Awful color. You can just about see it from the window. Carl Ness is about to disown his daughter."

"Molly," Eleanor said, "if you have finished your ice cream, we should be heading home."

"I wanna go see the purple store," Molly announced.

"Well…"

"And," her daughter added at the top of her voice, "I wanna go to the dance!"

* * *

That evening after the supper dishes were done Cord slipped into the space beside Eleanor on the porch swing. "We need to talk," he said.

"About?" Her voice sounded weary, and he felt halfway guilty about pressing her on a subject she obviously didn't want to talk about.

"About why you never want to go to a school shindig or a picnic without a lot of pushing from Molly and Danny. About why you don't want to go to the dance on Saturday."

"I don't like crowds."

"There was a big crowd at the Fourth of July picnic."

"That didn't matter so much. People were fairly well spread out along the river at the picnic."

"But at a dance, they're not, is that it? At a dance they're all bunched up together."

She gave the swing an extra-hard push with her foot. "Yes, they are."

He brought the swing to an abrupt stop and turned to face her. "Eleanor, I'd like you to explain why you feel so antisocial. Most women like being around other people."

"Why should it matter what most women like? I have never liked social gatherings. Why should I have to explain it to you?"

"Because it's hurting your kids," he said quietly.

She was silent for so long he thought maybe she hadn't heard him.

"Eleanor?"

"Oh, for heaven's sake, Cord. I...I feel uneasy around people. Other women, particularly."

"Why?"

She began twisting her hands together in her lap. "I've always felt that way, ever since I can remember. My mother... my mother was very society-conscious in Portland. I was extremely shy. I preferred reading books or fishing, things one did alone. But Mother said that I was not normal, that no daughter of hers should grow up being 'ingrown.' That was her word for it."

She broke off, and Cord pushed the swing back and forth for a full minute. "And?"

Eleanor pressed her lips together. "Mother was…critical. I still hear her voice in my ear sometimes. 'You are too independent. Too quiet. Too…everything.' I was never enough for Mother. She said I wasn't like other girls who had ladylike manners and could sing and play the piano. I didn't know how to make charming conversation, and I would never have any gentlemen callers."

Cord gritted his teeth. "Well, she was sure wrong there," he said under his breath.

"I grew up feeling that other people looked down on me, that I wasn't as good as they were."

"And you've been afraid of people ever since," he said.

Eleanor said nothing.

"Eleanor, that fear is hurting Molly and Daniel. Their mother's shyness shouldn't keep them from enjoying other people. Unless…" He gave the swing a shove with his boot. "Unless you want your kids to grow up afraid, too."

She remained silent, but when he sneaked a look at her he saw that her eyes were shut tight.

"Eleanor?"

"Yes," she said in a low voice. "I know you are right, Cord. I will try."

His throat ached so much he couldn't speak. Instead, he reached out and quietly touched her hand.

Chapter Seventeen

Eleanor spent all day Saturday fighting a battalion of butterflies that had flitted and bumped about her stomach since before breakfast. It wasn't that she had nothing appropriate to wear. Her friend, dressmaker Verena Forester, had created a truly lovely red-and-yellow-print calico dress with lace around the square neckline and a full gored skirt that swung wide when she moved. Molly's dress was the same except hers was blue and the skirt was only four gores. Still, Molly had spent every minute since supper twirling about the parlor and watching her skirt bell out.

Danny was disgusted by the whole idea of a dance, and no amount of man-to-man encouragement from Cord was making any difference. "Why do I want to go to a stupid old dance, anyway?"

"Well, son, there might be cakes and cookies and maybe even some apple pies."

"Aw, I can get cakes and cookies from Ma when she bakes. I bet they're not near as good as hers."

Eleanor was so jumpy with nerves she only half heard Danny's compliment. She felt faint already. Her mother had belittled her because of her lack of social graces, and as a result she had never really learned to dance well. And Tom had never encouraged her to come into town for any reason, much less a social or a dance.

She had never missed Tom when he went somewhere. She had always been happiest at the farm, by herself. In fact, in all the years he'd been gone since the War, she hadn't missed him.

Tonight she would be frozen with fear by the time they arrived at Peter Jensen's barn. Well, so be it. She had the worst case of the flutters she'd had in years, but somehow she had to get through this one evening for her children's sake. Then, she promised herself, she would never, never have to do this again.

She racked her brain for a plan, a strategy, for surviving this ordeal. And then an hour before they were to leave, Molly unknowingly supplied one.

"Mama, are you gonna teach me how to dance?"

Of course! It was the perfect solution. If she was busy teaching Molly all about two-steps and schottisches she would have no time to talk to anyone. Even better, she would be too occupied with her daughter to pay any attention whatsoever to her "male admirers," as Cord described them.

Mercy! The evening might not be as bad as she feared. She stiffened her backbone and climbed the stairs to her bedroom to brush her hair and don her new dress.

In the children's room, Molly could barely sit still while Eleanor brushed her hair and tied blue ribbons on the ends of her blond braids. Danny grumbled about everything, the too-tight cuffs on the sleeves of his clean shirt, his new leather belt, which was too stiff, even having to polish his shoes. By the time she herded both children downstairs her nerves were thoroughly frazzled.

Then Cord stepped in through the back door and she caught her breath. He wore his usual jeans and a crisp blue shirt she remembered ironing only yesterday, but droplets of water clung to his dark hair, and he had trimmed his moustache. He had refused to let her do it when she had given them all haircuts; apparently he'd sneaked her mending scissors out of her sewing basket and done it on his own.

"The wagon's ready," he announced. "Eleanor, could you spare an apple for the—" He stopped short and stared at her. "Horse?" he finished.

"I'll get one," Molly sang. She clattered off into the pantry and returned with a shriveled red apple and held it out. But Cord wasn't looking at Molly. He was looking at Eleanor.

Her cheeks got all pink, and she self-consciously brushed an imaginary speck off her red dress. He'd never seen her wear anything but blue or brown before; the red dress, with tiny yellow flowers sprinkled all over it, came as a shock. The low, lace-edged square neckline was a shock, too. He'd never seen so much as an inch of skin below her chin. The plain shirtwaists she wore revealed nothing, and seeing her bare forearms when she rolled up her sleeves was nothing like looking at the creamy smooth skin of her chest. The neck of her dress dipped down to the curve of her breasts, and suddenly he found his mouth had gone dry.

He scarcely noticed when Molly thrust the apple into his hand and gazed up at him. "Are you gonna dance with me, Cord?"

"What? Oh, why, sure I am, Molly."

"Are you gonna dance with Mama, too?"

Cord's eyes met Eleanor's over her daughter's head. A full minute went by, but neither one of them said a word.

"Well, are you?" the girl cried.

"Maybe," he said, his voice quiet. "That depends on your mama. I'll have to ask her first."

"I'm not gonna dance with anybody," Danny announced. "I think dancing is dumb."

Cord drew in a long, slow breath. He still held Eleanor's

gaze, and he was wondering why she didn't look away like she always did when he looked at her too long.

"Don'tcha think dancing is dumb, Cord?" Danny pursued.

"No, Danny, I don't. I think dancing is God's way of reminding us of something."

"Remindin' us of what? Boy, you sure aren't making any sense tonight."

"Reminding us that a man and a woman—"

"Can have a lot in common," Eleanor interjected.

Molly gave a squeal. "Is that like the boy cat and the girl cat? Like you told us before?"

Eleanor's burst of laughter at her daughter's question surprised him. "Um…maybe a little," Cord said. "But first they…um…dance together."

"Cat's don't dance!" Molly protested.

"But people do," he said. "There's an old vaquero saying about dancing. It's what a man does with a woman when he's thinkin' of doing something else."

Eleanor's cheeks turned an even deeper shade of rose.

All the way out to the Jensen place Eleanor and Cord sat on the wagon bench with a carefully maintained eight inches between them and didn't say a word. Molly sang snatches of songs she had learned from her mother and Danny grumbled about everything.

She didn't know why she was so jumpy this evening. A part of her couldn't help wondering when Cord would collect the kiss he'd won the day they'd bet on the laundry. Soon, she hoped. Waiting and wondering was making her nervous. *Oh, no, not soon.* The thought of his mouth touching hers again gave her the shivers.

When the wagon rolled into an empty space beside the huge red barn, Cord breathed a sigh of relief and Eleanor's shoulders tensed. He climbed down and lifted Molly out of the back, and the instant the girl's shoes touched the ground she raced off toward the barn door entrance. With a sullen expression on his face, Danny climbed down and trailed after his sister.

Cord then lifted Eleanor down from the bench. For some reason she couldn't look any higher than the buttons on his shirt, and after a long moment he removed his hands from her waist and they followed the sound of guitars and violins and a banjo or two into the overheated interior.

Jensen's barn overflowed with people, ranchers in clean jeans and pressed shirts and their best leather vests, wives in ruffled gingham or denim skirts and colorful shirtwaists with knitted shawls about their shoulders, townspeople and dozens of children, from babies in wicker cradles to adolescents, some of whom Eleanor recognized from Danny's School Night.

She set the plate of molasses cookies she'd brought on the already crowded refreshment table and searched for a quiet corner where she could sit out of the way of the noise and bustle and keep an eye on Molly.

Cord drifted off…somewhere, and a few moments later she saw him bend down to Molly's level, lift her little hands in his and step back and forth with her in time to the music. Every so often he would turn her under his arm and her skirt would flare out. Eleanor smiled in spite of herself. Molly would be lit up for days.

She chose a bench at the edge of the dance floor, half in the shadows, which suited her just fine. She scooted into the darkest part, folded her hands in her lap and settled down to watch.

Couples waltzed and two-stepped around and around on the sanded and polished plank floor, visited the refreshment table, changed partners and waltzed around and around some more. It was pretty to see. The women were decked out in their best "goin' meetin'" clothes, and it turned out to be quite a fashion show. She wondered if Verena Forester had played a role in the parade of finery that passed in front of her, everything from double-flounced peach silk to plain blue denim. She knew Verena often attended dances and socials to see her handiwork in action and to get ideas for more.

She began to relax a bit, and then something across the room caught her eye and she jerked upright. At the outer edge of the throng of dancers, there was Danny, laboriously two-stepping along with a very pretty little girl in a yellow striped dress and a matching pinafore. They weren't looking at each other; both were studiously watching their feet. The girl was talking and she seemed to be leading, which was understandable since Eleanor knew her son hadn't the foggiest idea what he should be doing on a dance floor.

She wanted to laugh, and then she wanted to cry. Dear grumbly, unwilling Danny was actually dancing with a girl! She closed her eyes. *My firstborn is growing up right before my eyes.*

It had all happened so fast! All at once she felt older and lonelier and more lost than she ever had in all her twenty-seven years. She clenched her hands in her lap and resolved she would not cry, not here in front of all these people.

"Miss Eleanor?"

She snapped her lids open to see Todd Mankewicz leaning over her.

"Would you care to dance, Miss Eleanor?"

She stared at him. He wasn't bad looking with his pale blue eyes and blond sideburns. He just wasn't very interesting to talk to.

"Oh, I… Actually, Todd, I am not dancing this evening. I am…watching over my children."

"Oh. Maybe some other night, then."

She watched him move away and head straight for Helen Landsfelter, the woman Doc Dougherty had sent out to take care of her when she'd had pneumonia. She had to laugh. Helen was over thirty if she was a day.

But you yourself are almost thirty. Your life is half-over!

Tears stung into her eyes. Oh, mercy sakes! Whatever was wrong with her tonight?

She focused on Danny and the girl in yellow, then caught sight of Molly and Cord coming toward her.

"Didja see me, Mama? Cord twirled me so my skirt went way out!"

"Yes, I did see you, Molly. You looked…very twirly, I must say."

Chuckling, Cord set a glass of lemonade on the bench beside her. "Guess you didn't think I looked 'twirly,' huh?"

She looked up at him. "You looked plenty twirly, Cord. More twirly than I've ever seen you!"

He laughed and handed her the glass. "The lemonade's for you, Eleanor. Molly and I already had our share."

"Thank you, Cord." She sipped a few swallows, then folded her hands around the glass.

"I saw what's-his-name from your Sunday porch crowd asking you to dance," he said.

"Todd Mankewicz. I told him I wasn't dancing this evening."

"Eleanor, you know it's a sin to tell a lie."

"But I wasn't—"

"Yeah, you were. Cuz you *are* dancing this evening."

"Oh, no, I'm—"

"With me." He lifted the lemonade glass out of her hand and handed it to Molly. Then he deliberately twined Eleanor's fingers into his own and pulled her to her feet. With his hand at her back he guided her onto the dance floor and turned her to face him.

She sent him a resigned look. "I haven't danced in so many years I'm not sure I remember how."

"It's been a lot of years for me, too. But you couldn't be worse than Molly. All she wanted to do was spin around so her dress twirled out."

"Would you like to see my dress twirl out?" she said.

He focused on the musicians for a moment. "Not sure you can twirl to that. It's a two-step."

She smiled. "I can two-step and twirl."

"Prove it." He swung her into his arms and started a determined two-step against the waltz rhythm the musicians had slipped into, and that made her laugh out loud.

Cord restarted their dance, swinging into what he thought was a waltz. At least he prayed it was a waltz. He glanced down into Eleanor's face and she looked quickly away. He went back to the two-step because it was slower and he could just hold her and move his body with hers.

She smelled good. The scent of her hair reminded him of the honeysuckle that trailed over the front porch post, and the subtle fragrance rising from her skin was faintly spicy-sweet, like roses, maybe. He could hear her breathing slowly in and out…in and then out again…

God help him, he could scarcely think!

She said nothing for a long time, and then she glanced up at him. "I didn't want to come to this dance," she said.

"I know."

"And I didn't think I wanted to dance."

"I know," he said again.

"And you know what?" She sent him a wobbly smile. "I think I'm glad."

Cord missed a step. *She's glad? About dancing with me?* That made him warm all the way down to his toes.

And at the same time it made him damn scared. He'd better get his mind off the woman in his arms in the next sixty seconds or he'd go up in smoke.

"Look at Danny over there," he said. "After all that complaining, he's dancing with that little girl in the yellow pinafore."

She nodded. "I think males are just like females."

"Not hardly."

"Oh, yes. They are very similar. Males, like females, complain about things that frighten them."

"Yeah? I'm trying to think if I complain about anything."

"Yes, you do, Cord. You complain about my Sunday visitors."

He couldn't think of a single thing to say to that. He did complain about them, he acknowledged. He didn't want to think about what that might mean. Was he scared one of them would lay a hand on her? Was he scared she might like one of them?

He couldn't stand to think about either possibility. In fact, with Eleanor in his arms he was having a hard time thinking at all.

"Cord, I should get back to Molly."

"No, you shouldn't. I see Molly over on the sidelines, talking to Edith Ness."

"Oh, dear. I hope she's not getting any ideas about painting the front porch green or purple or some awful color."

"Your front porch does need a coat of paint, Eleanor. Fact is, your whole house needs painting. You want me to—?"

"Cord, how long will you... I mean, aren't you going to California soon?"

"Not until after your apples are harvested. And," he added with a chuckle, "your front porch is painted."

"I wish I could pay you something. It isn't right for you to work so hard and not be paid."

"You *are* paying me. Just don't ask how."

"But... I don't understand."

Cord forced himself to look away from her upturned face. "Hell's bells, woman, neither do I."

They danced a full quarter of an hour without speaking another word. For a long time he managed not to look at her, either, but finally he couldn't stand it any longer.

"Eleanor."

She looked up, and he let himself study her small, heart-shaped face the way he remembered doing that first day when he'd stumbled, hungry and tired, through all those apple trees to her front door. He remembered thinking her eyes were like gray dove's wings, soft and kinda hurting somehow. They'd made his heart stop for an instant, and they were doing the same thing to him now, stopping his heartbeat like he'd been shot. All she had to do to bring him to his knees was look into his eyes that way.

Eleanor felt his arm tighten at her back. Cord was still looking at her, but the expression in his eyes had changed. "Cord, why are you staring at me like that?"

"I'm counting up all the good things about being here in Jensen's barn."

"Tell me some of them. It was very hard for me to come."

"Well, one of the good things is teaching Molly to dance so she could twirl around."

"She will never forget that, Cord. Neither will I."

"And then there's watching your son, Danny, dance with a pretty girl and grow up right in front of us."

"Amazing, isn't it? How life catches up with us no matter how hard we try to stop it."

"And then—" he swallowed hard "—there's dancing with you."

Her lips curved into a lopsided smile. "And then there's…" Her smile faltered. "Oh, no. Cord, Fanny Moreland is heading straight for you."

He didn't even look up. "Doesn't matter. Ladies don't cut in."

"I bet this one does," she murmured. She watched Fanny hover at Cord's back, waiting for a chance to pounce. What incredibly bad manners! If she had ever behaved like that her mother would have switched her until she couldn't sit down.

Fanny stepped forward and brought them to a stop. "Mrs. Malloy, your daughter needs you."

"No, she doesn't," Cord said.

Fanny blinked. "Oh, but she does, really." She laid her hand possessively on Cord's arm.

"Why does she need me?" Eleanor asked, her voice cool.

"Um…well, ah think she's thirsty."

"Can't be," Cord said. "We drank about a gallon of lemonade half an hour ago."

People were beginning to stare at the three of them. Eleanor saw that Fanny wasn't going to give up without causing a scene, so she stepped out of Cord's arms.

"The field is yours, Fanny," she murmured. She turned and walked away. Behind her she heard a bark of laughter from Cord and the chatter of Fanny's voice. From her tone it sounded as if she was trying to persuade Cord to do something. Dance with her, probably.

When she reached the bench where Molly sat with Edith Ness, she settled her skirts around her and scanned the crowded floor, looking for Cord and Fanny. After a long moment she realized they weren't there. Aha. Fanny wasn't persuading Cord to dance with her. She was persuading him to walk outside with her.

"What's the matter, Mama? You look all funny."

"I'm a bit tired, I guess."

No, you are not tired. She had had a long, busy day, but she wasn't the least bit tired. In fact, dancing with Cord, feeling the gentle pressure of his warm hand at her back and listening to the pleasant low rumble of his voice, she had felt extraordinarily well.

But something must be bothering her because Molly had noticed it. She set her mind to assessing what it was. She had already acknowledged she was jealous of Fanny's youth and the fact that she was so pretty, so that couldn't be it. But now…

Now, she had to admit, she was jealous. She was jealous because…because Fanny and Cord were taking a walk outside. Perhaps walking out behind the barn, which everyone understood was another way to say "for a kiss."

That was what she was jealous of—that Cord could be kissing Fanny Moreland!

* * *

The next morning at breakfast Molly stopped Cord in the middle of his explanation about storing garden tools. "Do you like that pretty Fanny lady?"

"Some," he said.

"Better'n me?"

"Nope."

"Better'n Mama?"

"Nope."

"A *big* 'nope'?" Molly persisted. "Or a little one?"

He chuckled and looked over at Eleanor, who sat across from him, drinking a second cup of coffee. "A big 'nope,'" he said with a grin.

Eleanor's cheeks turned pink.

Chapter Eighteen

The garden plot waited. It had been spaded and raked smooth, and Eleanor's fingers itched to poke in the nasturtium and zinnia seeds Rosie Greywolf had given her. The peas and beets and carrots she had planted in the backyard beds were already shooting up and were looking green and healthy.

She'd never tried to grow flowers before, but ever since her recovery from pneumonia she had hungered for more than the pink roses and honeysuckle clambering over the porch trellis. She wanted a riot of blooms in orange and yellow and scarlet, not organized in neat rows but all tangled up so the colors swirled together like a painting. The picture in her mind made her smile. So helter-skelter and unplanned. Like life.

All at once she remembered the day Cord had uncovered the gravestone that now stood at one end of the plot. And the kiss they had shared. It wasn't the "bet" kiss; she was still half expecting that. Maybe he'd forgotten all about it. Or maybe Fanny Moreland had taken his mind off the kiss Eleanor owed him.

Or maybe he was no longer interested.

The seeds made both her apron pockets bulge out, and she hurried out to the sun-drenched plot beyond the maple trees. When she reached it, she stopped short. At the far end of the spaded area she spied the gravestone. The encrusted dirt had been scrubbed off so the name and the dates were clearly visible, and it now stood upright, its base securely anchored in the earth. She clasped her hand over her mouth and dropped to her knees.

She would plant red nasturtiums at little Amanda's gravesite, she decided, and let them tumble at the base and trail over the upright stone. Taking a shaky breath, she set to work. She had planted the area halfway to the far end of the plot when a shadow fell over her shoulder.

"Figured you'd be out here," Cord said. "You're getting dirtier than Molly and Danny put together."

"No doubt I am, but I don't care. Ever since I was ill I've wanted to have masses and masses of flowers. I was so hungry for life and color and…happy things! You probably don't know what I'm talking about, do you?"

He was silent for a heartbeat. "I do know, Eleanor. I know what it feels like to wonder if you're going to live or die. And when you do survive, you wake up one morning hankering for all sorts of things."

"I wanted ice cream and perfume, of all things," she confessed. "And flowers. What did you want?"

"Steak. Whiskey. Strawberries. Sunshine. A pretty face." He laughed softly. "And apple pie."

"Sunshine? That's odd."

"Not when you're in…Missouri in the middle of winter. You miss funny things sometimes."

In prison everything was gray. Gray walls, gray uniforms, gray mattress, gray faces. Even the food was gray. That alone made it deadening. It had been a lifeless hell he never again wanted to experience.

Eleanor nodded and dug her fingers into her pocketful of seeds. "Thank you cleaning off that gravestone, Cord. I'm planting nasturtiums at the base."

"I'll fetch a bucket of water if you want the seeds watered in."

She watched him go off to the pump and fill the tin bucket, and when he returned he used his cupped hands to scoop water out onto the planted area. For the next hour they worked in tandem, Eleanor on her knees sprinkling her seeds and patting the soil over them and Cord moving behind her, splashing water onto the earth.

As she worked she could feel him watching her. It made her feel warm all over, warmer than was warranted by the temperature this afternoon. In fact, she felt warmer than she had felt since she was a girl at her first square dance. Even, she thought with a jolt, warmer than when she'd married Tom.

Cord's voice startled her. "Know what I think?"

"I'm sure I could never guess."

"I think you're getting tired, and—"

"Don't start telling me what to do!" she said.

He jerked, and water slopped over the edge of the tin bucket onto her apron. Furious, she slapped down her trowel and stood up. Her vision blurred and she took an unsteady step backward.

"What's wrong?" He touched her shoulder.

"I'm a little dizzy."

"Probably stood up too fast." He set the bucket down, turned her toward him and gripped her shoulders with both hands.

For some reason she couldn't think, couldn't utter a single word with him touching her that way. She swayed toward him and felt his fingers tighten.

"Eleanor."

"What?" she said in an uneven voice.

"You still feel dizzy?"

"N-no."

"Okay if I let you go?"

"N-no," she murmured. "I mean yes. Let me go."

But he didn't. Instead he stepped in close and pulled her into his arms.

"Cord—"

"Yeah, I know. I shouldn't do this. But you owe me a kiss, remember? I've been thinking about it for weeks. I liked thinking about it."

He bent his head and caught her mouth under his. For a long, heart-pounding moment she felt as if she were flying away toward the sun.

All at once he released her. "Eleanor, open your eyes."

She looked up into his steady gaze and drew in a shaky breath. "Yes?"

"You sure you're all right?"

"I th-think so. Why?"

"Not dizzy?"

"No."

"Finished planting all your seeds?"

"Yes."

"Good."

"Why?"

"Because I'm gonna kiss you again and I don't want you thinking about your zinnias."

She blinked, and then she laughed and tipped her face up to his. "Nasturtiums," she whispered. She rested her palms against his shirtfront. "Red ones."

Cord kissed her, and then he kissed her again, longer this time. Just when he thought about lifting her into his arms and heading for her bedroom, a voice in his head screamed into his brain, *Let her go. She doesn't belong to you. You have no right to her.*

"Oh, God," he groaned against her temple. "I don't think I can stand another Sunday afternoon watching you pour lemonade for some randy visitors from town."

"I can't stand it, either," she admitted.

"How about we go on another picnic instead?"

"We'll have to take Molly and Daniel with us."

"Maybe they'll fall asleep," he murmured.

She pulled out of his arms and bent to fluff out her apron. "They won't fall asleep. They'll want to play catch or make grass blade whistles or pick blackberries."

Cord chuckled. "If I make you a blackberry pie will you kiss me again?"

"Certainly not," she said. "But I bet Molly and Danny would."

"Not exactly what I had in mind."

"I know," she said, her voice quiet. "But you and I both know this cannot go any further. It's time to put a stop to it."

Chapter Nineteen

No amount of fried chicken and coleslaw could take up this much space, Cord thought, loading the last picnic items into the wicker hamper. He lugged it out through the apple orchard to a grassy spot by the stream and spread a blanket in the shade of a grove of cottonwoods. Out of breath, Eleanor flopped down and immediately propped her head on her bent knees.

Molly patted her shoulder. "Mama, does your head ache again?"

"No, honey. I'm just a bit out of breath. I've been frying chicken since breakfast. Wouldn't it be funny," she said with a little laugh, "if now I'm too tired to eat our picnic lunch?"

"Wouldn't be funny at all," Cord said, kneeling beside her. "Why don't you stretch out and rest while I rustle up some lemonade?"

She took his suggestion, lay back and gazed up through the leafy trees at the blazing blue sky overhead. Molly and Danny raced off to the stream to hunt for minnows, and Cord rooted around in the picnic hamper. "Keep an eye on the children, would you?" she murmured.

He folded her hand around a jar of cool lemonade and walked off toward the stream with the big water jug. She watched him wedge it among some rocks, say something to Molly and Danny and start back toward her. For a long minute he stood looking down at her, then he stretched out beside her and propped his head on his bent arm. Idly he plucked at the grass, stuck a blade between his lips and rolled it around with his tongue.

She watched his mouth move and listened to the sound of the children's chatter drifting on the still air. Surely she was crazy to like this man so much, to let him kiss her and, even worse, to enjoy it. It was scandalous.

But the truth was she had never been kissed like that before. Even married to Tom she had never experienced the rush of heat, the giddy, devil-may-care feeling that flowed through her when Cord touched her. How could that be?

She had liked Tom well enough when they were married. But she had never felt this unsteady thrum in her chest when she was near him, not even when she was lying next to him in their bed. Mostly she had felt grateful that he had taken her away from her parents' miserable, oppressive household.

But Cord... Cord was another matter. She couldn't begin to understand what she felt about him. She was miffed when he ordered her to rest, touched when he did small, thoughtful things like erecting Amanda's gravestone in her flower bed or baking an apple pie or drying the supper dishes. But, she acknowledged, when he stood near her, or when he touched her, she felt something much more basic. Much more...involving.

She liked him. She hadn't wanted to like this man, but she did. She trusted him. She trusted him with her children. She'd felt it instinctively from that first day when her eyes rested on his craggy, unshaved face and looked into those clear blue eyes that didn't look away no matter what she said.

She rolled over and sat up. "Nothing much bothers you, does it, Cord?"

He spit out the blade of grass. "Plenty bothers me, Eleanor. You have something specific in mind?"

"Well...you're not disturbed when the clean laundry blows off the clothesline and needs to be rinsed again. Or when the children escape after supper and leave you doing up the dishes. Or when Molly wants you to dress one of the kittens up in her doll clothes. Or—"

"Or when you snap at me and tell me to mind my own business when you're so tired you can't walk straight. Or when Danny begged you to let him ride the horse to school and you wouldn't listen, or—"

"Cord, what *does* bother you?"

He let a long silence lapse, during which Molly screeched at something they found in the creek and Danny yelled at her to stop being a sissy. Eleanor didn't think what they found was life-threatening because animated chatter followed. So she waited, watching Cord's face.

"Some things bother me a little," he said, his voice quiet. "Some things bother me a lot."

"Tell me about the 'littles.'"

He laughed. "Well, there's Mama Cat in my bed at night. And finding a raccoon print in the yard or a broken egg in the henhouse."

"What about the things that bother you a lot?"

He shifted to his other elbow and stuck another blade of grass between his lips. "Those Sunday-afternoon gents with their shiny shoes and bow ties lounging all over your front porch."

"Oh, that. Pay no attention to them, Cord. I don't. What else bothers you a lot?"

"Watching you."

"That's all? Just watching me?"

He smiled, an odd sort of half-contented, half-sad smile. "I do it a lot."

"Why?"

"Eleanor, I don't think you really want me to answer that question."

She sat up straighter. "Yes, I do, Cord. I want to know."

He hesitated. "I watch you because I want—"

"Mama!" Molly tumbled onto the blanket between them, Danny at her heels.

"*What* is going on?" Eleanor demanded.

"Danny pushed me in the creek and now my shoes are all wet and squishy."

Danny hovered at the edge of the blanket. "Well, you asked for it, you big sissy. It was only a frog."

"Maybe it's time for you two to play a game of catch," Eleanor proposed.

"Nah. I'm hungry, Ma."

Cord stood up and took the boy by the arm. "Lunch later, Dan. How about you show me this frog you spotted?"

"'Druther play catch," the boy muttered.

"After I see this frog. Must be a big one if it made your sister scream."

"Aw, she screams at everything."

They walked off together toward the creek. Molly watched for a minute, then darted after them and latched onto Cord's hand.

He watches me because he wants...what? Eleanor wondered. What does Cord want? Wages? Afternoons off? *Strawberries?*

All three of them returned with Cord carrying the lemonade jug in one hand and Molly's hand nestled in the other. He stopped at the blanket and nudged the lunch hamper with his boot. "Think it's about time for our picnic?"

Eleanor sat up and busied herself with the contents of the wicker hamper. But she couldn't stop thinking about Cord, about what he was about to say. About what he wanted.

After an hour spent eating fried chicken and coleslaw, along with fresh tomatoes and radishes, the children scampered off to play catch with a sock ball Eleanor had stitched up and Cord stretched out with his arms folded under his head and closed his eyes.

She sipped the last of her lemonade and found herself studying him. His chest rose and fell steadily, and his breathing slowed. *He must have fallen asleep.*

She studied his face, wondering about her hired man, Cord Winterman. Where had he come from? Missouri, he'd said once. But before that, had he been a rancher? A store-keeper? Why did he have no money when he arrived? Could he be on the run? She doubted that, though it might explain his lack of funds.

But he was too relaxed and at ease on her farm to be fleeing from the law. Besides, Sheriff Rivera always kept a stack of wanted posters on his desk, and when Cord drove her into town, the sheriff didn't give him a second look.

She began packing away the picnic things, then noticed that Cord's eyes were open.

"Kids still off playing catch?" he asked, his voice lazy.

She nodded. "It's funny how something competitive like catching a rag ball solves all squabbles."

"Doesn't work for grown-ups," he remarked with a grin.

"Grown-ups compete in other ways."

"Yeah?"

"Of course. My friend Verena Forester, the dressmaker in town, and I have been competing for years over who can sew better. She believes she is winning because for the last year I haven't had enough energy to make any dresses."

He chuckled. "Didn't realize women were so competitive."

"Oh, yes. Verena's always telling me my dresses are out-of-date, that my necklines are all wrong. Not low enough."

"What you're wearing today is buttoned up to your chin."

She fingered the buttons of her shirtwaist. "Well, yes, but this is daytime. My green dimity will be for evening."

"Yeah?" he said with a frown. "Evening where?"

"Another evening at the Jensen's barn next Saturday night. This time it's a square dance."

He sat up. "You want to go?"

"We are *all* going. As you say, it would be good for the children."

"Well, that's sure a switch. What changed your mind about social stuff?"

"Oh, I don't really know. Molly loves to dance now that you've taught her how to twirl. And maybe that little girl in the yellow pinafore will be there. That would please Danny."

Then she looked off across the meadow. She could never admit the real reason, that she felt safe and protected when she was with Cord. That she wanted to feel his arms around her again.

He sat up. "Last time we went to a dance Fanny Moreland crawled all over me and you got mad and wouldn't talk all the way home."

"I did not!"

"You did."

She looked down at the picnic basket for a long time. "Well, I'm over that now. With the children along, I'd need to take the wagon and I don't feel strong enough yet to handle it alone. So…would you come?"

Cord laughed out loud. "Well, now, Miss Eleanor, I thought you'd never ask!"

Chapter Twenty

Darla Bledsoe clutched Eleanor's forearm, eyeing Cord, who was just now entering Jensen's barn after parking the wagon. *"Who* is that delicious-looking man?"

Eleanor sighed. It was one thing to work up enough courage to brave another dance. It was quite another to fend off another hungry female.

"That's my hired man," she replied. "His name is Cordell Winterman."

"Your hired man? You mean he's helping to bring in your apple harvest?"

Eleanor edged away from the pretty red-haired widow. "Yes, that and more. He's been very helpful doing all sorts of things, repairing the barn, mending the pasture fence. He has even dug a flower bed for me."

"How nice," Darla said tightly. Her avid gaze followed Cord's loose-limbed progress across the floor toward them.

Molly dashed across the plank floor and grabbed Cord's hand. Eleanor watched him bend down to her daughter's level and listen to what she was saying. Darla watched, too, her eyes calculating.

Cord straightened, scooped Molly up in his arms and waltzed her around and around to the sound of guitars and a violin playing "Clementine." She flung both her little arms about his neck.

"Is he married?" Darla asked, watching him.

"No, he isn't." At least Darla wasn't as annoyingly obvious as Fanny Moreland. Eleanor sat down on a wooden bench on the sidelines and turned toward Sarah Cloudman beside her. The gray-haired boardinghouse owner sent her a raised-eyebrow look.

Cord danced past with Molly in his arms, and all at once Darla sank down beside Eleanor. "Call him over," she whispered.

"No, Darla. He's busy waltzing with my daughter. Molly will talk about it for days. He—"

Before she could finish her sentence, Darla shot off the bench and darted across the floor. Eleanor watched her bring Cord to a halt with a possessive hand on his arm, then push Molly off toward the sidelines. On second thought, Darla and Fanny were apparently cut from the same man-hungry cloth.

"Watch out," Sarah Cloudman murmured. "That one's got claws like the tines of a pitchfork."

Molly skipped over and Eleanor lifted her daughter onto her lap. "That lady said you wanted me, Mama."

"Hah!" Sarah huffed. "What'd I just say?"

Eleanor cuddled her daughter close. "Shall you and I have some apple cider?" At Molly's nod, the two of them stood up and moved toward the refreshment table. When they returned with two cups of golden apple cider, Eleanor asked Molly where Danny was.

"He's playing outside with my grandson, Mark," Mrs. Cloudman volunteered. "Rooney, my husband, is teaching them to toss horseshoes."

Horseshoes! Her son was turning into a man before she got used to his being a little boy playing with marbles.

Eleanor's gaze returned to the dance floor, where sets were forming for a square dance. Darla was tugging Cord into position in the first set when he stopped dead and lifted Darla's hand off his sleeve.

"Oh, please, Cordell." Darla's petulant voice rose above the violins. "I bet you've had a lot of square-dancing experience."

Eleanor gritted her teeth. On second thought, maybe she preferred Fanny Moreland.

Cord plucked the woman's hand off his sleeve. "Sure have," he said blandly. He took her elbow and purposefully steered her to the sidelines, where he left her standing with Jessamine and Cole Sanders, publishers of the *Smoke River Lark-Sentinel*. As he turned to leave, Jessamine winked at him and he chuckled. The woman had read his thoughts exactly.

He didn't want to dance with Darla. He scanned the crowd, praying Fanny Moreland wasn't present. He didn't want to dance with Fanny, either. He wanted to dance with Eleanor. She was sitting across the room next to Sarah Cloudman, with Molly on her lap. He crossed the room in long strides, walked up to Eleanor and held out his hand.

"Oh, Cord, I don't think I ought to do any dancing tonight. I'm not very good at square-dancing."

"I don't care," he said shortly. He lifted Molly onto the bench next to Mrs. Cloudman, pulled Eleanor to her feet and piloted her into an assembling set that was short one couple.

"Cord, I don't think…"

"Don't argue. I haven't been to a real square dance since… In a long time." He maneuvered her into position. When the call came to "swing your partners," he turned to her.

As Cord remembered from the first time she'd danced with him, Eleanor fit perfectly in his arms. After a minute he had to laugh. She said she wasn't good at square-dancing, but she was so light on her feet it was like dancing with a snowflake. Maybe she hadn't done very much recently, but she must have at some time; she knew every call, every tricky maneuver. She even added a double turn on the "promenade home."

Her gray eyes sparkled, and he felt absurdly pleased that she was enjoying herself. Correction, that she was enjoying herself *with him*. He blew out a long breath and swung her around and around until her long ruffled skirt got tangled up between his legs.

The square dance caller finished up two more sets and then announced that a slow two-step would be next. When the music started, Eleanor headed for the sidelines, but Cord caught her shoulder.

"Dance with me."

"But I *have* been dancing with you," she protested.

"Not hardly."

"But—"

"Eleanor, for God's sake, stop making excuses and dance with me."

"I'm not mak—"

"Yes, you are." He pressed his hand against her back and pulled her close. "Now hush up and dance."

She tried to stop moving with him, but he wouldn't let her. "Cord, you know I dislike it when you order me around."

"Yeah, I know," he whispered. He nestled her chin against his shoulder. "Dance with me. That's an order."

She laughed. And then she didn't say another word for the next twenty minutes, through "Red River Valley" and "Clementine" and maybe another song, but he lost track. He closed his eyes and breathed in the lemony-rose scent of her hair and listened to her breathing until he thought he'd go crazy.

He wanted her so much he ached. "Eleanor," he murmured.

"Hmm?"

"When will the apple harvest be finished?"

"Around the middle of October. Why?"

"You know that I'm staying until then."

She lifted her head and looked up at him. "Yes, I know."

"That's two months longer than I planned to be around when I came in the spring."

"Oh." She was silent for a long minute. "Yes, I remember now. You are going on to California."

"I was, yes."

"And now you're not?"

"Now I don't know." He didn't want to tell her what his plans were because he no longer knew what they were. The only thing he knew was that he couldn't stay on as her hired man. He wanted more than that. And Eleanor was married to someone else.

He pulled her closer and felt the nagging hunger he'd known ever since the first day he'd laid eyes on her. As the washtub bass thumped and the violins dipped and soared, they slowly circled around the plank floor and he held her close and stopped trying to think rationally.

The music filled the noisy barn, rising above the sounds of crying children, the good-natured laughter of storekeepers and wrangling rival ranchers. Eleanor closed her eyes. She wouldn't think about the apple harvest or October or Cord's leaving, not tonight. Not here in his arms, inhaling the scent of shaving lotion and sweat and whiskey.

Whiskey? Had he been drinking? Underneath everything she detected the laundry soap smell of the blue chambray shirt he wore. The sleeves were rolled up almost to the elbow; his bare forearm rested against her upper back. She pressed against it, not to move farther away from him but to feel his warmth.

He folded her right hand into his and lowered their intertwined fingers so her knuckles rested in the middle of his chest. His heartbeat thumped steadily under her palm. In his arms she felt protected. Valued. Almost…cherished.

At night, when she allowed herself to examine her most secret feelings, what she felt for Cord Winterman was decidedly unsettling. She drew in a long, uneven breath. *What is wrong with me? I should not be feeling these things in another man's arms.*

Suddenly she felt Cord's pulse jump into an erratic rhythm. Surely he couldn't be reading her thoughts, could he? Oh, heavens, she was growing far too warm.

"Darla Bledsoe is stalking us," he whispered.

She looked at him sideways and laughed. "Darla is stalking *you*, Cord. Not me."

"Let her. I'm not interested."

"Darla is quite wealthy," she couldn't resist saying. "Like Fanny Moreland. When Darla's husband died she inherited a lumber company."

"Not interested."

Another question popped into her head and she opened her mouth, and then immediately closed it. Mercy sakes, she couldn't possibly ask him that! Not in a million years. First of all, it was none of her business. And second, she wasn't sure she wanted to hear the answer. After all, a man's private life was…private.

But she wondered about it just the same. And she spent most of the night thinking about it. After the apple harvest, would Cord stay and court one of the hungry females who lusted after him?

And how would she feel if he did?

The following morning Cord awoke to Danny's anguished voice from the barn door below him. "Cord! Come quick! Ma's collapsed."

He swept Mama Cat and the kittens off his blanket, yanked on his jeans and climbed down the loft ladder.

"Hurry!" Danny cried.

He raced out the door after the boy and pounded up the porch steps. The front door stood ajar. "Where is she?" he shouted.

"In the kitchen. She was standin' at the stove and she just kinda crumpled up all of a sudden."

Eleanor lay sprawled awkwardly on the kitchen floor, facedown, inches away from the hot stove. A sobbing Molly knelt beside her.

Cord crouched beside her and felt for a pulse in her neck. It was there, but it was faint. Gently he rolled her over and began rubbing one of her hands. Her face was dead white.

"What's wrong with her?" Molly wept.

"Don't know yet. Danny, get a wet dish towel." He bent over her. "Eleanor? Eleanor, can you hear me?"

Danny pressed a sopping towel into his hand and he slipped his hand under her to raise her head a few inches off the floor, then pressed the towel against her neck.

"Is Mama gonna die?" Molly wailed.

"No, honey. She's breathing and her heart's beating. She's gonna be just fine." He began to undo the top buttons of her blue gingham dress and spread the bodice wide. Thank God she wasn't wearing a damn-fool corset. "Danny, get me another cold towel."

He slapped this on her upper chest. "Eleanor, can you hear me?" He thought she gave a little moan, but Molly was crying so hard he couldn't be sure.

He lifted Eleanor into his arms and started for the staircase. "Danny, run ahead and open her door. And bring those towels."

Cord climbed the stairs after the boy. "Don't cry, Molly," he called over his shoulder. "Your mama's going to be fine."

The girl trailed him all the way up, snuffling loudly. At the top of the stairs he headed for the last room on the right and angled Eleanor's body through the door. Danny smoothed out the rumpled quilt and Cord carefully laid the limp form down on the bed.

Her face still looked white as fresh plaster. He replaced the wet towel at her neck, swung the second one in the air to cool it and again laid it on her chest.

Molly crawled up on the bed beside her mother. "Mama, wake up. Please wake up."

"Danny, go down and check the stove, see if there's anything left on it that could burn."

"Ma was makin' coffee," the boy volunteered.

"Good. Fill a big cup and dump in a couple lumps of sugar and bring it on up."

Danny thumped down the stairs and Cord laid his hand on Eleanor's forehead. Cold. "Molly, help me get this quilt over her." Together they worked the blanket out from under her shoulders, then her hips, and spread it over her inert form.

"How come she doesn't wake up?" Molly asked in a small voice.

Cord didn't answer. He was wondering the same thing. Danny reappeared with the coffee in Eleanor's favorite mug. "It might be too hot," he said. "It was boiling."

At that moment Eleanor opened her eyes. "What happened?" she said.

"You fainted," Cord said. "Danny came and got me and I carried you upstairs."

"Oh, yes, I remember now. I was setting the coffeepot on the stove and all at once things got gray and spotty and I couldn't see clearly."

"You just crumpled up by the stove," Danny volunteered.

Molly scooted closer. "You scared me, Mama. You looked all funny."

Eleanor tried to sit up but Cord pressed her shoulders down and offered the coffee. "Drink some of this," he ordered.

"I can't when I'm lying down," she said, her voice weak.

He helped her sit up and folded her hands around the mug.

"Danny brought the coffee from the kitchen."

At her first sip she wrinkled her nose. "Too sweet. Danny, you know I never use sugar."

"Cord said to—"

"Drink it anyway," Cord said. "I figure you fainted because you were plumb out of strength. Maybe you've been overdoing it the last few days."

"I have a farm to run," she countered. "But I did feel extra-tired after all that square-dancing last night. And then I didn't sleep much."

Cord looked at her sharply. "How come?"

"I…" She looked down at the quilt covering her. "I must have been overtired and keyed up. Anyway, I couldn't sleep. And this morning I felt perfectly fine until I went to set the coffeepot on the stove and things went all gray."

"Lucky you didn't crack your head on the stove or a corner of the kitchen table."

"It's lucky I didn't fall on top of Molly or Danny! They were standing right there next to me, helping with breakfast."

"You probably just folded from the bottom up. I saw plenty of that threshing wheat in hot weather."

Danny perked up. "Where was that, Cord?"

"Kansas. Hotter 'n—" He caught himself. "Hotter than blazes."

"It wasn't that hot in my kitchen this morning," Eleanor said.

Cord stood up. "Maybe not, but you've had enough activity today. I'll finish cooking breakfast and you catch up on your sleep."

She pressed her mouth into a line. "Cord, I hate it when you order me around."

He gave her a long, amused look, and then he grinned. "One egg or two?"

The rest of the day felt perfectly decadent. Eleanor ate the scrambled eggs and bacon that Danny brought up on a tray, and then she slid down under the blue quilt and lazed away the morning. After a few hours she got up, slipped off her half-unbuttoned dress and curled up under the quilt again.

She was deeply asleep until she heard voices coming from the front yard. She stumbled to the window and pulled the curtain aside to see what was going on, and there was Cord, standing squarely in front of Todd Mankewicz and two others, Red Smalley and someone she couldn't identify because his back was toward her. Her hired man wasn't saying anything, but the three male visitors were being plenty vocal. She raised the window so she could hear what they were saying.

"Look here, Winterman, you got no right to tell us Miss Eleanor isn't receiving visitors." The speaker was Todd.

Red echoed his words. "This ain't your house, hired man. You got no place tellin' us to shove off."

"Yeah," the third fellow, Gus Garner, shouted, his blond beard quivering. "Let her tell us herself. Where is she, anyway?"

"She's upstairs, asleep."

"How come?" Red bellowed. "It's two o'clock in the afternoon."

Cord stepped to the edge of the yard. "That's none of your business."

"Heck, yes, it's our business," Todd shouted. "We're keepin' an eye on Miss Eleanor."

Eleanor bit back a bubble of laughter. Keeping an eye on her molasses cookies would be closer to the truth. Then she heard Cord's low voice.

"Mrs. Malloy—" she liked the subtle emphasis he achieved by using her full name "—doesn't need you or anyone else to keep an eye on her. She's managed on her own for the last seven years with no one's 'eye on her.' Plus she's got an almost grown son and a hired man."

Todd puffed out his chest. "You're out of line, Winterman. You got no right to speak for Miss Eleanor. Got no right to even be here, far as I can see."

Cord advanced a step. "I work here, Mankewicz. Mrs. Malloy hired me to work for her."

Todd edged back a step, followed by Red. Gus, the pudgy blond one, stood his ground, shaking his fist in Cord's face. Cord reached out and brushed the meaty arm aside, then took another step forward. All three men edged back toward the front gate.

Danny appeared at Cord's side, and Eleanor's chest tightened. Her son was trying to protect her right along with her hired man.

Red stopped and lifted his bristly chin. "Just what's your interest in Miss Eleanor, Winterman?"

"My interest? Doing the chores she can't manage. Keeping an eye on her children. And right now I'm interested in protecting her."

"From what?" Todd shot. "From us?"

Cord made no answer, just took another step forward.

Eleanor almost cheered. Maybe her hired man would permanently discourage her stream of Sunday-afternoon visitors. Wouldn't it be wonderful to sit on the porch swing without being invaded by visitors and having to pour lemonade all afternoon?

Red's back was now pressing into the gate. "I'm not leavin' 'til Miss Eleanor herself tells me to leave."

At that, Eleanor raised the window even higher and leaned out. "I want you all to leave!" she cried.

The three male faces tilted upward and she ducked behind the curtain. Then she peeked out to see the men shake their heads, yank open the gate and crowd through. After a moment they all climbed into the buggy in which they'd driven out from town and rolled back onto the road.

Cord followed them, swung the gate closed and bent to ruffle Danny's hair. He said something to her son, but his voice was so low Eleanor couldn't hear the words.

Smiling for the first time all day, she tiptoed back to the bed and crawled under the covers. It was simply wonderful to feel protected! Her two brave knights, one tall and lean and one short and bony, deserved a special dessert after supper tonight. Blackberry cobbler, maybe.

But by suppertime Eleanor found she could scarcely drag herself out of bed again. Cooking supper was out of the question. She curled up and tried to think.

What was wrong with her? Was Cord right, that she had simply overdone it on Saturday? Or was it something more serious?

She got her answer an hour later when another buggy rattled up to the gate and a few minutes later Doc Dougherty mounted the stairs. She heard a tentative knock on her bedroom door and Danny peered in.

"Ma? Cord rode into town and got the doctor. Can he come in?"

The tall, dark-haired physician walked to her bedside, plunked down his leather bag and withdrew a stethoscope. He checked her pulse and her breathing, listened to her heart and thumped her on the back, then listened to her chest again.

"Eleanor, I don't need to tell you how difficult it can be to recover from pneumonia, and you had a particularly bad case. Getting your strength back can take months."

"That's too long," she moaned. "I can't wait months!"

He patted her shoulder. "I suspect that's the problem. You've been working too hard, doing too much. And there's something else I'd like to say. Maybe it'll wake you up. If it weren't for your hired man, you'd probably be dead."

Eleanor stared up at him. "But I feel perfectly well, really I do. Except for this morning, I mean."

"I believe you. But I want you to pay attention to what I've said. When you've been seriously ill, as you were last winter, recovery will be slow. It's a 'two steps forward and one step back'. proposition. I want to be very clear about this—if you want to live to see your children grow up, you must, absolutely *must*, take better care of yourself. Do less. Rest more."

"I have a farm to run, Doc. And children that need attention."

He leaned closer. "Eleanor, are you listening to me?"

"Y-yes. But I honestly thought I was doing better."

He smiled. "Don't be too hard on yourself. Just be more careful, all right?" He folded up his stethoscope and dropped it in his medical bag. "I think you did a smart thing to hire that man downstairs in your kitchen."

Eleanor sat up. "In the kitchen? Whatever is he doing in the kitchen?"

Doc Dougherty chuckled. "I'd guess he's making supper. See that you eat some of it. And," he added in a mock serious tone, "do *not* wash up the dishes tonight."

She heard his laughter all the way down the stairs.

Well! Cord was making supper? Her curiosity built until she threw off the quilt, found her blue gingham dress and crept downstairs on bare feet to see what was going on in her kitchen.

She found Cord standing at the stove pouring pancake batter onto the griddle. Molly and Danny were setting plates on the table, followed by two milk glasses.

Danny caught sight of her just as he was laying out the forks. "H'lo, Ma. Are you all better?"

"I am much improved, Danny. I thought I would come down and see what was going on."

Cord spoke from the stove. "Supper is 'going on.' Are you hungry? We're having jelly roll-ups."

"Jelly roll-ups? What on earth is that?"

"You'll have to wait and see."

"Very well, I'll wait. The name, jelly roll-ups, sounds very appetizing."

Cord sent her a grin. "Molly, set a place for your mama." He turned back to the stove, grabbed the spatula and started flipping the pancakes.

"I've, um, never heard of jelly roll-ups," she ventured.

"Cord knows how to make 'em, Mama, and I found the strawberry jam in the pantry."

Eleanor sank down on her usual chair to watch. "I can't imagine what a 'jelly roll-up' is."

Cord sent her another grin, wider this time, and scooped up three large pancakes, which he stacked on a plate and put in the oven. "Never had a jelly roll-up, huh? Danny, pour some milk for you and Molly."

While her son filled the two glasses, Cord set a plate of very thin, lightly browned pancakes on the table. "Quick, now, take one of these and spread it all over with jam and roll it up tight."

Danny speared one, followed by Molly, and both smeared on strawberry jam. "Come on, Ma, grab one!"

"Yeah, grab one," Cord echoed from the stove.

She did, slathered the delicate pancake with jam, rolled it up and took a bite. To her surprise it was delicious, the pancake light and slightly sweet and flavored with something, maybe vanilla? She cut off more bites with her fork while the children ate theirs with their hands and licked the oozing jam off their fingers.

Cord set another plate of the thin pancakes on the table and sat down across from her. He spread jam on one, then laid another on top and spread that one, too. Then he rolled it up into a double-thick creation that made Eleanor smile.

"Oooh," Molly cried. "I want one like that!"

"Go ahead," Cord urged. "That's called a double jelly roll-up, and only members of the Malloy family are allowed to eat them. And me," he added.

While they constructed their double roll-ups, Cord poured coffee for Eleanor and himself. "Kind of a funny supper, I guess, but it's all I could think of. Anyway, it's keeping them busy instead of worrying about their mama." He tipped his head toward Molly and Danny; their jam-smeared faces looked intent.

She caught his gaze. "Thank you, Cord. For getting the doctor and for making supper."

"Doc says you need to rest more."

Eleanor nodded. "I will try," she said. "But it's hard. I look around and see so many things that need doing that I get carried away."

"Have you always been like that? Or is it just since you've been alone on the farm?"

"Always. Before I was married I needed to keep busy because…" She glanced at Molly and Danny, still absorbed in rolling up their pancakes. "That was a way to escape."

"Escape what? Were you mistreated?"

She sipped her coffee. "Not in the physical sense, no. But there were other things I needed to…not be aware of. My father and mother argued and bickered and shouted at each other, and at me, and…" She lowered her voice. "I needed to escape."

Cord tipped his chair back. "Molly? Danny? If you've finished your supper, why don't you gather up the plates and put them in the dishpan. I'll wash them up later."

"Sure, Cord. Kin we go outside, Ma?"

Eleanor nodded and the children tumbled out the door into the backyard.

Cord sent her a penetrating glance. "I don't know which is worse," he said slowly, "parents who argue all the time, or parents who whip you, or parents that die. At least when they die, it gets real quiet at home."

She blinked. "Cord, what are you saying?"

"I'm saying that even bad parents might be better than *no* parents. But then again—" he clunked his chair back onto the floor "—bad parents are pretty hard to take."

Eleanor sucked in her breath. "Were you beaten as a child?"

He didn't say anything for a long while, and when he did speak, his voice was low and hoarse. "Don't ask me anything more, Eleanor. I don't want to talk about it."

She said nothing, just reached over and briefly touched his hand. The sound of the children's laughter drifted through the open back door.

After a while Cord stood up and moved to the sink, where the dishpan full of plates and soapsuds waited.

"I think I'll finish my coffee on the front porch," Eleanor said. "Now that you've cleared it of unwanted guests," she added with a laugh. She pushed through the screen door and settled herself in the porch swing.

After a while Cord joined her, bringing with him the coffeepot. He filled up her cup and then his own and set the pot on the porch, then eased down onto the swing beside her and pushed it into a slow back-and-forth motion.

They rocked away for over an hour without saying a word. Eleanor thought it was the most peaceful evening she could ever recall.

Chapter Twenty-One

"Blackberries are ripe in the cow pasture," Danny announced the next afternoon. "And the apple trees are loaded with big red apples!"

Cord hoisted the water bucket and headed out to water Eleanor's flower bed. "Guess summer's really here," he remarked.

"Already," Eleanor added.

Her flower bed had burst into a riot of color. Looking at them in the evening after supper made her giddy with joy, especially when the red nasturtiums began to twine over the gravestone at the far end of her garden.

She picked lush bouquets for every room in the house, even the kitchen, where a fat mason jar of black-eyed Susans, blue delphiniums and frothy white baby's breath appeared on the kitchen table at supper one evening. Molly wanted to make a daisy chain of the black-eyed Susans, so Eleanor went out at dusk and picked another handful. When she returned, Cord had stuck one blossom in his buttonhole and Danny was washing up the supper dishes while Molly worked on her daisy chain.

Cord poured a second cup of coffee for each of them. They didn't talk, just sat at the supper table and listened to the children's sporadic chatter. Eleanor was feeling stronger than the day she had fainted. She was resting more, and she felt in increasingly good health since the pneumonia had sapped her strength and her spirits. And she was feeling happier.

Especially pleasing was the thought of picking bushels of Anna and Fiesta apples and taking them into town to sell. Already Carl Ness at the mercantile was asking when he could expect them. His storefront was now painted a rich turquoise blue, and Edith Ness was spending the summer painting the fronts of other establishments up and down Main Street. Even the sheriff's office now sported a bright sunshiny yellow facade. Eleanor laughed every time she and Cord drove past in the wagon.

Today Cord was delivering a wagonload of apples, eight bushel baskets, to Samson Northcutt at the mercantile in Gillette Springs. He left at dawn, and drove the hot, dusty forty miles. It took him all day, and by the time he unloaded all the apples he was dead tired. He thought about staying at the hotel in town, then decided he didn't want to be away from Eleanor and the kids all night.

He collected Samson's payment for the apples, grabbed a steak and a beer at the Shady Lady Saloon and fed the horse a hatful of oats. Then he headed for home.

Dusk threw lavender shadows across the road and he worked to keep his eyelids open. Probably shouldn't have had that beer—it cost two bits of Eleanor's hard-earned money—and now he regretted not topping off his meal with a few cups of strong coffee to help him stay alert.

This was the loneliest damn road between Smoke River and Gillette Springs, and it was studded with potholes deeper than one of Eleanor's dishpans! Made him wish he'd brought Danny with him for company, but he knew Eleanor would have had a fit if he'd even suggested it. She coddled the boy too much. Cord felt halfway guilty about secretly teaching him to ride, even though Eleanor now knew what they'd been doing, but he had decided it wasn't safe for Eleanor to live miles out of town with no way to get help in an emergency. Soon the boy would need a horse of his own.

He tightened his hands on the reins. After the apple harvest drew to a close and he moved on to California…

Oh, hell. He wasn't ready for it to come to a close, not yet. He urged the horse to pick up its pace. Chances were he wouldn't reach Smoke River until three or four in the morning, but he wanted to be there, not here on this endless road.

It grew black—dark, with no moon. He passed a stand of Douglas firs and thought about reining up for a few hours of sleep, then decided against it. He blinked hard and kept going.

Danny, you're coming with me on the next trip to Gillette Springs. His ma wouldn't like it, but so what? The kid was almost ten years old; it was time for him to take on more responsibility, especially since Cord planned to leave as soon as… Well, soon. Besides, Danny's chatter would help keep him awake.

Eleanor finished drying the last supper plate and stacked it in the china cabinet. She could hear Molly and Danny arguing about something on the porch; their voices rose and then faded away as they raced off toward the barn.

She hung the damp dish towel by the stove, slipped her garden shears into her apron pocket and walked out through the screen door and down the steps. She headed out past the maple trees to her flower garden, where she intended to pick more black-eyed Susans for the kitchen table and a fresh bouquet of fragrant alyssum and pinks for her bedroom.

When the sun went down, the heavenly sweet scent of the white nicotiana filled the evening air. Each time she passed the gravestone at the far end of the garden plot she said a brief prayer for little Amanda Martin. She bent to snip a handful of blooms, then thought she heard a horse.

Surely Cord couldn't be back so soon? She stepped through the maple trees and her entire body went cold.

A horse she didn't recognize was tied to the porch rail, and a man was tramping up her front steps. He wore a high-crowned hat and his spurs jingled at each step. She didn't recognize the horse, or the man, and she suddenly realized that this stranger stood between her and the revolver she kept above the front door.

The man peered through the screen and rapped on the wood, then turned toward her.

"H'lo, Ellie."

Her breath choked off. "Tom!" Then her vision went gray and her knees threatened to buckle. "Tom, what are you doing here?"

He barked out a harsh laugh. "I live here, remember?"

She would never have recognized him in a hundred years. His skin was sun-leathered, and the shadow of a beard darkened his chin. She worked to steady her voice. "You've been gone over seven years! Where have you been?"

He sent her a sidelong look. "Didja miss me?"

Eleanor bit her lip. "The War ended and months and months went by, and then years passed with no word. Not one word came from anyone with news that you'd been killed or captured or... You didn't desert, did you?"

He worked the toe of one boot into the dirt. "Nah, I didn't desert. Sure wanted to, though."

"Why didn't you write? You could at least have let me know you were alive. Why didn't you?"

He started down the porch steps. "Aw, c'mon, Ellie. I'm home now. Aren'tcha glad to see me?"

"I— It's been so long I don't even know you."

"Ellie..."

"Don't come near me!"

"Can I at least put my horse in the barn?"

"No, you cannot. You ride on back to town and leave me alone." Some instinct told her she didn't want him to know she and the children were alone out here. "Go on, get on your horse and ride out."

He swore, strode over to his horse and swung into the saddle. Instantly she dashed up the porch steps and made a beeline for the revolver over the door. Then she called the children into the house, locked the front door and sent them up to bed.

When she heard their bedroom door shut, she began to shake uncontrollably. The rest of the night she sat rigid on the settee in the parlor, positioned so she could see out the front window.

And she kept the loaded revolver in her lap.

Chapter Twenty-Two

Cord guided the wagon in through the gate and walked the gray gelding into the barn. It must be almost dawn and he was so tired he couldn't see straight. He unhitched the wagon, rubbed down the mare and fed her some oats, then climbed up to his pallet in the loft. In an instant he was asleep.

Late the next morning the sun streamed in through the small loft window and he sat up, rubbed his unshaven chin and pushed Mama Cat and her three kittens off his chest into the straw. He'd better hurry or he'd miss breakfast.

Just as he stepped out the barn door, an unfamiliar horse turned in at the gate. The rider's face was hidden by a new-looking wide-brimmed black hat, but Cord couldn't help noticing the man's fancy tooled boots and the jinglebobs on his spurs. The saddle looked Spanish.

The stranger dismounted, tied his horse to the fence rail and tramped up onto the porch. He didn't stop to knock, just pushed on through the screen door. The hair on the back of Cord's neck prickled.

He followed the man through the door, noting that his hat had been carelessly tossed onto the settee in the parlor. Cord moved on into the kitchen and stopped dead in his tracks.

Eleanor stood at the stove, cracking eggs into a ceramic

bowl, and the stranger was seated in Cord's chair at the kitchen table.

He cleared his throat and Eleanor spun toward him. "Oh, Cord, you're back! I——I'm glad."

Her face looked anything but glad. She looked exhausted, like she'd been awake all night, and her eyes looked funny. Uneasy. "Eleanor? What's going on?"

She waved a fluttery hand at the man sitting at the table. "Cord, this is my… This is Tom Malloy."

He stared hard at the man for so long he stopped fiddling with his fork and looked up. "Cordell Winterman," Cord said at last. He didn't offer to shake hands.

"Um… Tom has just returned from…?" Eleanor sent her husband a questioning look. "From…?"

"Mexico."

Cord lifted his eyebrows at Eleanor. She turned back to the bowl of half-beaten eggs and at that moment the kids thumped down the staircase.

"Cord!" Danny yelped. "You're back!"

Molly clasped his trouser leg and lifted her arms to him. He bent to pick her up, took the chair across from Malloy and settled the girl on his lap. He noticed that a fifth chair had been drawn up to the breakfast table.

"Danny," Eleanor began. "Do you remember your…" She tipped her head toward the stranger. "Your father?"

Danny's face went white and he studied the man. "You're my pa?" he said in a doubtful voice. "Ma says I was only two when you went away, so I guess I don't recognize you."

"And who's this?" Malloy boomed, looking at the girl Cord held on his lap.

"This is your daughter, Tom. Molly. She was born nine months after you left."

Malloy said nothing. Molly snuggled closer to Cord, and he patted her bony spine. Eleanor gave a final vicious frothing of the eggs with her fork and turned toward the stove.

"I don't believe you're my pa," Danny muttered. "Prove it."

Malloy raised his hand as if to slap the boy. "Tom!" Eleanor shouted. "Don't you dare touch my son!"

"Aw, c'mon, Ellie. A little discipline never hurt a kid."

Cord set Molly on her feet, stood up and shoved her and Danny behind him. "You heard her, Malloy. You lay a hand on either of these kids and you'll answer to me."

"Oh, yeah? Just who do you think you are, mister?"

"I'm the hired man."

"Well, Mr. Hired Man, this is my farm. I'm home now, and I don't need any hired man."

Eleanor moved to face her husband. "This is *my* farm, Tom. The deed is in my name."

"Huh! You're still my wife, Ellie. And I'm still your husband. What I say is the law around here, and I say your hired man rides out of here before the sun goes down."

Cord clenched his jaw. "I'm not riding anywhere, Malloy. Eleanor hired me and I'll go when she fires me."

Eleanor poured the beaten eggs into the skillet and stood at the stove, poking at them and biting her lip. She guessed it was a standoff, but she knew things weren't finished between her hired man and her husband. Or between Tom and herself. It left her with a hard knot in the pit of her stomach.

With a shaking hand she dumped the scrambled eggs onto a platter and lifted a dozen slices of crisp toast from the oven rack. "Sit down and eat, Cord. Molly, Daniel, have you washed your hands?"

Both children nodded and scrambled back onto their chairs. She poured coffee for Cord and her husband and took a seat between them, putting Molly and Danny on either side of her. Neither child, she noticed, spared a glance at Tom. On impulse she folded her hands and bent her head.

"Dear Lord…" Out of the corner of her eye she saw Cord send her a puzzled look. In all the months he'd been here, she had never once said grace. She gave him what she hoped was a significant look and went on.

"We thank You for the food we are about to eat and for our many blessings, for the hens that lay our eggs, for the apple trees that provide our income, for the good health of Molly and Daniel." She paused and swallowed. "And we thank you for Cord Winterman, my hired man. Without him, this farm would not have survived these past months. Amen."

"How come you didn't mention me in your blessing, Ellie?" Tom growled.

"Because," she said calmly, "I don't know whether you are a blessing or not. You've been gone so long I hardly know you. You're like a stranger."

"We'll get to know each other soon enough, Ellie. Tonight, maybe."

She stiffened. "No, we will not, Tom. You will be sleeping in the barn."

"The barn!" He reached for the platter of scrambled eggs and she rapped her fork sharply on his knuckles. "In this house, the children eat first." She spooned eggs onto Molly and Danny's plates, then passed the platter to Cord.

"The hell I'm gonna sleep in the barn," Tom muttered. "A man has his rights."

Cord shoved the platter of scrambled eggs in front of him. "She said you're sleeping in the barn, Malloy. If I was you I'd take that as a polite request."

"Well, you're *not* me, hired man. I'll sleep where I damn well please."

Eleanor clanked her fork onto the table. "You will sleep in the barn, Tom. Or you will sleep in town."

"Huh!" He eyed Cord. "I wonder where your hired man sleeps."

"In the attic," Cord said quickly, with a questioning look at her.

She swallowed. "Yes, Cord sleeps in the attic."

A long, awkward silence fell. Finally Cord picked up his spoon and began stirring some milk from Molly's glass into his coffee. Eleanor shot him a puzzled glance; Cord always drank his coffee black.

"I'm going to be picking apples today," he announced. "Later I'll load them into the wagon to take into town. Anybody want to help?"

"I will!" Danny sang out.

Molly looked at her mother. "I wanna play with my dollies. Can I?"

Eleanor smiled at her. "Yes, honey. Your dollies need you to dress them up nice. I will be helping Cord in the orchard." She pushed a bite of scrambled egg into her mouth and forced herself to swallow it down. It tasted like shoe leather.

Tom pursed his lips. "Me, I'm gonna mosey on into town. Got some catching up to do."

Nobody said a word.

Cord heaved the bushel basket into the back of the wagon, grabbed an empty one and handed it down to Danny. "Take this to your ma, over behind that ladder." He picked up another and followed the boy to where Eleanor sat on the bottom rung, one hand over her eyes.

"Getting tired?" he asked.

"No. What I'm getting is worried."

He pointed to where he wanted Danny to drop the empty basket, and the boy moved away. "Worried about what? Looks like it's gonna be a real good apple harvest."

"I'm not worried about apples, Cord. I'm worried about Tom."

He went down on one knee in front of her. "What about Tom?"

"There's something odd about him. Something I can't put my finger on."

Cord nodded. He wouldn't describe Tom Malloy as odd, exactly. More like obnoxious. Maybe even violent.

"Could be he's just throwing his weight around. You know, testing the waters."

"The waters have been tested. He thinks he owns everything he sees, including me. I'm afraid of him, Cord."

"Eleanor, he doesn't own you. And if I remember right, he doesn't own this farm."

"Just think," she said quietly, staring at the ground. "I am afraid of my own husband."

He waited, saying nothing.

"Cord, I do want you to sleep in the attic. It's probably dusty up there and full of cobwebs, but I'll clean it up before tonight."

"I'm not worried about a few cobwebs. To be frank, I'm more concerned about Tom, even if he *is* sleeping in the barn."

She knew she was frowning, but she couldn't seem to stop. Never in all the years she had known Tom Malloy had she felt this uneasy.

"Eleanor, does your back door lock?"

"I don't know. I've never locked it before, or the front door, either, until last night. I guess you were right when you said I should."

"I'll pick up a lock set in town this afternoon."

She lifted her head and stared out into the orchard, then turned toward the soft thudding sound of Danny's tossing apples into the bushel basket. "This basket's full, Cord," Danny yelled. "I need another empty one."

Eleanor stood up and smoothed out her blue denim work apron. "I need to keep busy." She moved to the wagon and grabbed an empty basket, then tramped back toward Danny while Cord lugged the full bushel of apples to the wagon and set it in the bed.

He liked the idea of sleeping in the attic. But he couldn't help wondering how Tom was going to like sleeping in the barn loft with Mama Cat and a passel of kittens. Not much, he figured. Probably not at all. Good.

He also liked the idea of locking both front and back doors at night. But if he was honest with himself, what he liked best was the idea of sleeping just a few steps away from Eleanor.

Eleanor pushed open the door to the attic and peered into the gloom. She hadn't been up here for so many years she'd all but forgotten the tiny room that housed unused trunks and old books and the children's outgrown cradle. A narrow bed stood under the small window, with a worn mattress that no doubt needed turning. The windowpanes were so covered with dust and spiderwebs that precious little sunlight filtered through.

She studied the task ahead of her, then went back down the stairs to fetch her broom, cleaning rags and a bucket of hot water. When she had lugged it all back upstairs, she sat down to rest, then made a point of dusting off not only the window but the trunks and all the books, which she stacked on one oak-paneled trunk that served as a night table. Then she scrubbed the windowpanes until they shone and made up the bed with clean sheets and an unused quilt from her own bed, fluffed up the feather pillow she'd found in the linen closet and heaved a tired sigh.

Three hours later she dumped the filthy water on the pink rose by the back porch and collapsed on the settee in the front parlor. She was too exhausted to even brew a cup of tea. Doc Dougherty was right; recovery was two steps forward and one step back. Right now she felt like "one step back."

But the little attic room at the top of the stairs was as clean and dust-free as she could make it. Now that she had brushed all the spiderwebs off the window, there was even enough light to read by. Did her hired man read? she wondered. All at once she realized she actually knew very little about Cord.

But she was certain of one thing: she felt safe when Cord

was near. Now that he would be sleeping just a few feet away from her at night, she felt even more protected.

It was strange that Tom's presence had stirred up such uneasiness. There was something different about him, something she had never seen before. It was a kind of sly look she glimpsed at odd times, and he now walked with an unmistakable swagger. She had never seen arrogance in Tom before, and she wondered at it.

Chapter Twenty-Three

The next afternoon, after skipping their usual noon dinner and devouring hurry-up sandwiches of bacon and ripe tomatoes from Eleanor's vegetable garden, Cord set off for town with Danny and a wagonload of apples for Carl Ness at the mercantile. Tom had disappeared right after breakfast.

They had barely cleared the front gate when Danny started in with the questions.

"Cord, if that man's my pa, how come I don't like him?"

"Maybe because you haven't seen him for seven years. Your ma hasn't seen him, either."

"But I never even laid eyes on you before you came to work here for Ma, and I like *you*. Don't make sense."

"Some things in life *don't* make sense, Dan."

"I don't think Ma likes him, either," the boy blurted out. "D'you think she does?"

God, he hoped not. Tom Malloy wasn't worth Eleanor's little fingernail. "Well, she might not like him right now, but maybe she will in time."

"Boy, I sure hope not!"

Cord groaned inwardly. *I sure hope not, too.*

"How long are you gonna stay, Cord? Until after the apple harvest?"

Cord flapped the reins to pick up the gray's pace. A

month ago he'd planned to stay only until August, and then he'd planned to be off to California and the gold fields. Now he didn't know. Late at night when he couldn't sleep, he admitted to himself that he didn't want to leave at all.

He flapped the reins over the gray's broad back. "I thought I might stay around until things here are…resolved, so to speak."

Danny shot him a look. "'So to speak' how?"

Cord heaved a long sigh. If he knew the answer to that, he was a smarter man than he'd ever thought he was. "Resolved in a way that keeps your ma safe and happy."

"Aw, that ain't never gonna happen with *him* around."

Cord flicked the boy a sidelong glance. Danny's statement might be something he'd have to consider. "Yeah, maybe that's not going to happen. Guess we'll have to wait and see." After seven years, a husband was considered legally dead, wasn't he? So maybe Eleanor wasn't still married to the man. Legally.

Maybe.

Danny said nothing. Then he surprised Cord by scooting closer to him and laying his head against Cord's arm. His chest felt like it had just got pumped full of warm air.

"Cord?"

"Yeah?"

"Will you teach me how to fire Ma's revolver?"

He didn't answer until they reached the outskirts of Smoke River. "I will teach you on one condition, Dan. You have to promise not to tell your mother."

He slowed the horse as they entered town. Ness's mercantile storefront was a pale apple green today, which might explain why Carl Ness was extra-brusque when he and Danny walked in.

"Yeah, yeah, more apples, like I wanted. I never get a minute's peace at harvest time. Corn comin' in. Tomatoes all over the place. Bush beans and… God knows what else. Yeah, you can unload them bushel baskets out back."

When Cord finished stowing the apples where Carl indicated, he bought a bag of lemon drops for Molly and two long licorice whips for Danny and himself. But what he learned while they stood on the sidewalk out front nibbling the candy down to a nub and leaning against a big sugar maple tree made the trip to town worth more than delivering Eleanor's apples and sharing a treat with Danny.

Next to the mercantile the door of Whitey Poletti's barber shop stood open, and every word spoken inside was audible. One voice sounded high and whiny; the other was muffled, as if it was coming from under a pile of hot towels on the speaker's face.

"Mexico, that's what I said," a man's voice said. "Plenty of gold mines and plenty of pretty women."

"Yeah? You get any?"

"Any what? Gold or women?"

"Both. Yeah, tell me about both."

Cord thought about covering Danny's ears, but that would alert the boy that there was something he shouldn't be hearing. At the moment he seemed plenty distracted by his licorice and the handsome horses tied up at the hitching rail. Cord, however, kept listening.

What he learned sent a chill up his spine, and it had nothing to do with pretty women. When he'd heard enough, he pushed off the tree trunk and laid his hand on Danny's shoulder.

"Come on, son. Let's go visit Sheriff Rivera. I saved a big juicy apple for him and his deputy."

In spite of its lemon yellow front, the interior of the sheriff's office had dingy white walls and a worn plank floor. When Cord and Danny walked in, the man behind the desk looked up from his newspaper but didn't remove the boots from his desk.

"Sheriff Rivera?" Cord began.

"That's me," a low voice came from behind the paper. "What can I do for you?"

"I'm not too sure, Sheriff. My name's Cordell Winterman, and this here is Daniel Malloy, Eleanor Malloy's son. I'm her hired man."

"Yeah? I'm acquainted with Miss Eleanor." The newspaper rustled and a lean, tanned face emerged from behind the headline.

JAILBREAK NEAR MISSOULA MINING CAMP

He studied Cord and Danny for a minute and grinned. "You two commit any crimes lately?"

Danny's spine went rigid. "No, sir!" he blurted out. "My ma would tan my hide good if I committed anything!"

Sheriff Rivera chuckled. "Well, then, what can I do for you?" He tipped his head toward the jail cells. "Sandy?" he called. "Any coffee left back there?"

A voice came from behind the door. "Only a dribble, Hawk. You want it?"

The lawman gave Cord an inquiring look. "You care for a dribble of my deputy's coffee?"

Cord shook his head. "No, thanks. Plan to have some with Rooney Cloudman over at the boardinghouse."

Rivera nodded. "Good man, Rooney. Good tracker, too. His coffee's always good."

"It's Sarah Cloudman's coffee," said the young blond fellow emerging through the door. "Sheriff, you want me to brew up another pot?"

Rivera shook his head and gestured at the two wooden chairs behind the desk. "Since you two haven't committed any crimes, would you care to sit down?" He removed his boots from the desk and pushed one of the chairs toward Cord, then glanced at Danny.

"Sandy, maybe Daniel here would like to see the jail?"

Danny grinned. "I sure would, sir. Never seen a real jail before, only in picture books." He followed Sandy through the door next to a large bulletin board plastered with wanted posters.

"Now," Rivera said, giving Cord a nod, "didn't figure you wanted the boy to hear whatever bad news you're bringing. So let's have it."

"It's not news, Sheriff. More like a question."

"Yeah? What about?"

Cord bent toward the man and lowered his voice. "You know anything about gold robberies down in Texas?"

"Funny you should mention that, Winterman. I know a few Texas Rangers down that way. They've been chasing some clever thieves over the border into Mexico, where they can't follow 'em."

Cord rose. "Mind if I look at your wanted posters?"

"Help yourself. Not all of them are current. The oldest ones are underneath."

Cord looked at all of them, including the yellowed fliers dated four and five years past.

"You lookin' for anyone in particular?"

"No. Mostly I wanted to make sure someone's face is *not* on a wanted notice."

The sheriff gave him a sharp look. "Like I say, new posters come in every few days. You might want to drop by again in a week or so."

"I'll do that, next time I'm in town." He extended his hand across the cluttered desk. "Thanks, Rivera."

"Glad you stopped by, Winterman." The sheriff gripped Cord's hand in a firm handshake and grinned. "You tell Miss Eleanor hello for me. But don't tell her I let her son into the jail."

Cord laughed. "There's a lot of things I don't tell Mrs. Malloy."

Rivera nodded just as Danny emerged from the back, his eyes big as one of Eleanor's pie plates. "Seen enough?" Cord asked.

"Gosh, sure must be scary to be in jail. Those cells are real tiny and there's nuthin' in 'em to sleep on or…"

Both Cord and the sheriff laughed out loud. "Guess you're gonna be a lifelong law abider, Daniel," Rivera said. "You come back and visit anytime you feel tempted to do anything shady, you hear?"

"Yessir, I sure will. Only thing I've been tempted by are those caramels at the mercantile, and I guess I won't ever steal one."

"Well, son, you're too young for wild women, so I guess you're gonna be a straight shooter for a few more years yet." He stood up and walked around his desk to shake Danny's hand.

Cord thought the boy would pop off a shirt button.

Molly begged Eleanor to sew some new clothes for her favorite doll, so when Cord and Danny left for town, she set up the treadle sewing machine and gathered some scraps left over from her own dressmaking and whipped together a tiny green dimity nightgown and a new red calico dress with a ruffle around the hem. She hoped the garments wouldn't end up on one of the kittens.

When Cord returned from town, Danny helped him install a shiny new lock on the back door. Now her hired man sat across the supper table from her, slowly cutting his fried chicken with unusual care and deliberately smashing his already mashed potatoes down with the tines of his fork.

Eleanor thought he seemed distracted. Not just distracted, but oddly distant, and that wasn't like her usually unflappable hired man.

Tom, on the other hand, was strangely jolly all during supper. Had he received a piece of good news while he'd been in town? If so, why did he not share it with her?

She hoped her husband's unusually high spirits and his genial mood would last through the evening, though she knew he was angry about having to sleep in the barn. But on that issue she was relying on her instincts. She didn't feel comfortable with Tom anywhere near her.

Her husband was hunched over, wolfing down his food without raising his eyes from his plate. Watching him sent another uneasy chill up her backbone. Something was different about her husband, but she couldn't begin to guess what it was.

"Ma, can I have more chicken?" Danny asked. "I worked hard today pickin' apples and helpin' Cord in town."

"You certainly did, Danny." She moved the platter closer to him.

"Cord worked hard, too, Ma."

"Cord," Eleanor said with deliberation, "still has half a chicken breast on his plate."

Her hired man sat studying his supper plate but not eating a single bite, and that made Eleanor frown. Usually he ate with gusto. Tonight he seemed to have no appetite.

"Is there something wrong with your chicken, Cord?"

"What? Oh, no. Chicken tastes fine."

Still he made no attempt to finish his meal. It wasn't like him to have no appetite. Something was wrong, but she couldn't ask him about it with Tom sitting at the table. She would have to wait until everyone finished their supper and gobbled down the blackberry cobbler she'd baked for dessert.

Finally the children asked to be excused and raced off to play hopscotch in the backyard while it was still light. Tom stalked off to the front porch for a smoke. Cord stayed behind to help her with the dishes.

She filled the enamel dishpan with the water she'd heated on the stove, shaved in some soap and added the five greasy supper plates. "While you were in town, I dusted your room in the attic and swept out the rest of the cobwebs on the ceiling."

"Thanks, Eleanor."

"It must get awfully hot up there with only the one window."

He didn't respond.

"Oh, and I put a pillow on the bed and—"

"I'll be fine," he said shortly. "I'm used to the heat at night. The loft was plenty warm, especially with Mama Cat and her kittens curled up on my belly."

She laughed. "You'd been adopted by Mama Cat, and you didn't complain once!"

"Oh, I complained, all right, just not to you."

"Really? Who did you complain to?"

He unfolded the dish towel from the rack by the stove. "Amanda Martin."

Her hand stilled on the wet dishrag. "You mean you talked to that gravestone out in my garden?"

"It was kinda nice, actually," he said. "Amanda never talks back."

Eleanor splashed a handful of soapsuds at him, then reached to brush them off his shirtfront. He caught her hand, but instead of releasing it, he closed his fingers around hers.

"I don't plan to go up to the attic until you and the kids are in bed, all right? I want to check around outside and lock both the doors."

She looked up at him. "Check around for what?"

"Don't know, exactly. Just want to make sure everything's all right. You know, the apple orchard, your flower garden, that kind of thing."

"And Amanda Martin," she said with a smile. She tried to pull her hand free, but he tightened his grip.

"Eleanor."

There was something in his voice she hadn't heard before. "Cord? What is it?"

"I want you to sleep with your revolver beside your bed."

She gasped. "But why?"

"And make sure it's loaded."

She pulled her hand free. "Tell me why," she demanded.

He looked everywhere but at her, the ceiling, the coffeepot still sitting on the stove, even the dish towel he'd stuffed under his belt. "Because," he said carefully, "I don't like your husband."

She shrugged. "I admit Tom is different from before he went away, but—"

"And I don't trust him."

She swished the dishrag over a dirty plate and slipped it into the hot rinse water. "I see. But Cord, you said you'll be leaving soon, after the apples are harvested."

"Yeah, that's what I said, all right. But I don't want to leave you and the kids while he's here." He grasped the clean plate and whipped the towel from his belt. "Don't ask me why, Eleanor, because I don't know."

She scrubbed off two more plates while she digested his words. Part of her was elated that he wouldn't be leaving right after the harvest. Another part of her felt vaguely disappointed that he wasn't staying because of *her*. Because of his feelings for her.

He *did* have feelings for her, didn't he? She admitted that she didn't really know. Maybe she was just another woman to him. Maybe a few kisses didn't mean the same thing to a man as they did to a woman.

A dull pain lodged in her chest. She gazed out the double window over the kitchen sink and rapidly blinked her stinging eyes. *Eleanor Malloy, you are a very foolish woman.*

She dropped her gaze to the sudsy dishpan. Not only that, she was a very foolish *married* woman.

At her elbow, Cord laid the dish towel on the sideboard, then picked it up again. He wanted to put his arms around her so bad the muscles in his forearm twitched. A week ago he'd held back because she was married. A week ago he'd planned to leave after the harvest. But then her husband had returned, and now she was even more married.

Well, maybe she was married and maybe, after an unexplained seven-year absence, she wasn't. But he had a bad feeling about the man anyway. He couldn't just ride away and leave Eleanor to an uncertain future. Maybe even a dangerous one.

So what in blazes was he going to do?

Chapter Twenty-Four

Eleanor lay in the dark staring at her open bedroom window, which looked out onto the front porch. After supper Tom had drifted to the porch swing, but she knew he was no longer sitting there because she couldn't smell any cigarette smoke. Tom had never smoked before; when had he become addicted to tobacco?

Earlier, when she stepped outside after supper, the swing had been littered with the small white papers he used to roll up his cigarettes. Apparently his hand was none too steady because a good number had fluttered onto the plank floor. He hadn't swept them up, either, but had left them for her.

She crept out of bed and moved to the rocker and tucked her bare feet up under her nightgown. *My life is all wrong.* She had known that for a long while, but she'd been so proud and stubborn she couldn't admit it. Until now. Until Tom had tramped through her front door all smiles and blandishments, as if he hadn't been away for seven whole years.

She lifted her face to the slight breeze ruffling the curtains and breathed in the nicotiana-scented air. Why did she always learn things too late? Six months into her marriage she'd realized she didn't like Tom well enough to lie beside him each night and enjoy what a wife was supposed to enjoy, but by then she was pregnant with Danny.

Last winter when she'd caught pneumonia, Doc Dougherty had wanted to put her in the Smoke River hospital in town, but she'd been too stubborn to see the sense of it. She didn't want to be separated from Molly and Danny, even for a week or two. She'd decided she could manage.

And she *had* managed, but only up to a point. Little by little the farm had suffered.

She rocked back and forth, trying to sort everything out and think clearly and sensibly about her life. She supposed she had done the best she could, but she'd done everything wrong anyway. Well, maybe not everything. She had Molly and Danny. And she had this house and her farm and all those beautiful, healthy apple trees.

And she had Cord. She was grateful for his help and his protection, but she knew he would be leaving eventually, and what then? *Oh, God, what then?*

Cord tossed the quilt and the top sheet off onto the floor and padded over to the door of the tiny attic room. The single window was open as far as it would go, but the air inside was still stifling. Maybe if he left the door open some cool air could circulate.

The hallway was bathed in shadows, and no light showed under either of the two bedroom doors that faced each other. From behind one came the soft breathing of the sleeping children; from behind the other he could hear nothing but the rhythmic *creak-creak* of a rocking chair. Eleanor was awake. Thinking, maybe. Or worrying.

He propped his door open with one of the books he'd found stacked on a trunk in the corner. Couldn't read the title in the dark, but he hoped it wasn't the Bible. Just as he turned back toward his bed, a figure passed in front of the parlor window downstairs.

He waited. After a moment the front doorknob rattled. Quickly he dug his Colt revolver out of his saddlebag, crept silently down the stairs and positioned himself on the other side of the door.

The knob turned twice more, and then fell silent. Heavy footsteps clumped across the porch and down the steps, and Cord pulled aside the window curtain to see a dark, bulky figure moving across the yard toward the barn. Tom Malloy.

He lifted his finger from the trigger and turned to find Eleanor at the top of the stairs, her revolver clutched in her hand.

"It was Tom," he said quietly as he moved toward her. He lifted the gun out of her hand and checked the chamber. Empty. "Just what were you going to do with an unloaded revolver?"

"I—I didn't know it was unloaded." Her voice shook.

"What are you doing down here?" he asked.

"I heard you go down the stairs and I thought you might need help."

He couldn't help his low laugh. "Hot damn, Eleanor, I'm not so green that I'd check out a noise in the middle of the night without a loaded weapon in my hand. Besides, you can hardly lift that revolver of yours."

"I know," she said in a quavery voice, "but I can shoot it. You showed me how, with both hands and I— Oh, for heaven's sake, Cord, why are we standing here arguing?"

Cord looked past her into the darkened kitchen. "Maybe because we're both standing here in the middle of midnight dressed in not very much and we don't know what else to do."

She choked on a bubble of laughter. "I am wearing a good deal, as a matter of fact, a long nightgown that buttons up to my chin and has long sleeves." Her eyes flicked downward. "You, however, are wearing only your drawers."

He was silent for a full minute. "That nightgown is damn sheer."

She laughed again. "I must say, your eyesight in the dark is very good."

He couldn't think of a darn thing to say to that, and then she fired off another barb. "Besides, I've seen men's drawers many times before. Yours are not that unusual."

He stifled a grin. Discussing each other's nightwear seemed kind of crazy. "Next time you figure on helping me, make sure your revolver is loaded. And," he added with a smile, "I don't care what you're wearing."

That wasn't exactly true, he acknowledged. He couldn't help noticing that her filmy white nightgown was so sheer he could see every dip and curve of her body. Even worse, he was drinking in the sight like a thirsty man in the middle of the desert.

"Eleanor, go back to bed."

Without a word she turned away. He followed her into the parlor and watched her climb the stairs and disappear behind her bedroom door.

And then he poured himself a double shot of whiskey and sat nursing it until the sky turned pink.

The next morning, Cord and Danny loaded six more bushels of ripe shiny apples into the wagon and drove them to Rose Cottage, Sarah Cloudman's boardinghouse in town. Her husband, Rooney, helped lug them into the root cellar, where it was cool and dry, and then invited them to stay and share a fresh pot of coffee.

Sarah invited Danny inside to join her grandson, Mark, for milk and molasses cookies, then brought a tray with the coffeepot and two blue ceramic mugs and set it down on the wide porch railing for Rooney and Cord.

"Got somethin' to show you," Rooney said when Sarah

and Danny disappeared into the house. He handed Cord a page from the *Smoke River Lark-Sentinel.*

THEFT RING SUSPECTED IN
TEXAS MURDERS

"Whaddya make of that, Winterman?"

Cord studied the gray-haired man for a long moment. "Suspected of stealing what?" he asked.

"Gold, I'd guess."

"Funny thing to be reporting so far from Texas, don't you think?"

Rooney's bushy eyebrows rose. "Oh, that newspaper lady Jessamine Sanders is one smart cookie. She keeps up with most everything that goes on in the western half of the country and reports it in the *Sentinel.* Uses the telegraph, ya know. She sure doesn't miss much."

Cord accepted the mug of coffee Rooney filled. "You mind telling me why this caught your eye?"

The older man blew into his cup and gave Cord a steely-eyed perusal. "Well, now, I'll tell ya. In the last six months, there's only two new fellers come to town. One of them's you, and the other's Miz Malloy's husband, Tom. Now, I know for a fact that Miss Eleanor ain't payin' you wages to work as her hired man."

"That's true, she isn't paying me. I came to town dead broke and I'm gonna leave the same way."

"How come? Now that she's bringin' in her apple harvest she could afford to pay her hired help."

Cord leaned against the porch railing and studied Rooney for a long moment. "I'm not accepting any money from her. She needs it for herself and those kids of hers. And besides—"

"Besides," Rooney interrupted with a twinkle in his blue eyes, "you're in love with her."

Cord dropped his coffee mug, which tumbled off the railing into the yellow rose bush. "Just how do you figure that?"

"Son, I watched you at Jensen's dance a coupla weeks back. Now, in my time I've seen a hundred or so twosomes movin' around a dance floor in each other's arms, but I never saw one like you and Miss Eleanor. You're so deep in love with her you couldn't dance straight."

"Guess there's nothing sensible I can say to that." Cord moved off the porch and busied himself fishing around in the rosebush to find his mug.

When he came back up the steps, Rooney sat grinning at him. "Brush the dirt outta yer cup and I'll fill it up again." He topped up his own mug and then pinned his keen eyes on Cord.

"Now, you tell me all about yerself, and I'll just set here and listen."

Cord talked for a quarter of an hour before Rooney raised a leathery hand to stop him. "That's enough, Cord. I reckon there's lots more, but it ain't none of my business."

Cord stared at him as a growing suspicion dawned on him. "Mr. Cloudman, are you thinking what I'm thinking about Tom Malloy?"

"Prob'ly. And call me Rooney."

"I'm teaching Danny to shoot Eleanor's revolver," Cord said casually.

"Fine idea. Every young lad oughta know how to handle a gun. Last summer I taught Sarah's grandson, Mark, how to fire my Walker Colt. Scared him silly. I told him I might not always be around to protect Sarah, and the kid fell to wailin' like a scalped Indian."

"I figure Danny's gonna do the same," Cord said. "Can't be helped."

"Aw, hell, life's like that, ain't it? Too much that can't be helped."

The two men exchanged a long look, and an hour later, after he and Rooney shared a firm handshake, Cord and

Danny climbed onto the wagon bench and started down the street. Before they turned the corner, Cord looked back at Rooney Cloudman one final time.

The older man stood on the boardinghouse porch, a grin on his weathered face, and gave him a thumbs-up.

Cord focused on guiding the wagon down the road leading out of town and decided the time had come. "Next time we come to town I'm bringing your mother's revolver, Dan. I'm gonna show you how to fire it."

The following week Cord and Danny made another trip to town with a wagon load of apples, and this time Cord had sneaked Eleanor's revolver into his waistband. After unloading half a dozen bushel baskets of apples at Ness's mercantile, they walked across to the sheriff's office for a quick visit.

Both jail cells were occupied. "Drunk and disorderly," Rivera explained. "I ought to charge the Golden Partridge rent on Saturday night."

So Danny thumbed through the sheriff's newspaper while Cord inspected the wanted posters. He didn't know whether he wanted to find a familiar face or not. Maybe not. He didn't want to bring even more heartache for Eleanor, and with the apple harvest in full swing, she had no energy for anything else.

Tom was still sleeping in the barn and grumbling loudly about it, but ever since Cord had installed not only a lock on the back door but a dead bolt on the front door, he'd paid Eleanor's husband less attention at night. When Tom was out of sight, Cord tried to keep him out of mind.

Most nights Tom wasn't even around. Often he rode off somewhere after supper, and sometimes he didn't turn up for supper at all. And, Cord noted with increasing disgust, Tom never appeared in the apple orchard to help, even though he could sometimes hear Eleanor and her husband's arguments about it when Eleanor thought no one was listening.

Most of those arguments occurred after breakfast, far away from the house or behind the chicken house in the backyard.

Eleanor never prevailed. He thought about getting her a little derringer to slip in her apron pocket, but he knew she'd never carry it for fear of accidentally hurting one of the children. All the more reason, he thought as the empty wagon rattled out of town, why Danny should know how to handle Eleanor's revolver.

He turned off on the road that led to the river, pulled to a stop in a grove of leafy cottonwoods and loosened the cinch on the gray gelding. Danny bobbed at his side.

"How come you do that, Cord? It's a lot of botheration to get her cinch tightened up in the first place, so why do it twice?"

"We're gonna be here awhile, son. So while we work, the horse gets to rest." He walked the boy a good thirty yards away from the road and set an empty lima bean can on a flat rock with a wall of boulders behind it. Then he showed him how to hold the gun in both hands and take his time sighting down the barrel. "It's gonna kick hard when you fire it, Danny. So if you have to fire more than once, let it settle down first, then take aim again."

"Okay," Danny breathed. He brought the revolver up, aimed and squeezed the trigger. The can flew off the rock and Danny did a little dance of triumph.

"Whooee, Cord, look what I did!"

Cord retrieved the can. "Looks like you put a hole right dead center. You shot the he— Heck out of that can, all right." He replaced it on the rock. "Think you could do it again?"

"Sure. I never liked lima beans anyway," the boy quipped.

Cord laughed, and after Danny's next successful shot he recognized a potential marksman. After seven more accurate shots, the tin can was so torn up it would no longer stand upright.

The boy's grin was so wide it showed all his teeth. "I learn fast, huh, Cord?"

"We're not done yet." He showed him how to clean the revolver, check to see whether it was loaded, and how to carry it in the waistband of his jeans. He knew Eleanor would never let her son have a proper holster. He also talked to him about how to decide when to use a firearm in the first place.

"Not all situations call for a gun. Most disagreements with folks aren't important enough to risk a life for, but for those that are life-threatening, the rule is you don't shoot unless you have to. Fire only to save your own life or somebody else's."

"Did your pa teach you all this stuff?"

Cord flinched. "No, he didn't. If he had, I'd have grown up a lot smarter."

"You ever kill anyone?"

God in heaven, where did that come from? "Yeah. I'm sorry to say I've killed a lot of someones in my life. Spent a lot of years regretting it."

"Wish we'd brought another tin can so's I could practice some more."

"Next time we'll bring two cans," Cord promised. "What else don't you like besides lima beans?"

Chapter Twenty-Five

Eleanor floured the chicken pieces and dropped them into the Dutch oven to brown, then started chopping up two onions and enough carrots for her stew. Ever since Cord and Danny had returned from town she couldn't help the feeling that they were keeping something from her. But with supper to cook and bread dough to mix up and set to rise, she couldn't worry about it now.

Her hired man and her son had rumbled through the gate, bringing the supplies she'd ordered and a bag of lemon drops for Molly, but when Cord and her son walked up on the porch she sensed something was different. Danny couldn't seem to stop smiling, and then he refused to play jacks with his sister. "That's sissy stuff," he pronounced. And for the rest of the afternoon he swaggered self-importantly about the yard until Eleanor's concern turned into genuine worry. What had gotten into her son?

Oh, Lordy, had Danny and Cord had a man-to-man talk about the facts of life?

Cord was acting different, too. Moody and silent and so thoughtful she wondered if there had been some trouble in town. But when she questioned him about it, he clammed up. It made her downright furious the way males stuck together.

At supper, the tension grew even thicker. Tom tramped

in, impatient for his meal and short-spoken to the point of rudeness. He yelled at Molly when she accidentally slopped milk on the table, and when her blue eyes filled with tears he'd made it even worse. "Just like a girl," he snarled. "Cryin' over every little thing."

At that, Eleanor's backbone went rigid. Molly rarely cried about anything, even skinned knees, and Eleanor, who prided herself on her own stiff upper lip, could not recall the last time her daughter had shed tears.

"Tom," she said in a firm voice, "do not discipline Molly by speaking sharply or saying something hurtful."

"Oh, yeah? I'll say whatever I damn please in my own house!"

That made Molly cry even harder.

Cord rose from the table, picked up his bowl of chicken stew and walked out onto the front porch. Then Danny hurriedly slurped down his milk and asked to be excused, followed by Molly. Both children made a beeline for the front porch.

Every bone in Eleanor's body wanted to do the same thing. But she couldn't.

"Tom, do you want more stew?"

"Nah. Tastes kinda paltry compared to steak."

"I cannot afford steak, not until the apple harvest is finished."

He leaned forward and planted both elbows on the table. "When will that be?"

The question surprised her. "Surely you remember farming the orchard before you went away? The harvest finishes in October. Sometimes as late as early November."

"Oh, yeah. Guess I forgot. Ellie, how long is that hired man gonna stay around?"

"It depends."

"Depends on what? What're ya paying him, anyway?"

She hesitated. "I am not paying him until the end of the season. As for how long he stays, that depends on him."

"Huh! What kind of hired man decides how long he's gonna stay around and work?"

My kind of hired man. "Cord is his own man, Tom."

Her husband shot to his feet. "Well, I'm gonna get rid of him."

"Sit down, Tom," she said quietly. "Cord does not work for you. Remember, this farm belongs to me now."

She stood up, snatched up his half-eaten bowl of stew and stalked to the sink. The children had already added their dishes to the pan of hot soapy water; she added her own, then plunked in Tom's plate and silverware and his coffee cup."

"Guess supper's over, huh?"

"Yes," she said through gritted teeth. "Supper is most definitely over."

He looked at her for a long time, as if deciding something. "It's still light outside, Ellie. I'm gonna ride into town for…for a while."

He tramped out the back door, and through the kitchen window she watched him cross the yard to the barn. A few minutes later that black horse of his galloped out the gate.

She walked out to the front porch, where Cord sat rocking in the swing. Molly was snuggled under one arm; Danny sat on his other side, fiddling with his jackknife.

"I'm washing up the dishes, Cord. May I have your bowl?"

He handed it over, then nudged Danny. "Dan, you think you and Molly could wash up the dishes tonight? I'd like to talk to your mother."

"Sure, Cord." Danny grabbed the dish out of his mother's grasp, and both children streaked through the front door. Eleanor sank down beside Cord, leaned her head back and closed her eyes.

He pushed the swing into motion. "Tired?"

"Not physically, no. Emotionally, I'm a wreck. And don't ask why."

Cord gave a short laugh. "I don't need to ask why."

She rocked in silence for some time. Their shoulders weren't touching, but every nerve in his body was aware of her. She smelled good, like fresh bread and cinnamon, and her warmth made him want to roll his sleeves up higher so her bare skin would touch his.

"Eleanor, I need to tell you something."

"Oh, not now, Cord. Let me enjoy being out here in peace and quiet just for a few minutes."

His chest tightened. "It's not about me. It's about Tom."

Her lids snapped open. "What about Tom?"

"I think I know why he was gone for so many years."

She jolted upright so fast the swing jerked. "Why?"

He took his time answering. "I think he might have been in prison."

"Prison!" She twisted toward him. "What on earth makes you say that?"

This was the part he'd struggled with, not how to tell her he suspected what he did, but *why*. He drew in a long breath.

"I've been watching him, Eleanor. The way he walks, the way he eats. Especially the way he eats. He kinda hunches over with both his arms around his plate."

"I have noticed that, too. He never used to eat that way."

"Prisoners eat that way to guard their food. It keeps someone else from snatching it away."

"Prisoners? How on earth would you know—?" She broke off. "Oh, no. Oh, Cord, no." Her voice sounded funny.

He wanted to touch her so bad he clenched his fists. "Eleanor, listen. There's something else I need to tell you."

"Yes? Go on."

Oh, God, if he told her why he knew it would be the end of everything. She would never look at him in the same way again. She would probably ask him to leave.

A suffocating sense of loss swept over him. But he had to tell her. He had to.

He drew in a long, slow breath. "Eleanor, I've spent time in prison. Eight years."

"Whatever for?"

"For killing the man I found in bed with my wife."

Her gray eyes looked dazed. "You were never going to tell me this, were you?" she said dully.

"No, I wasn't. I was going to help you out on the farm until you were back on your feet, and then I was going to move on to California. I spent eight years behind brick walls, thinking about California, thinking about green fields and trees."

He thought she'd be screaming at him by now, but she didn't say a word.

"Why did you stop here, at my farm?" she said at last.

"I told you once before, Eleanor. When I saw your apple trees in bloom I couldn't bring myself to ride on past. It was like I was hungry for something."

"Why have you stayed?"

"To be honest, I'm not real sure. Well, that's not exactly true." He swallowed over a lump the size of a peach pit, cleared his throat and swallowed again. "I stayed because you were here."

She stared at him. He wished she would close her eyes or look at the porch floor, or the maple trees, anywhere but straight at him like she was doing at this moment.

"I might be able to explain it better if I understood it myself," he said quietly. "But for now I wanted you to know about Tom, and if that meant knowing about me, well, I figured I had to risk it."

"Cord," she breathed.

Damn, damn, *damn*. He hadn't wanted to tell her. Right now he'd give up all the gold in California to go back an hour in time and take back his words.

"You're going to leave, aren't you? Soon, I mean?"

He'd give his right arm if she'd stop looking at him that

way. "The honest truth is that I don't think I *can* leave until this thing is resolved."

She pushed the swing into motion again. "By 'this thing,' you mean Tom, don't you?"

He nodded.

Eleanor kept the swing gliding back and forth, trying to steady her breathing. Why was he telling her this, warning her about her husband in one breath and talking about leaving in the next? What did he mean by "this thing is resolved"? When she and Tom are "married" once more? They would never be married, but she also knew she could never divorce him. Under Oregon law, if a woman sued for divorce, any children were awarded to the husband.

She realized her arms were clasped tight across her midriff, her fingernails biting into the palms of her hands. She shot a glance at Cord's face and saw that the muscles in his jaw were working.

"What else did you do in town today?" she asked at last.

"Stayed and talked with Rooney Cloudman while Danny and Mark played… I don't know what they played, come to think of it. Checkers, maybe."

"Danny hates checkers. He says he always loses."

Cord's shoulders relaxed. "I'm a champion checkers player. Never been beat. Maybe I'll give Danny some pointers."

"After they finish up the dishes," she said wearily. "Sometimes I feel I can't keep up with things the way they keep happening."

"Anything in particular?"

She half laughed, half groaned. "Oh, just everything. Tom. Danny growing up so fast. Molly's fascination with putting doll clothes on kittens." She paused. "And you."

"The kittens will grow out of doll clothes and Danny will end up being Danny, just older."

"And Tom will…what?"

He shifted to face her. "Wish I knew. In poker we call Tom a wild card." He touched her arm. "Before I turn in I'm gonna walk the property, check to make sure everything's okay. You want any flowers from your garden?"

"Yes, maybe a few black-eyed Susans, those daisy-like things with black centers. And while you're out there, say a prayer for Amanda Martin."

The swing jerked when he stood up, and then he disappeared into the darkness. She sat rocking in the soft evening air until Danny and Molly emerged from the house.

"The supper dishes are all done, Ma. And we put 'em away, too."

"Thank you both. Now, upstairs to bed with you."

"You gonna read us a story, Mama?"

She sighed. "Not tonight, Molly. I seem to be extra-tired."

When she heard them climb the stairs she closed her eyes and told herself she wasn't frightened, that everything would turn out all right. She didn't believe that, not really, but she couldn't let herself contemplate anything else.

Ten minutes later Cord came up the porch steps to find Eleanor sound asleep. He laid the yellow flowers on her lap and she didn't even twitch, so he settled himself on the top porch step and waited, unable to stop looking at her.

Her mouth had relaxed into an almost-smile. Her lashes were sooty against her too-pale cheeks, and her deep, even breathing told him she was not about to wake up anytime soon.

He waited half an hour, then an hour, and still she didn't move a muscle. Finally he decided she shouldn't be found dozing in the porch swing when Tom returned, and he stood up and bent over her.

"Eleanor." He touched her shoulder. "Eleanor, wake up. You need to go to bed."

Her eyelids fluttered open and immediately drifted shut.

"Eleanor."

"Don't wanna move," she murmured.

He chuckled. "Come on." He grasped the bunch of flowers in one hand, and slid it beneath her shoulder, then slipped his free arm under her legs and lifted her into his arms. Then he manhandled the screen door open and stepped into the dark house.

Chapter Twenty-Six

Cord climbed the stairs slowly to avoid jarring the drowsy woman in his arms. She weighed next to nothing, probably because she didn't eat any more than Molly and she was still working from sunup until dark doing everything but lifting heavy bushels of apples into the wagon.

He bent at the knees to open the door to her bedroom, maneuvered her through it and laid her on the bed with the bouquet of flowers next to her. Her bedroom smelled like her, roses and lemons and soap. The room was soft, somehow. Feminine. Only a woman would put ruffled blue muslin curtains on a second-floor window nobody could see. Or sleep with a bouquet of flowers scenting the warm air.

It was too warm to cover her with the blue-and-yellow flowered quilt, so he pulled off her shoes and straightened her wrinkled blue denim work skirt. He thought about loosening the top two buttons of her shirtwaist, then decided that would be dancing too close to the devil. He'd have a hard time stopping at just two buttons.

But the air in her bedroom was stifling. Why did women insist on wearing high-necked garments on a steaming hot day like today? He went ahead and unbuttoned her shirtwaist until he glimpsed the lacy top of her camisole. At least she wasn't wearing a corset. Then he moved to the window and shoved the sash up.

Fresh air wafted in. He turned back to the bed to find her eyes open, studying him.

"Are the children asleep?" she asked in a sleep-fuzzy voice.

"Guess so. Their bedroom door's closed."

"Check on them, would you? Danny is good at faking it."

"Faking it to do what?"

"Reading something he knows I would not approve of."

"Eleanor, he's a growing boy. He's gonna find out about the world outside your farm no matter what you do, so maybe you should let him do some exploring instead of squashing his natural curiosity."

She giggled sleepily. "I can certainly see how *you* were raised."

"No, you can't." She stretched her arms over her head and he tried not to stare at the creamy skin he'd exposed.

"Cord, tell me how you were raised."

"Like he— Heck I will. Some things are private."

She propped herself up on one elbow, then noticed that the top of her shirtwaist was gaping open. He expected her to screech, but she calmly undid one additional button and flapped the fabric against her chest. "It's too hot," she muttered.

Cord stuffed his hands in his back pockets to keep from touching her. "I'll go check on the kids."

"Do it later," she said. "If you won't tell me about your childhood, tell me about your wife."

He jerked up as if he'd been shot. "No." He hadn't thought about his wife for eight long years, and he wasn't about to start now. He made a move for the doorway but she caught his hand.

"I'm sorry, Cord. Really sorry."

"For what?"

"For everything. I'm sorry about Tom and for being so

weak after the pneumonia, and I'm sorry about your wife. I'm sorry you saw my apple trees in bloom on your way to California. I'm sorry you stopped."

He sucked in a breath and held it, eyeing the daisy things he'd laid on the quilt beside her. Then he exhaled in one long, slow stream. "Eleanor, I'm sorry about Tom, and about you being sick. But I'm not sorry about your apple trees, and I'm sure as hell not sorry I stopped at your farm."

Her eyes went wide. "Really? Why aren't you sorry?"

"You can't ask me that."

"I can, too, ask that. Tell me."

He picked up the bunch of daisies. "I need to put these in water," he muttered.

When the door closed behind him, Eleanor lay staring at it for a long time, thinking of Cord's mouth on hers, his lips asking questions she couldn't answer.

She stood up, stripped her clothes off down to her drawers and camisole, and poured a pitcher of tepid water into the basin on the bureau. She was bone-tired, but it was too hot to sleep, so she bathed her sticky skin and stood in front of the open window to cool off. She grimaced at the thought of sitting up for another night, rocking back and forth in the wicker rocker.

Two weeks ago she would have sat out in the porch swing, enjoying the fresh night air. Two weeks ago she would have rolled herself up in the quilt and slept out in the backyard under the stars. Now she felt like a prisoner in her own house.

She stretched out on the bed, then sat bolt upright. This was *her* farm. *Hers! She* was in charge here. Something had to be done about Tom. And, she thought with an inward sob, something had to be done about Cord.

Danny and Cord sat hunched over the checkerboard in the shade of the maple trees. Eleanor was working nearby in her flower garden, deadheading yellow daisies with her garden shears, while Molly crooned to one of the captive kittens.

Tom was blessedly absent. There had been a scene at breakfast when Cord had asked for his help loading up the bushel baskets of ripe apples to take to Gillette Springs.

Got things to do in town, Tom had blustered.

Eleanor had confronted him, pancake spatula in hand. *What things?*

It's Sunday, right? I'm...going to church.

She had laughed out loud at that. *You haven't seen the inside of the church since the day we were married!*

But he'd stormed out to the barn anyway, saddled up that black gelding of his and clattered off down the road. She and Danny had helped Cord load up the baskets of apples, and now she was cutting flowers for bouquets, grateful the peace and quiet of a morning broken only by a meadowlark somewhere in the pasture. And Cord's voice.

"Next," Cord said to Danny, "you force my piece into the corner, like this. And then you..." Eleanor heard four crisp clicks as Cord apparently did something clever and Danny laughed.

"Gee, that's real swift, Cord. I bet Mark Rose doesn't know that trick!"

"Don't be too sure, Dan. Mark has Rooney for a grandpa, and you can be sure that foxy old man is giving him some pointers."

"When did you learn to play checkers, Cord?"

"When I was a kid, about your age."

"Whereabouts was you?"

A pause. "Oh, here and there."

"Yeah? Where's 'here and there'?"

Eleanor stopped her flower-snipping to listen more closely.

"Where was you borned, Cord?" Molly's voice.

"Uh, Virginia."

"Where's Ginia?" Molly asked.

"Does your school map show the Southern states, Dan?"

"Sure. Virginia's right next to Kentucky. What'dja do then?"

Cord cleared his throat. "When my ma died, my father took me to live with an aunt in Charleston. I didn't like it much, and neither did Pa, so when he died I struck out for the West and ended up in Kansas."

"How old were you?" Molly asked.

"Twelve. Almost."

Eleanor dropped her shears. Twelve! Why, that was hardly older than Danny! Against her better judgment she moved closer and found herself shamelessly eavesdropping.

"Didja have a girlfriend?" Molly questioned.

"Yeah, Cord," Danny echoed. "Didja?"

Cord laughed. "Hey, you want to learn to play killer checkers or not?"

"I wanna learn about *you*," Molly sang.

Eleanor nodded in agreement. Girls were always more curious than boys.

"Didja have a girlfriend, Cord?" Danny asked again. "I won't tell anybody, honest."

"Well, not until I was older. Now, Dan, back to checkers. When you get a king—"

"How old was 'older'?"

There was an awkward pause. "About fifteen, I guess. Almost."

Eleanor almost laughed out loud. He'd been only fourteen years old! She would bet Cord had left a string of broken hearts all the way to Kansas. *Ask him when he fell in love*, she silently urged. *When he got married.*

"Cord, didja ever read a book called *David Copperfield*?"

"That what you're reading in school?"

"Aw, heck, no. Miz Panovsky would prob'ly have a fit if she knew."

"Why's that?" Cord lowered his voice. "Strong language?"

"N-no, not really."

"Naked ladies?" Cord's voice sounded as if he would laugh if given half a chance.

"Huh? Shoot, no."

"Then how come Miss What's-her-name doesn't like it?"

"Ma doesn't like it, either," Danny said.

"Why not? What's this book about?"

"It's about this boy who gets adopted by a rich lady."

"And?"

"He gots a girlfriend," Molly crowed. "A real pretty one."

"Aw, how would *you* know?" Danny shouted.

"Cuz," the girl announced, "I can read, too!"

Eleanor jerked upright.

Molly is reading? She's reading David Copperfield? *Molly is only seven years old!*

Cord redirected the conversation. "Molly, can you play checkers, too?"

"No. I like playing with my dollies better."

"Cord," Danny interjected. "Maybe later you can tell me about some naked ladies, huh?"

Cord chuckled. "Years later, maybe. That's for grown-up boys. Fourteen at least, okay?"

"Sixteen!" Eleanor blurted out aloud.

There was a long, quiet pause. "Okay, sixteen," he called.

Eleanor pressed her lips together. "That's still awfully young for naked—"

Cord gave a hoot of laughter. Eleanor's face went hot and she dropped her shears into a patch of nicotiana.

"Why don't you come on out, Eleanor?" Cord called. "You could hear even better over here."

She bit her lip.

Cord listened for a moment but heard nothing but the *snip-snick* of her garden shears. He figured Danny was ready to give Rooney's grandson a run for his checker money, so he drew the lesson to a close. But Molly wasn't finished with him yet.

"Cord, d'you like boy dollies or girl dollies better?"

He hoped Eleanor was still listening. "I like girl dollies, honey."

"How come?"

"Well…" He listened for the sound of snipping shears and when he heard nothing he couldn't help smiling. He knew she was all ears.

"Girls are special," he said loudly. "They look pretty and they smell good and they're soft and warm. And they can do all kinds of things boys can't."

"What things?" Danny and his sister said in unison.

"Well, for one thing, girls can make cookies."

"Boys can make cookies, too!" Danny said. "I can make oatmeal cookies bigger'n saucers."

"Okay, let's see. Another thing girls can do is dance."

"Boys can dance, too!" Molly shouted.

Cord frowned and stroked his chin dramatically.

"Well…" *Eleanor, are you listening to this?* "Girls can make you feel better when you're hurt."

"Oh, yeah, I guess so," Danny murmured.

"And girls can…uh…rock you to sleep at night," he added.

Molly nodded her head so vigorously her curls bobbed.

"And girls can—" Cord closed his eyes briefly "—leave you all hot and bothered so you can't sleep at night."

"Huh?" Danny tugged his forearm. "What does 'hot and bothered' mean?"

Cord listened again for the sound of shears in the flower garden behind the trees, took a deep breath and answered the boy's question. "Hot and bothered is something special that happens to grown-up boys. It means you can't breathe right and you feel a funny kind of ache below your belly."

"How 'grown-up' is a grown-up boy?" Danny wanted to know. And then he immediately added, "What kinda ache, Cord?"

Cord grinned. "It's an ache that happens every time a

special girl is near you. Not just a pretty girl, but a special one."

Danny lowered his voice. "You mean a *naked* lady?"

Cord laughed. "Well, no. A lady doesn't have to be naked to make a boy feel that ache."

"Well, what does she have to be?"

"Don't you dare answer that!" Eleanor shouted. She flew out from behind the maple trees and confronted him, fists propped on her hips.

Danny looked up, his expression bland. "Oh, h'lo, Ma."

"Mama, you wanna play with my dolly?"

Cord got to his feet. "We were talking about *David Copperfield*, and one thing led to another."

She glared at him. "Have you read *David Copperfield*?"

"Yeah, actually. When I was in, uh, Missouri I did a lot of reading. Some books I wouldn't recommend for Daniel just yet. Come to think of it, Eleanor, have *you* read *David Copperfield*?"

"Certainly not!"

"Why not?" he asked, keeping as straight a face as he could manage.

"Because it's…it's… Well, I don't have the time."

He couldn't help grinning. In the middle of a tense week, the last hour had been halfway enjoyable. Arousing, even. Just talking about a male reaction to something exciting had gotten him swollen and achy in a place he didn't dare look at.

Girls can tie a man in knots.

"Dan, why don't you and your sister go get some lemonade from that pitcher on the front porch?"

When the kids galloped off, Cord stepped toward Eleanor. "Okay, I admit I knew you were listening, and I was having some fun teasing you."

"Fun! It was downright embarrassing!"

"Yeah, maybe it was. But there's nothing wrong with

David Copperfield. And maybe you shouldn't get so hot and both— So het up about a book you haven't read."

"Don't you tell me how to raise my son."

"I'm not telling you how to raise him. I'm telling you not to criticize something you don't know anything about."

"Oh."

Her furious scarlet face told him his remark had hit home. She stalked toward him. He stood unmoving, and when she got within two feet she began pelting him with the flowers she'd picked. At first he tried to catch them, but as the rain of asters and daisies and little furry-looking pink things pelted him, he gave up. When her hands were empty, he stepped in close and pulled her into his arms.

Her whole body was shaking. He pressed her head against his shoulder, noticing that her hair smelled of carnations. "Eleanor, don't cry."

"I—I'm n-not crying. I'm just mad."

"What about?"

"What about!" she sobbed. "How can you ask that?"

He waited, not saying anything.

"About everything, I guess," she said in an unsteady voice. "I just f-feel overwhelmed."

He walked her to the front porch and poured a glass of cool lemonade. "Drink this." He folded her hands around the glass. After she downed three good gulps, he propelled her up the steps and settled her in the porch swing.

"I threw away all the flowers I picked," she said.

"I noticed," he said with a smile. "You want me to go gather them up?"

She shook her head. "I was deadheading."

"What's that?"

"Snipping off the spent flowers. It makes them bloom even more."

"Kinda like shaving, I guess."

She gave a choked laugh. "I never thought of it like that,

but yes. I guess shaving makes a man's whiskers grow even more."

He sent her a sharp look. "That's true of other things, too."

"Really? What other things?"

"Well, how about this. Someone told me once that if something doesn't kill you, it makes you stronger. I thought about that a lot in prison."

Her head drooped. "Oh, Cord, some days I feel like I'm in prison on this farm. And it's *my* farm."

"You're not in prison," he said bluntly. "You have no idea what being in prison is like. It changes you."

She frowned down at the glass in her hand. "This summer is changing me. I'm not sure who I am anymore."

Cord said nothing. *This summer is changing me, too.* And it scared him.

Chapter Twenty-Seven

The next trip Cord and Danny made to town with a load of fresh-picked apples resulted in an unexpected growing-up experience for Eleanor's son. The wagon rolled down Main Street, headed for Ness's mercantile, and just as they reached the Golden Partridge, Danny grabbed Cord's arm. "What's the Golden Partridge, anyway?"

"It's a saloon, Danny."

"Where they drink liquor?" He twisted to study it as they drove past.

"And do other things," Cord said.

"What kinda 'other things'? Do they have naked ladies?"

Cord laughed. "Nope. No naked ladies. They play poker and faro and gamble with dice."

"Where do they have naked ladies?"

Cord coughed. "You sure you want to know?"

"Yeah, I'm sure!"

"And you won't breathe a word to your ma that I told you?"

Danny nodded and sketched a big X over his chest with his forefinger. "Cross my heart."

"Okay. We'll drive by the naked lady place on our way out of town."

"Gosh," Danny breathed. "Maybe I'm gettin' too old for lemon drops, huh?"

"Lemon drops are for Molly. I thought you liked caramels."

"I like 'em both. But I'm sure not gonna steal any, not after I saw that jail cell in back of the sheriff's office."

Ness's mercantile now sported a painted mural of winding vines and flowers against the same pale green background Cord had seen last week. Maybe young Edith Ness was expanding her artistic streak. Or maybe she was getting more serious about it.

Carl Ness, however, still exhibited his usual surliness, despite the fact that the store was jam-packed with people buying hoes and rubber boots and ribbons and chicken feed.

"Unload yer apples around the back, why don'tcha, Cord?"

Cord wondered why Carl never volunteered to help him and Danny wrestle the heavy bushel baskets out of the wagon and into the back of his store. Maybe he had a bad back. Or maybe he didn't feel comfortable leaving his cash register untended. Or maybe the man was just plain lazy.

"Cord, look!" Danny jostled his arm. "Over there, behind the shovels."

He turned, half expecting to see Tom Malloy. Instead, Darla Bledsoe and Fanny Moreland stood in the aisle, debating the merits of a bolt of calico. The two women spied him at the same instant.

"Cordell!" Fanny reached him first. "Why, you sweet thing, ah wager you're bringing Miz Malloy's apples to market."

Darla managed to cut in front of her. "I haven't seen you in town lately, Cordell. And just when I—"

"How is Mrs. Malloy, Cordell?" Fanny interrupted. "Is she still—?"

"Despaired of seeing y'all again," Darla finished.

Fanny elbowed her to one side. "Is she still managing that farm all by herself?"

Cord opened his mouth to reply, then snapped his jaw shut. He sure didn't want to get in the middle of the catfight these two ladies looked like they were working up to. He dropped one hand to Danny's shoulder and gave it a squeeze. "Go get some caramels for the trip home, Dan. And some lemon drops for Molly."

"Sure, Cord."

Darla attacked again. "I was just remarking to Mr. Ness that…"

Fanny jerked to attention. "What were y'all saying about…?"

"The flowers painted on the front of the mercantile look so beautiful. I am partial to roses, myself," Darla purred. "What about you, Cordell?"

"Miz Malloy's apples? There surely seem to be a lot of them this season, don't there?"

"Yeah, lots of apples. And sure, roses are real nice." He couldn't remember which answer went with which lady, so he smiled at both of them and turned toward the candy counter, where Danny was choosing caramels and lemon drops.

Fanny followed them all the way out to the boardwalk, and Darla was close behind.

Cord put his hand on Danny's shoulder. "Come on, Dan." He steered the boy toward the Golden Partridge. *Thank the Lord women aren't welcome in saloons!*

Inside it was dim and smoky and blessedly quiet. In one corner a poker game absorbed the attention of four men gathered around a grimy-looking table. "Okay, Dan, this is what a saloon looks like." He stepped up to the bar. "One whiskey and one sarsaparilla."

One shot glass and one dark bottle slid along the smooth mahogany bar. "Lemme taste your whiskey, Cord."

He looked down into the eager face of a kid real anxious

to do his growing up in a hurry. Well, what the heck? He passed the whiskey over.

"Sip it," he ordered.

Danny swallowed down a mouthful, grimaced and shut his eyes tight.

"I said to sip it," Cord said with a grin.

The boy opened his mouth, but no words came out. Cord slapped his back two or three times and after a moment Danny sucked in a guttural breath. "I think I like sarsaparilla better," he said, his voice hoarse.

Cord tried hard not to laugh. He bit his lip and downed the rest of his whiskey while Danny gulped the fizzy liquid in the bottle of sarsaparilla.

"Okay," the boy wheezed. "Now do I get to see some naked ladies?"

The bartender's russet eyebrows went up. Cord spilled some coins onto the bar top, snagged the pop bottle and ushered the boy out onto the street. Once they were settled on the wagon bench, Cord leaned over. "You're not actually gonna see any naked ladies, Dan. Just where they live, all right?"

"All right, I guess." He took a big swig from his bottle of pop. "Do you have to be all growed up before you can see them naked?"

"That's right," Cord lied. "You have to be at least thirty years old."

"How old are you, Cord?"

"Thirty-two. Old enough to know better."

"Know better about what?"

"Everything, son. Young men do foolish things."

Danny peered up at him with interest. "What'd you do that was foolish, Cord? You know, when you were young. What'd you do after the War?"

Cord looked out at the distant hills for a long moment, then ruffled the boy's hair. "Well, I got tired of yellin' at herds of cattle so I worked as a gunsmith for some years. Settled in town. Got married."

"Didja ever have any kids?"

"No."

"How come?"

"One reason is that my wife was…interested in other things. Another reason was…" He broke off. He figured Danny didn't need to know the rest. His wife… Oh, hell, he didn't need to rake up that old pain.

He turned the wagon down a short side street and the gray gelding clopped slowly past a rambling brown house with blue cornflowers growing in the front yard.

"You sure this is the right place, Cord? Looks just like all the other houses. They even got flowers, just like Ma does."

"Yep," Cord said. "Naked ladies are just like other ladies in lots of ways."

"'Cept they're naked, huh? Sure wish I could see one."

"Chances are you've seen one already. They dress just like other ladies."

"You think that pretty Fanny lady is a naked lady?"

Cord grabbed the sarsaparilla bottle out of Danny's hand and downed a swallow. "That pretty Fanny lady is a lot of things, but a naked lady isn't one of them."

"I bet she is underneath all them ruffles."

Cord coughed and grabbed the bottle again.

"Do you think Ma is a naked lady, too, underneath?"

"No." *Well, yes.* Eleanor was most definitely naked underneath her work dress and her petticoat and her camisole and her… He closed his eyes. He couldn't let himself think about it.

"Time to head for home, Danny. Remember, not a word to your ma about this afternoon."

"'Course not, Cord. Us men got to stick together, huh?"

Cord bit the inside of his cheek and again closed his eyes.

* * *

"You saw Darla and Fanny in town?" Eleanor queried. "Danny said they were both at the mercantile when you delivered the apples."

"Yeah," he said, keeping his voice noncommittal. "Forgot to tell you."

Eleanor studied the tanned face of her hired man across the supper table. Surely any red-blooded male would remember meeting a pretty woman in town. Especially *two* pretty women.

But, she reflected, it was Tom and not Cord who usually went into town after supper. For some reason she didn't really care what Tom was up to at night. Cord was another matter.

Oh, dear God, that was all backward. Backward and upside-down. And confusing. *And maddening!*

"What's the matter, Ma? Don't you like that pretty Fanny lady? Or that other one with the red hair?"

Eleanor bit down hard on her bottom lip. "Hush up and eat your potatoes, Danny."

Chapter Twenty-Eight

⦚⦚⦚⦚⦚⦚

"Ellie, you got any more beans?"

Without a word Eleanor ladled a dollop of baked beans onto Tom's supper plate and added a square of corn bread.

"Where's the butter?" he barked.

"You ate it all," Danny shot back.

Eleanor laid her hand on her son's thin shoulder. "I will be churning tomorrow. There will be plenty of butter by suppertime."

"What about breakfast?" Tom grumbled. "Can't you churn some tonight?"

"No, she can't," Danny protested. "Ma's worked real hard all day an' she's tired."

Tom lifted both elbows off the table and leaned back in his chair. "You talkin' back to me, son?"

"I'm not your—"

Cord's hand shot out to clamp onto the boy's other shoulder.

"Son," Danny said under his breath.

Tom hunched forward, his fist raised. "Why, you little—"

In the next second, Cord was on his feet. He grabbed the front of Tom's shirt and yanked him up out of his chair. "Malloy, you lay a hand on the boy and I'll kill you."

"Yeah? Well, I'm just waitin' for you to try."

"Tom! Cord! Stop it this instant!" Eleanor tipped a full glass of cold milk down Tom's trousers. "You will not kill anyone in my kitchen! Now, sit down and hush up, both of you."

Danny watched them, his eyes wide with fear. Molly began to cry.

"Shut up!" Tom shouted at the girl.

Eleanor smacked the baked bean ladle hard across his knuckles.

"Ow! What'ja do that for?"

"You do not yell at my children. Ever. Do you understand?"

Tom glared across the table at Cord. "What're you lookin' at, boyo?"

"I'm looking at a bad-mannered supper guest who's about to get hell beat out of him."

"Children," Eleanor interjected, "go upstairs to bed. Now."

Tom lurched to his feet, and suddenly Cord realized the man was drunk. He collared him, pushed his bulky frame across the floor and out the screen door, and flung him down the porch steps.

"Cord," Eleanor whispered when he returned to the kitchen, "he'll kill you."

"No, he won't. He's drunk."

"But tomorrow he'll be sober."

"Won't matter. He won't kill me."

"What makes you so sure?"

"His hands shake. Probably drinks too much."

"But if he tries… Cord, you can't kill him. He's the children's father."

"I'll keep that in mind," he said tersely.

She sent him a stern look and began gathering up the dishes.

Cord stepped out onto the porch to confront Malloy, but there was no sign of him. Or his horse, he discovered when he strolled over to the barn. Where did the man go during the day? Apparently he had enough money for barbershop shaves and whiskey, but where did he get it? He sure wasn't helping Eleanor around the farm, and if he thought the land still belonged to him, why didn't he take on some responsibility? The only thing Tom seemed to be interested in was Eleanor, and Cord could see his frustration in that regard.

He knew it was foolish to think that a drunken or a cowardly man wasn't dangerous. A drunk or a coward was even more dangerous. But there was more at stake here than just besting Tom Malloy. Danny and Molly must be kept safe.

And there was Eleanor. He blew his breath out through tight lips. Guess it was time to get his priorities straight.

Eleanor stared at Cord across the breakfast table in disbelief. "You want me to what?"

"Come with me to Gillette Springs to deliver the apples."

"That is an absolutely scandalous idea! A woman just cannot—"

"Sure beats tangling with a drunk man who could turn violent in a heartbeat. We can take Molly and Danny with us."

"No," she said quickly. "There are too many uncertainties on the road. I would rather leave them with Sarah Cloudman in town."

"You could stay with Sarah, too," he pointed out. "It would be safer than being here, alone, on the farm."

She hesitated. "Yes, I guess I could, but…"

"Eleanor, listen to me. I don't want you alone out here at night. Tom is dangerous. He threatens Molly and Danny, and it's only a matter of time until he threatens you, too."

He waited, studying her face. She hated it when he did that. He saw all sorts of things she wanted to keep hidden, all her questions about Tom, about why he hadn't come back after the War; why he seemed to have money for his fancy vest and shiny spurs; where did he get it? It made her feel…vulnerable.

"What if Tom follows us?"

"Why would he? He won't know you're with me, and he's not fool enough to confront me."

She worried her bottom lip between her teeth. It was her final delivery of apples to Samson Northcutt in Gillette Springs. Yesterday they had picked the last of this year's crop, and even though it was more than a forty-mile trip, Northcutt's mercantile paid the highest price of the season. Not only that, in past years, the proprietor had put her up at the Royal Springs Hotel at his expense. Last year she'd hired Sammy Greywolf to make the trip with her, but this year Cord had taken over.

"Eleanor, you're dead tired and strung up tighter than new barbed wire. It will do you good to get away."

She bristled and glared at him across the table. "I am not 'strung up,' as you put it!"

"Oh, yeah? That why you sent Danny off to school this morning?"

"Of course. His education is important."

"It's Saturday. There's no school on Saturday."

"Oh." She looked down at the half-eaten pancake on her plate.

"Danny and Molly are upstairs, working on a jigsaw puzzle I found in the attic," Cord said. "We can drop them at Rose Cottage on our way out of town. Sarah and Rooney will look after them, and Danny can play checkers with Mark."

Eleanor leveled a long look at the man facing her, watched him refill her coffee cup and then his own. She studied his long-fingered hands. Tom had not returned last night, and it was the first breakfast in the last month she had felt relaxed enough to be even halfway hungry. The thought of being able to breathe freely for an entire day, not worrying every hour about what mood Tom was in or what would anger him, punched a little hole in the cloud of despair that hovered over her.

"What about it, Eleanor?"

His softly spoken words jerked her attention back to the kitchen and the fact that another day of worry and tension was beginning.

"Very well. I'll wash up the dishes and pack a few overnight things for the children while you hitch up the wagon."

She had to laugh at how quickly he bolted for the back door. "Pack a lunch, too," he called as he strode down the wooden steps.

She made bacon sandwiches and fresh coffee, poured it into a mason jar and double-wrapped it in dish towels to keep it hot. When she'd filled her canvas travel bag with clean underclothes for Molly and Daniel, she suddenly noticed she was still wearing her apron over her denim work skirt and she had on her oldest shirtwaist, a frayed blue muslin with four cracked buttons.

Oh, bother. This was a working trip, not a holiday. She should dress like the farm woman she was. She changed only her shoes, trading her plain black leather walking oxfords for the scuffed work boots she wore in the apple orchard.

By eight o'clock she guessed she was ready, or as ready as she would ever be. She didn't really like Gillette Springs, with its grain elevator and the county courthouse and the fancy women's hat store. It was busy and noisy, and it lacked the quiet, small-town feeling of Smoke River, where everyone knew you and people were mostly friendly, even mercantile owner Carl Ness. Most days, anyway. Lately, Carl had been looking at her oddly and his words were more clipped than usual. She was sure Tom had something to do with it.

"Hurry up, children!" she called. "Cord is waiting in the

wagon." She untied her apron, folded a clean shirtwaist and her hairbrush into a clean flour sack and grabbed her wide-brimmed straw sun hat. When she closed the front door she noted that the revolver was missing from the shelf. Cord must have taken it.

Chapter Twenty-Nine

By the time they rolled into the bustling community of Gillette Springs, Cord's forearms ached and Eleanor's nose was sunburned in spite of her broad-brimmed hat. It had been a long, hot ten hours since they left Smoke River, and the short respite among the stand of fir trees where they stopped to devour the sandwiches and coffee seemed like days ago. Eleanor's shoulders slumped and her head drooped with fatigue. Cord's own shoulders were feeling the sting of overworked muscles.

They unloaded seven bushel baskets of apples at the Gillette Springs mercantile, then drove on down the street and parked the wagon in front of the Royal Springs Hotel. Cord unhitched the horse, fed and watered it and then turned to Eleanor.

"How about some supper?"

"Later," Eleanor countered. "For the last ten miles I've been thinking about a bath."

"Right out here on Main Street?" he joked.

She said nothing. He guessed she was too tired to fight back. He guided her up the hotel steps to the registration desk and punched the bell, and the shiny-faced clerk looked up.

"Ah, Miz Malloy! You've come to visit us again, I see. More of those good apples, I bet."

"You are correct, Mr. Barnaby. This is my last delivery of the season."

"Sign here, ma'am." He slid over the hotel register. "Dining room's open 'til nine."

"Could I have a bath brought up to my room?"

"Sure thing, Miz Malloy." He slapped a room key down on the polished counter and turned to Cord. "And for you, sir?"

"I'm with her," he said.

The clerk's eyebrows shot up. "In the same room, you mean?"

"Yes," Cord said.

"Certainly not," Eleanor retorted. "He will be sleeping elsewhere." She bent her head close to Cord's. "Sammy Greywolf always slept in the stable," she intoned.

"I'm not Sammy Greywolf." He swiped the key off the counter and took Eleanor's elbow.

"Well!" Mr. Barnaby's face looked almost purple.

Cord pinned him with a look. "I'd appreciate it if you'd close your mouth and bring up the lady's bath."

He piloted Eleanor up the stairs. "What do you think you're doing?" she hissed.

"Getting you a bath and then some supper, and then I'm getting some sleep."

She shot him an exasperated look. "Certainly not with me!"

"Not exactly 'with you,' no."

She stopped dead at the top of the landing. "Well, *what* exactly? I expected you to sleep in the stable, like Sammy Greywolf did. Or at least in a separate room."

"Separate rooms cost money." And he couldn't protect her from a separate room. He lifted the room key out of her hand and unlocked Number Six. "I'll be down in the bar," he said, gently pushing her inside. "Leave me some bathwater."

An hour later Cord settled himself across from a still weary-looking Eleanor Malloy in the hotel dining room.

Both her hands were wrapped around a delicate-looking cup of tea.

"Bathwater was still warm," he said. "Thanks."

She just stared at him, so he signaled the waitress for some coffee. "I know you've been looking at this shirt all day, Eleanor, but I didn't bring a clean one."

"You don't have a clean one," she said absently. "Wash day isn't until Monday."

He nodded and gulped down a swallow of the coffee the waitress set at his elbow. "We need to talk."

"Oh?" Her eyebrows went up. "What about? Please make it quick, because I am starving."

"Okay, here's 'quick.' We need to talk about tonight."

Eleanor unfolded the menu and bent forward. "All right, I'm listening. What *about* tonight? Cord, are you sure you know what you're doing?"

He leaned back in the plush upholstered chair and gave her a long look. "I know exactly what I'm doing."

"Oh?" she said primly. "Explain it to me, then."

"I thought it'd be...safer."

"Safer? Whatever do you mean?" He hesitated so long a chill went up her spine.

"Tom will know I took the wagon to Gillette Springs today. When he finds you gone, he'll figure you came with me, and there's no telling what he'll think. Or do. He might be in town right now."

She stopped running her forefinger down the menu items and looked up. "What should we do?"

"Nothing. Let's eat supper."

She gave him a quick glance and tapped a fingernail on one supper item. "Steak," she said to the frilly-aproned waitress who approached, order pad in hand.

"I'll have steak, too," he said. Eleanor noted the admiring look the girl gave him.

"Potatoes, sir?"

"Yeah. Fried. Lots of 'em."

"Would you care for wine?"

Cord sought her eyes. She didn't dare. Wine befuddled her senses. She shook her head.

"Sure," he said to the girl. "Make it a big glass."

All through the meal Eleanor found herself watching his face. There were so many things she couldn't begin to understand about this man. Now she had to admit she was beginning not to understand herself.

She felt no loyalty toward Tom. Even if he was her husband, she had ceased to care about him years ago. Even so, she still felt bound by her wedding vows.

She liked being close to Cord. She valued his help and she had to admit she enjoyed his company. She liked talking to him, and she even enjoyed his occasional teasing. She would miss him when he left her farm and rode on to California. Tom or no Tom, she knew Cord would be moving on, and her life would continue.

Their meals came, along with another glass of wine for Cord. She ate slowly, savoring every bite of a supper eaten in peace with no sullen looks or sharp words from anyone. Neither she nor Cord said a word for some minutes, and then Cord laid his fork aside.

"Why do you stay with him, Eleanor? He's no good for you."

"I know," she said slowly. "But Tom is the children's father. If I left him, he could claim Molly and Danny."

"I don't think he'd want them. He hasn't shown much interest in being a father."

"I can't risk it, Cord. Besides, I have to live in Smoke River. My farm is there. And Molly and Daniel have to live there, too. If I did the unthinkable and just left Tom, I would become known as a loose woman. It would hurt the children. It would be terrible for them if their mother became a pariah in town."

"It's dangerous, both for you and for your kids. Leaving him might be better," he said, holding her gaze.

"No, it would not be better. Small towns can be narrow-minded."

He picked up his knife and slowly, deliberately, cut three perfect squares of steak, looked at them for a few seconds, and then laid the knife down again.

Eleanor studied him. "Cord?"

"Yeah?"

"What is wrong?"

"Nothing." Then he looked straight into her eyes. "Oh, hell, everything's wrong."

"Do you want to tell me what 'everything' is?"

"Yeah. But not now. I want to tell you later."

Whatever was bothering him was tightening his jaw muscles in a way she had never seen, not even when he'd confronted Tom and tossed him down the front porch steps. But she wasn't going to let whatever was bothering Cord spoil the delicious freedom-from-care feeling she felt tonight. She hadn't felt this happy or this lighthearted since Molly was born.

She folded her hands in her lap and watched Cord across the table. The haircut she'd given him some weeks ago had grown out, and the shock of dark hair falling across his forehead made her smile. When he brushed it back she noticed his hand was shaking.

Something was wrong. In all the months she'd known Cord Winterman she had never seen his hand shake. She had never before seen him unnerved about anything.

The waitress cleared their plates and brought coffee, but before she had finished stirring in some cream Cord reached across and captured her hand. "Eleanor, drink your coffee and let's go upstairs."

"Don't you want dessert?"

He shook his head and started to rise, but she caught his arm. "Could I have some peach pie? I'm so sick of apple pie and apple turnovers and apple dumplings and applesauce…

apple *everything.* I bet you are, too. Let's mark the end of the harvest with something that's *not* made of apples."

His expression softened and he signaled the waitress. "You have any peach pie?"

"Oh, yes, sir. Made fresh today."

"Bring us a couple of slices, could you? And put some ice cream on top."

The girl spun away toward the kitchen. "Ice cream!" Eleanor exulted. "Thank you for indulging me, Cord. I feel like celebrating, don't you?"

"Nope."

She narrowed her eyes. "You're not really worried about Tom, are you? About his maybe being here, I mean?"

"Some," he admitted. "Not a whole lot, though. Not enough to spoil peach pie and ice cream."

"But there is something on your mind," she pursued. "I can see it in your eyes."

He took his time downing a swallow of his coffee. "Yeah, there's something on my mind."

"Is it a *big* something?"

"Big enough." Their desserts arrived, scoops of vanilla ice cream melting on top. Cord watched her take big bites of the pie and little bites of the ice cream while his plate sat untouched in front of him and the *à la mode* turned to soup.

"Oh, this is delicious!" she cried. "Maybe I should plant some peach trees for next summer. What do you think?"

"You figure you could manage a bigger orchard?"

Her smile faded. "I suppose not. Not alone, anyway. Somehow I keep thinking that Tom—"

"No. Eleanor, Tom's not in this with you."

"How do you mean? Oh, never mind, I know what you mean. I know exactly what you mean. I just don't want to think about it."

"Ever?" he asked carefully.

"Well, at least not tonight. Tonight I feel lighter than air, away from everything."

Away from Tom she meant. Suddenly he noticed the ice cream puddle on his plate threatened to spill over onto the tablecloth and he grabbed his spoon. Yeah, the pie was good, even with the melting mess on top. He polished off half of it before he became aware of her laughter.

"What's so funny?"

"You. Eating peach pie with a spoon, like a little boy."

He grinned in spite of himself and downed another bite. "Sometimes little boys have the right idea—grab it before it gets away."

"Or melts," she said.

"Or melts," he echoed. He considered that idea in ways he could never share with Eleanor, and they finished their coffee in silence.

Upstairs in Number Six, Eleanor flew to the window and raised the sash while Cord lit the kerosene lamp on the night table separating the two narrow beds. Music drifted in from the saloon down the street, tinkly notes from a badly played piano, but it seemed to make no difference to Eleanor, who was humming along. "Oh, my darling Clementine," she sang, peering out the window. "You are lost and gone for—"

She turned toward him and broke off. "Cord? What's wrong?"

"Nothing," he managed. *Everything* was wrong. It was eating him up. He had to say something. And he had to say it now.

Chapter Thirty

"Eleanor..." he began.

"Oh, Cord, let's not talk now. Not after such a nice supper."

"We've got to talk sometime. I've got some things to say to you."

"Later. Please, Cord."

He snapped his jaw shut.

In the heavy quiet Eleanor moved to open her overnight bag and lifted out the hairbrush and the clean shirtwaist she had brought. Cord, she noticed, had brought no luggage at all, no clean shirt, no shaving kit, nothing. She guessed he planned to sleep fully clothed.

And so would she. She hung the shirtwaist in the small armoire in the corner and began to loosen the hairpins in the bun at her neck.

Cord turned away. He couldn't watch her do things with her hair; made his groin ache. To distract himself he slipped the Colt from his belt and laid it on the nightstand, poured some water into the ceramic basin on the bureau and splashed some on his face. Then he made a mistake.

He turned around and saw her standing at the window, her arms raised, brushing her hair.

"Dammit, don't do that!"

She pivoted toward him, wide-eyed. "Don't do what?"

He reached her in three long strides and lifted the brush out of her hand. "Don't brush your hair."

She stared at him so long he thought maybe he had ice cream on his chin. "Why?" she asked in surprise. "I brush my hair every night."

He stood facing her, taking slow, deliberate breaths until the roaring in his head stopped. "I sure hope you're gonna understand this, because I'm not sure I have a good grip on it."

"Understand what? I don't—"

He closed his hands around her upper arms. "Eleanor, for once in your life just hush up and listen."

Her gray eyes widened even further. "Very well, Cord, I'm listening."

"I—" He stopped himself. He couldn't say that to her, not in a million years. He swallowed and began again.

"Eleanor, you know I like you. And you know I like Molly and Danny."

She nodded, keeping her eyes on his.

"But there's two things you *don't* know." He stopped and swallowed hard. "The first thing is that I've wanted you from the minute I laid eyes on you. And I want you right now so bad I can hardly breathe."

"Oh, Cord," she whispered.

"Don't talk," he ordered. He swallowed again and went on. "The second thing you don't know is that I am not going to make love to another man's wife, even a man who's a drunk and a bully. But, dammit, I'm having a devil of a time remembering that."

"Oh," she said, her voice quiet. "I see."

He groaned. "Hell, no, you don't see. You have no idea what it's like to lie awake half the night aching because you're only a dozen steps away and I can't…won't…"

"Is this like being hot and bothered, as you explained to Danny?"

The question was so matter of fact he wasn't sure he'd heard her right. "'Hot and bothered,'" he repeated. "'Hot and bothered' isn't near strong enough. Try 'half-crazy.' Out of my head half the time because I can't think straight watching you. Wanting you."

"I see," she said again. "Well, there is something that I want *you* to know, Cord."

His breath stopped. "Yeah? What's that?"

"I do not ever intend to betray my marriage vows, no matter how drunk or how…whatever my husband is."

Cord stared at her. "Guess that solves our problem, then, doesn't it?"

"Yes," she said, her voice quiet, "I believe it does. Since you won't have another man's wife and I will not break my marriage vows, it seems clear that we are perfectly safe from each other tonight."

He barked out a laugh. "Yeah, I guess so. God help us."

"And," she continued calmly, "if you will stop looking at me like that, I will stop brushing my hair."

He couldn't make his hands release her, so he drew her into his arms and tucked her head under his chin. "Eleanor, you know something? If I live through tonight, maybe I'll start going to church."

"No, you won't, Cord," she whispered. "You will go to California." She pulled his head down to hers and brushed her lips over his cheek.

"And I will miss you every single day for the rest of my life."

A more sleepless night Cord could not remember. Not even in prison had his thoughts bumbled about in his brain like drunken cats. He couldn't go on like this much longer, but…

Well, there it was, the big *but*. He couldn't leave Eleanor in danger, and if he'd learned anything in his thirty-two years, it was that Tom Malloy spelled danger. But neither could he stay around watching Eleanor fry bacon and hang out the laundry and smile at her children, listening to her breathing at night, aching for her. He wondered how long he could continue like this without going stark raving mad.

And as much as he wanted to, he knew he couldn't kill Tom Malloy. They'd slam him back in prison so fast his head would spin.

But you're caught in a prison anyway, one you can't escape from.

He tried not to think about it. He stared up at the darkened ceiling, moved his gaze to the single window through which a faint light shone and counted the number of holes in the lace curtains. He almost missed Mama Cat and her kittens snuggled up next to his body. After a while he noticed that he couldn't hear any breathing sounds coming from Eleanor.

Her bed was maybe three feet from his, pushed up against the wall under the window. He'd heard the bedsprings give when she lay down, but she hadn't said anything, not *good night* or *sleep well* or *see you in the morning.* Nothing. In the dark, which she insisted on while she took off whatever it was she took off, he couldn't see her face, just the glimmer of her bare arms.

But he knew she was awake. She was lying still and real quiet, just like he was. So maybe she was trying to figure things out, just like he was.

And then he heard her draw in an uneven breath, and he knew she was crying. Dammit anyway. He couldn't stand it when she was unhappy. He lay motionless for a long time, listening, and finally he'd had enough. A man could take only so much of a woman's pain.

He rolled off the bed, made his way across the darkened room to where she lay, and without a word stretched out beside her and gathered her into his arms. Her face was wet and her body shook with sobs, but she didn't make a sound. He pressed her head into the hollow of his shoulder.

Her arm crept across his bare chest and she clung to him until her breathing gradually slowed and evened out and her arm went slack.

He smiled into her rose-scented hair. He wasn't making love to another man's wife, and she wasn't breaking any marriage vows, but right now none of that mattered. What did matter was that they were together. And no matter what happened in Smoke River tomorrow or next week or next year, Eleanor Malloy would know that he cared about her.

Ever since that night in Gillette Springs, Eleanor had been acutely aware that she and Cord were closer in some undefined way. They were more careful of each other, more protective. They no longer teased each other. They didn't argue. They looked at each other across the supper table with understanding and acceptance, even when Tom was present. Which wasn't often.

But there would come a breaking point, and they both knew it.

Late summer melted into fall so seamlessly that Eleanor scarcely noticed. Afternoons were still scorching, especially when she worked outside in the hot sun scrubbing shirts and jeans on the wooden washboard or picking bush beans and pulling up carrots for chicken stew. The balmy evenings settled over the farm like a benediction, and darkness spread over the apple trees and the front porch like black velvet.

Danny started school again, riding Cord's bay mare, which he saddled for him each morning, and returning with homework to struggle over each evening. Molly was learning to churn butter and try her hand at hemming handkerchiefs and the doll clothes Eleanor stitched up on her treadle sewing machine. She was also helping Molly with her reading and teaching her to knit tiny blankets for the doll cradle Cord had made for her.

And Tom was spending more and more time away from the farm.

As the long, hot days passed, Cord said less and less. To-night she sat on the porch swing, sorting through the pock-etful of flower seeds she'd gleaned from her garden, asters and black-eyed Susans and sweet alyssum. Next summer she would put bouquets everywhere, even in the barn, in the cow's stall and the tack room Cord had reorganized. Next month she would do more sewing, she decided. Make a pretty pink dress with ruffles for Molly to start school in and a new gored calico skirt for herself.

She dreaded the coming of winter. The weather would turn cold, too cold for Tom to ride back and forth from the farm to wherever he went every day, and that meant he would spend more nights on the farm. She and the children would see more of him, and she couldn't bring herself to think about what that would mean.

As the weeks went on, the leaves on the maple trees turned gold and orange and began to drift onto the ground, and Tom grew more and more short-tempered. Tonight at supper he had been so unpleasant Cord had finally picked up his plate of beans and corn bread and finished eating on the porch. Later, Tom stormed out the front door and with a vicious jab of his fist purposely knocked Cord's plate up-side down into his lap.

But what upset Eleanor most was what her husband said. "You're still here, huh, hired man? Guess I gotta do something to get you off my farm." He said other things, too. Terrible things about drifters and men with no right to decent treatment.

Cord waited until Tom had ridden off, then he stood up and walked off into the dark. She tried to put the ugly words out of her mind, sent Molly and Danny up to bed and sat rocking on the porch swing.

She couldn't help wondering why Cord seemed so dis-tant lately. She had thought and thought about that night they spent together in Gillette Springs, wondering what she might have done differently, wondering if that was what was bothering him.

Cord walked his nightly route through the apple orchard and around the perimeter of the farm, then checked out the barn. He didn't know exactly what he was looking for, but tonight he had an uneasy, crawly feeling that nibbled at the base of his spine. Finally he tramped back through the gate to find Eleanor sitting in the swing, sorting seeds into the cups of a battered muffin tin.

She looked up as he drew near the porch steps. "Is everything all right?"

"Far as I can tell. Tom's gone. Kids go to bed?"

"Yes. Danny has school tomorrow."

"What about you?"

"I'll go up in a minute. I thought I'd sit here a while and cool off. It's awfully hot in the kitchen."

He came up the steps but made no move to sit down beside her. "Guess I'll turn in." Then he hesitated. "Don't sit out here too late, Eleanor. Tom was in a funny mood when he rode off."

"Yes," she agreed quietly.

He put his hand on the screen door. "I locked the back door. Be sure to lock this one, all right?" Without waiting for an answer, he moved through the doorway, and the screen slapped shut behind him.

An hour later she still sat rocking back and forth, lost in thought. She shut her eyes tight.

Dear God, I am so lonely. I ache to talk to Cord. Or not talk. I just want to be near him.

She must be a disloyal wife for wanting this. But dear heavenly God, she knew she would suffer when Cord was gone.

With a jerk she stopped the motion of the swing, stood up and marched into the house. She locked the door and went up the stairs to her bedroom. She'd go crazy if she let herself think about it.

Chapter Thirty-One

⁓⁓⁓

Cord jolted awake and lay unmoving for a moment, wondering what had wakened him. The house was quiet. He knew it was buttoned up tight because he'd double-checked the locks on both the front and back doors. Eleanor and the kids slept nearby, and his ears were attuned to any noise from downstairs.

The house had the middle-of-the-night stillness that was usual between midnight and 4:00 a.m. So what had brought him out of a sound sleep? He started to roll over when he saw an odd flicker of light through the window.

Fire!

He scrambled off the narrow bed, pulled on his jeans and jammed his boots on his bare feet.

"Fire!" he yelled. He raced out of the attic and pounded on Eleanor's bedroom door. "Eleanor, wake up!" He pushed the door open to see her white-clad figure sitting up in bed.

"Get dressed!" he ordered. "The barn's on fire!"

By the time he reached the front porch, red-orange flames were shooting fifty feet into the sky. The unearthly growl of an unchecked fire shot a chill up his backbone.

Eleanor banged through the screen door wearing a white nightgown with a baggy plaid shirt over it and her work boots.

"Fill a bucket!" he shouted. "I'll check on Tom and get the animals out."

He closed his ears against the high-pitched screams of the horses and headed toward the burning building. The wide barn door was hot to the touch. He bunched his shirt around his fist, rammed the wooden latch free and shoved the door open.

Black, eye-stinging smoke roiled out. He sucked in a lungful of air and plunged inside. "Tom! Tom!"

No answer. He climbed the ladder into the loft, but Tom was gone.

He found the milk cow, smacked her on the flank, and she lumbered out into the yard.

The stalled horses were panic-stricken and refused to budge, so he stripped his shirt off and tied it around the gray gelding's eyes. Fighting against the heat, he slipped a rope around its neck and dragged it forward into the cool night air. He paused only long enough to yank the covering from its head and plunge it into the bucket of water Eleanor held.

He sloshed handfuls of the cool water over his face and bare chest, then grabbed his wet shirt and ran back into the barn. His bay mare was squealing in her stall, snorting in fear and rearing up to bang her hooves against the wall. Cord sidled over, stretched his wet shirt over the mare's rolling black eyes and grabbed a handful of coarse hair.

"Come on, girl," he urged. "Move! You can do it. Just come with me." He tugged hard, but the horse balked again. By now flames were nibbling around the edge of the barn door; if they didn't get through it in the next few moments they would be trapped.

At last the quivering animal took a step forward, then two. Cord slapped her rump hard and she bolted through the burning doorway and into the yard, where he hoped Eleanor could catch her mane and bring her to a stop. He heard the splash as Eleanor tossed a bucket of water on the mare's singed hide and heard her voice.

"Cord!" she screamed. "The horses are safe."

He ducked back into the smoke-filled tack room, grabbed the two saddles and all the harnesses he could and heaved the armload out the barn door.

Eleanor watched the barn door, now a mass of flames. Why did Cord not follow the animals outside? Oh, dear God in heaven, was he trapped?

"Cord!" A sickening feeling flooded her stomach. The fire had consumed most of the structure. Nothing was left but two walls and the roof, and flames were now eating their way along the eaves. *Dear God, Cord will die in there!*

Without thinking she dumped the water bucket over herself, grabbed up her nightgown in one hand and started forward. Just as she reached the barn door, Cord stumbled through with Mama Cat under one arm and his hands full of squirming kittens. Smoke rose from his trousers, and the ends of his hair were frizzy.

She grabbed him around the waist and knocked the kittens away. With a yowl Mama Cat skittered off into the dark, and Eleanor mopped at Cord's soot-streaked face with the hem of her sopping gown.

"Are you burned anywhere else?" she demanded.

Water dribbled down his cheeks and dripped off his chin. "Don't think so," he panted. "Water feels good. Thanks."

All at once she began to tremble. He could have died! And if it weren't for him, all her stock, the horses and the milk cow, would have been incinerated.

Cord touched her shoulder. "You all right?"

"Y-yes, just shaky. I usually get scared *after* an emergency," she wept. "And th-then I have a g-good cry."

He propelled her up onto the porch and settled her in the swing, where she curled her legs up under her wet nightgown and bent her head.

"I smell like smoke," he rasped. "I'm gonna wash off at the pump."

She sat sobbing and trembling while he doused his head

under the faucet and dumped a bucket of water over his smoke-singed jeans. When he returned he slid onto the swing next to her and wrapped his arm around her shoulder.

After long minutes without saying anything, he pulled her to her feet and walked her into the house. At the foot of the staircase he stopped her and touched her shoulder.

"Eleanor…" He steadied her body against his. "Listen to me."

"Yes? Wh-what is it?"

He waited, feeling her frame shake. "That fire was set on purpose."

Her sharp intake of breath made him pause. He didn't want to frighten her, or the children, but he did want to make sure she understood what had happened.

"Cord, how could you possibly know that?"

He started to speak, then bit his tongue and waited a long moment, searching for the right words. "I found a blackened pile of straw inside the tack room. And four burned matches. Someone intended to set your barn on fire."

She swayed into him and swiped tears off her glistening cheeks. "Oh, no," she moaned. "I don't believe that. I can't believe anyone would do such a thing."

Tom would. But Cord wouldn't say it.

He turned her toward the stairs and started up ahead of her. "Come on. Let's check the children, be sure they're all right."

He reached one hand back to grasp hers and slowly led her up the steps until they stood together outside Molly and Danny's bedroom. Eleanor twisted the doorknob, pushed the door inward and quietly stepped inside. After a moment she backed out.

"They're both still sound asleep," she whispered. "You'd think if they heard any of the commotion outside they'd be wide-awake and full of questions."

"Give thanks to God your kids are sound sleepers."

She closed the door and leaned her head against the

painted wood. "I can't think about it. I can't…" Her voice choked off.

Cord guided her across the hallway to her own bedroom. The door stood ajar. He led her over to the bed, sat her down and knelt to pull off her boots. When he looked up she had buried her face in her hands and her shoulders were shaking.

"Eleanor, it's all over now. You're safe. Molly and Danny are safe. And your cow is probably eating your petunias."

"N-no, she wouldn't be," she said in a hiccuppy voice. "Betsy doesn't like petunias."

She couldn't seem to stop crying, so he tried to distract her. "Your nightgown is all wet."

"I kn-know."

She tipped onto her side and curled up in a tight ball.

"Don't leave," she whispered.

He settled his tired body beside her and smoothed her hair.

"Cord," she murmured. "Stay here with me."

"My jeans are filthy and I smell like smoke."

"Stay anyway."

He knew it was fear talking, but he stood up, toed off his boots and peeled off his water-soaked jeans. They dropped onto the rag rug beside the bed with a wet-mud sound, and then before he could stop himself, he threw caution out the window and stripped off his drawers. He wondered if she would even notice, much less care, but right now he didn't give a damn. She'd asked him to stay and by God he would stay.

She rolled toward him, her closed eyes leaking tears. He noticed she still wore that too-big plaid shirt over her night-gown. Gently he began to undo the top button. "You need to get out of this, Eleanor. It smells like smoke."

Her head dipped in a nod, so he continued, unbuttoning it all the way and spreading it open so she could shrug out of it. He slipped one hand under her shoulder, pulled the garment down her arms and tossed it onto the pile of wet clothes on the floor. When he glanced back up he found her eyes were open. He reached to pull the quilt up over her shaking body, but she stopped him.

"My nightgown is all wet."

"Yeah?" He held his breath.

She began to undo the buttons, starting at the high neck and working slowly downward. Her trembling fingers had trouble with the buttonholes.

"Eleanor, you sure you know what you're doing? Your gown will dry out in an hour or so."

"I kn-know exactly what I'm doing," she said.

"No, you don't. You're scared and exhausted and not thinking clearly." He caught her hand to stop her, but she deliberately moved it away and continued with the buttons.

"I am also cold and lonely and so glad you are here with me I could cry."

"You're already crying," he said, his voice quiet. "You haven't stopped crying since I brought Mama Cat out and chased your cow into the pasture." He leaned over and pressed his mouth to her damp eyelids. "Eleanor Malloy, you are one helluva woman."

She wriggled free of the muslin gown, and when he'd added it to the pile on the floor, she laid her forefinger on his lips. "Remember when I said I would never break my marriage vows?"

"Yeah. I've thought about that a lot. Keeps me awake most nights."

She touched his face. "Cord, I have a confession to make."

"Oh, yeah? What's that?"

She stretched out beside him on the bed. "I lied."

Chapter Thirty-Two

Cord laughed aloud. "You lied? You *lied*?" He brushed aside her hand and bent to kiss her. When he lifted his head his breathing was uneven.

"First of all, I don't believe you lied. And second, we're lying here next to each other buck naked, and whatever you said that night doesn't matter." He kissed her again, moving his mouth slowly over hers, then behind her ear, her closed eyelids, the hollow of her throat.

The tips of her breasts began to swell. She wanted him to kiss her there, touch her there. She ran one finger across his bare chest, trailing it over his shoulder and finally circling one of his nipples. When he thrust his head back she knew it was what she ought to do. She had no idea how to make love to a man. Tom had never done more than roughly knee her legs apart and plunge inside her.

But *this*... Cord had barely touched her and she wanted to do all sorts of things. *This cannot be wrong. Being with this man is too glorious to be wrong.*

And then his kiss changed. It went on and on, deeper and more demanding. His tongue slipped between her lips, inviting and teaching; it made her light-headed. He was showing her things she had never dreamed of, inciting feelings she never knew she had, responses she never knew existed.

His mouth found her nipples. She felt them ache as he touched her breasts, then moved his hand down to her belly and below. No one had ever touched her in such an intimate way. She had never known about such things, this sharp sweetness that flowed through her body like a hot, lazy river of sensation. She moved in his arms and heard his breathing catch.

His warm breath washed over her breasts. "Remember that night in Gillette Springs when we talked about all the reasons we weren't going to do this?"

"I remember it very well," she whispered. "I lay awake a long time that night, watching you while you slept. I kept wondering if we were wrong to deny ourselves this."

"I didn't do much sleeping that night. Maybe it was wrong that night, Eleanor, but it's not wrong now."

She reached her arms around his neck, pulled his head down to hers and pressed her lips on his closed eyelids. He gathered her against him. "I want to touch you," he murmured. "All over."

He combed his fingers through her hair, then began smoothing his hand over her naked back and down over her hips. His mouth followed, his tongue hot and searching. His breathing grew ragged.

Cord touched her hesitantly at first, afraid to be too intimate too soon, afraid that in his hunger he might be too rough. When he entered her she cried his name and moved with him until her body stilled and he heard her gasp.

"Eleanor," he whispered. "I love you. *I love you.*"

His body convulsed in one star-filled explosion, and tears stung into his eyes. God in heaven, he knew he was never going to be the same after tonight.

For more years than he cared to count, his past mistakes had haunted him. Bad decisions. Bad choices. Bad years in prison paying for them. But ever since he'd laid eyes on the woman beside him he'd felt himself start to come back to life. It was scary. He didn't really know how to stop drifting and get his life back, and for the past six months he'd been running on instinct. It was scary. At times it felt unreal. Overwhelming.

And tonight…

This beautiful, extraordinary gift would last him for the rest of his life.

After a long while he rolled to one side, taking her with him, and wrapped her tight in his arms. "If I live to be a hundred years old," he murmured near her ear, "I will never forget this night. Never."

Chapter Thirty-Three

Cord turned from the stove, where he was frying bacon, to see Danny standing in the kitchen doorway. "Where's Ma?"

Molly popped up behind him. "Are we gonna have pancakes?"

"No, honey. We're having scrambled eggs and bacon, all right?"

"Oh, goody! Where's Mama?"

Cord hesitated. "She's...still asleep."

"Is she sick?" Danny asked.

"No, she's just tired. She was up late last night."

"How come?"

Cord laid the spatula down and turned to face both children. "Go look outside, Dan. You, too, Molly."

They streaked into the parlor and barreled through the front door. In half a minute they were back, their eyes big as soup bowls. "Golly gee whiz, Cord, what happened to our barn?"

"It burned down last night, Dan."

"Where's Mama Cat and the kitties?" Molly cried.

"How come it burned down?" Danny pursued.

Cord forked over a slice of bacon. "I don't really know, son. Molly, you want to break some eggs into this dish?" He pointed to the china bowl beside the stove.

Eight eggs splatted into the bowl, and Cord whisked them around with a fork, added some milk and poured the mixture into the skillet. Too late he realized the pan was too hot; scrambled eggs should be cooked slowly.

"Where's Mama Cat?" Molly repeated.

"Mama Cat is just fine, Molly. I think you'll find her and all the kittens under the front porch. But how about waiting until you've had breakfast before you go find her?"

The girl grabbed three plates from the lowest shelf of the china cabinet and a handful of spoons and forks and spread them out in a haphazard circle. "I'm gonna eat real fast, all right?"

Danny settled himself at the table. "Whooee, wait till the kids at school hear about our barn! Did any of the horses get hurt?"

"All the horses are safe. Saddles, too. And the cow."

The boy sent him a startlingly adult look. "What started the fire, Cord?"

"I don't know exactly," he lied.

"Sure smells smoky outside."

Cord set the speckleware coffeepot over the heat, portioned out the overcooked eggs and bacon slices, and hooked his boot heel on the rung of his chair. While Danny gobbled his breakfast and Molly daintily, but quickly, spooned eggs past her lips, Cord kept his eye on the coffeepot. As soon as he saddled his bay mare for Danny and got the boy off to school, he'd take a cup of coffee up to Eleanor.

The boy slurped down the last of his milk, and Cord made a bacon sandwich and put it and a rosy red apple into his lunchbox. Then he walked outside, caught his horse and laid the saddle onto her back.

When Danny was mounted, Cord slipped the lunch into one pocket of his saddlebag. Then he slipped Eleanor's revolver from his belt and settled it in a separate pocket. He made sure Danny watched him do it.

"I'm putting this in along with your lunch, Dan."

"How come?"

"Just for general protection. You know how to fire it now, so I figured you might need it someday."

"Yeah?" Danny frowned. "Why would I?"

Cord didn't answer. "It's loaded. Don't show it to anyone."

"Oh. Right."

He caught the boy's eye. "Do I have your word on that?"

"Yeah, Cord, I promise."

Cord patted the mare's neck. "You break my trust and I'll thrash you so hard you won't sit down for a month. Got it?"

"Got it."

He slapped the animal's rump, the horse jolted forward and he stood watching the boy canter off with a tight feeling in his throat. When he turned back to the house he found Molly down on her hands and knees about to crawl under the porch. Oh, boy, Eleanor would sure scream about that! No telling what the girl would find under there besides kittens. He should have put a pinafore on her, or at least an apron.

"Molly, let me look so you won't get dirty." He bent and scraped his arm in a semicircle, and three orange kittens tumbled out, followed by Mama Cat.

Before he could stand up, Molly flung her arms around his neck. "You're all dirty now, Cord. Bet you're sorry."

"Nope," he said quietly. "Not by a long shot."

Back in the kitchen he gathered up the breakfast dishes, dunked them into the pan of hot soapy water and filled up a cup of coffee for Eleanor. She ought to be awake by now.

Or maybe not. When he considered why not, he felt hot all over.

The tap on her bedroom door was so tentative she thought it must be Molly or Danny. When Cord stepped inside she blinked.

"Where are the children?"

"Danny's on his way to school. Molly's on the front porch, playing with the kittens." He sat on the edge of the bed and handed her the cup and saucer. "No sugar and lots of cream, right?"

She smiled up at him. "This morning I wouldn't notice. Or care."

He leaned forward and pressed his lips against her hair.

"Did Danny take a lunch?"

"Yep. Bacon sandwich and an apple."

Cord had an odd look on his face, but she didn't want to ask.

"Is there any bacon left?"

"You hungry?"

She nodded. "I am absolutely ravenous this morning!"

"Eleanor…"

"Yes, I know," she said. "I'll have to tear down the rest of the barn before I can rebuild it, won't I? The prospect makes me sick to my stomach."

"No, I wasn't thinking about that."

"About what, then? About last night?" She knew her cheeks were getting red, but she didn't care.

He gave a quiet laugh. "You know you just turned the color of ripe raspberries? Makes me—" he grinned "—damn hungry."

The look in his eyes made her want to slide down and pull the sheet over her head.

"Don't know what to say, huh?" he said quietly.

She shook her head. The truth was she did not know what to say, or do, or even think. Yesterday she'd been sane, sensible Eleanor Malloy. Today…well, she didn't know about today.

Or tomorrow.

"You don't suppose the children heard us last night, do you?"

He laughed. "No. They slept through the fire, didn't they? Let's get back to a real problem."

"Only two things are certain, Cord. The barn will have to be rebuilt and I am absolutely starving!"

"Eleanor, rebuilding your barn isn't the real problem."

"What? What is the real problem?"

"We'll talk about it later." He lifted the cup away and set the saucer on the nightstand, tossed her discarded nightgown at her and waited while she slipped it over her head and buttoned it up to her chin. Then he walked her downstairs to the kitchen and sat her down at the table. When he set a plate of eggs and toast in front of her she looked up.

"No bacon?"

He chuckled. "I put it all in Danny's sandwich." He poured her another cup of coffee and pushed the cream pitcher toward her. She ate steadily while he washed and dried the dishes, then poured himself a mug of coffee and sat down across from her.

"We need to talk."

"Oh, Cord, I don't want to talk. I want to sit here with my coffee and pretend that my barn is still standing. Of course, with you frowning at me across the table, there's not much chance of that, is there?"

"I can't blame you for wanting to go back twenty-four hours and pretend it never happened, but—"

"But?"

His clear blue eyes held hers with a don't-you-dare-look-away expression in them, and he added some pressed-together lips to his frown.

"Cord, I would never want to go back twenty-four hours and pretend it didn't happen."

"By 'it' you mean…?"

Her cup clicked onto the saucer. "Of course I do. Do you imagine that a woman ever wants to forget something like that?"

"Not your barn on fire, huh?"

She shut her eyes. "Well, that, too. It was Tom, wasn't it?"

Cord hesitated. "Yeah, I think so."

"But why? Just for revenge?"

"Who knows? I wouldn't put anything past the man. Maybe he thought if he got rid of the barn he could sleep in the house. With you."

"Oh, Cord, I no longer know what to do about Tom, or you, or anything."

"Seems to me it's obvious, Eleanor. You have to rebuild your barn."

"Oh. But the thought of hiring men to work on it means—" she wrinkled her nose "—more Sundays with lemonade and cookies on the porch."

"You don't have to hire any men. I'll rebuild it. I don't drink much lemonade."

"But you'll be leaving! It's the end of the apple season and you're going to California."

He lifted her hand from around her coffee cup and folded his own around it. "I'm not leaving. I sure don't know what you're gonna do with a hired hand who's in love with you and a husband who's not, but one thing is certain, you do need a barn, and I can build one."

A small groan escaped her. "I feel caught smack-dab between a thundercloud and a lightning bolt."

"Eleanor, there's something else I want you to know. Working here on the farm as your hired man has given me a sense of purpose, a way to put my old life behind me and start believing that no matter what's happened in the past, life can be good."

"Lately I've felt so mixed-up and frightened I can't think straight. Do you really believe that, Cord? That life can be good?"

"I do believe that. You need my protection. You need me. That's sure as hell giving me something worth living for."

He released her hand and stood up. "Get dressed. You and Molly and I are going into town."

"What for?" she said suspiciously.

"We're gonna buy some lumber at the sawmill and some lemon drops for Molly at Ness's mercantile. And then I'm gonna stop in and have a talk with Sheriff Rivera."

Chapter Thirty-Four

Three days later Cord went into town alone. In all the months he'd been buying supplies at the mercantile, Cord had never seen Carl Ness look so interested in anything.

"I hear Miss Eleanor's barn burned down," the store owner said. "That why she wants a derringer?"

"Nope. She found a rattlesnake under the porch one day and 'bout screamed her head off 'til I killed it." He'd bet Eleanor had never screamed her head off about anything in her entire life, but where Carl Ness was concerned, a lie was better than the truth.

Carl nodded knowingly. "Women are like that. About the barn, Cord. You gotta be real careful with them kerosene lanterns, the barn bein' full of dry straw and everything. I bet Miss Eleanor's plenty het up 'bout you bein' so careless."

Cord coughed. "She's het up, all right. Things haven't been the same since that night." He tried to hide his smile.

"Ya know, her last hired man, ol' man Isaiah, quit on her sudden-like. I'd sure hate to see you go before she gets a new barn."

"Me, too," Cord said shortly. "Carl, add a box of cartridges and a bagful of lemon drops, too."

"Say, how's old Tom Malloy gettin' along on the farm? Heard the apple harvest was the best yet."

Cord let out a long breath. This week the mercantile storefront was painted an eye-blinking lime green; maybe that was why Carl was so talkative this morning. "Haven't seen much of Tom lately."

Carl grinned in an unfriendly way. "I reckon you've been too busy rebuildin' Miss Eleanor's barn."

"Yeah. Been plenty busy." Eleanor and Danny were helping him rebuild the barn. Tom had been conspicuously absent. But if Carl thought Eleanor's husband was spending his time out at the farm, it was obvious Tom wasn't spending much time in town. The sheriff said he hadn't seen Malloy, either. Made Cord wonder where he was. It also made him uneasy.

When Cord rode through the gate, Eleanor was in the yard, her hands on her hips and her "assessing expression" on her face.

"You deciding whether you want the barn square or round?"

"I'm deciding whether to add a special stall for the…" She lowered her voice to a whisper. "For the pony I'm getting Danny for his birthday next week."

"Pony, huh?" he said in an undertone. "I'd say yes. I'll make a separate stall for it."

"Wash Halliday is coming this evening. Maybe you could help me decide on the pony?"

He dismounted and walked toward her. "Brought some lemon drops for Molly. Where is she?"

"Under the porch with the kittens. As usual." Eleanor opened her mouth to call her, but Cord stepped forward and put a finger against her lips.

"Not yet. I…uh…brought you something from town, too. Not sure you're gonna like it."

"Oh? Why not? Does it bite or talk back or taste funny?"

He laughed, as she'd meant him to. "Doesn't taste funny unless you lick it." He rummaged in his saddlebag and brought out the smallest gun she'd ever seen and slipped it into her apron pocket.

"Cord! I'll shoot off one of my toes!"

"No, you won't."

"Why do I need this?"

"Because the revolver is too heavy for you."

"And?"

"I think you should be armed, in case of…uh…you know, snakes."

"And?"

He studied the tips of his leather boots. "Danny has the revolver."

A sinking sensation bloomed in the pit of her stomach. "He's too little for that revolver. I can scarcely lift it myself."

"Exactly. He'll have to think three times if he ever wants to aim it at anything."

"Oh, good heavens, my son is growing up right under my nose!"

"He's going to be ten years old, right?"

She nodded.

"Old enough to have a pony of his own?"

"Ye-es."

"Then he's old enough to carry the revolver in his saddlebag."

She looked at him askance. "Cord, what is it you are not telling me?" He looked everywhere but at her, so she knew he was keeping something from her. Finally he cleared his throat.

"Your son needs to have a way to protect himself."

"From what?"

"From…" Again he wouldn't meet her eyes. "From Tom."

"Tom! But Tom is his fath—" Suddenly she understood. She wouldn't have dreamed such a thing in a lifetime of Sundays, but Cord had a point. She hated it, but he did. In fact, her hired man had the *only* point: Tom could be violent.

Since her husband had returned after his unexplained

seven-year absence, he had been short-tempered and downright mean. And now Cord thought her son needed her revolver? And that she needed a weapon, as well? "For snakes," he said. She didn't believe that for a single minute.

It was Tom who set the barn on fire. That man was not the man she had married.

A funny prickle went up her spine. What was happening to her life? Along with that question another thudded into her consciousness. What was happening to *her*? Part of her felt happier than she had in years; but another part of her sensed a menacing gray cloud thickening around her. She couldn't bear to think too far ahead.

That night after supper, after she read Molly and Danny a story and they climbed the stairs to their bedroom, a pregnant silence fell in the kitchen. Ever since the night of the fire, when Cord had come to her bed, he had slept in the attic room as he had before. Tonight, however, he seemed restless, and he had the oddest look on his face.

She looked at him questioningly, and he reached across the table and took both her hands in his. Very quietly he said, "I'm leaving it up to you."

She knew what he meant by "it." He knew she wanted him. At night she ached to be with him, to be close to him. But she also knew he wouldn't be staying much longer.

She sucked in a shaky breath. She had to protect her heart. When Cord left she would have to go on living.

He stood, pulled her to her feet and kissed her, his lips gentle. "You go on up to bed, Eleanor. I'll wash up the supper dishes. I'll see you in the morning."

He waited, and when she nodded, he turned her toward the stairs and gave her a little push.

Chapter Thirty-Five

The next afternoon Eleanor stepped out the back door to take the clean clothes off the clothesline to find a familiar figure sitting under the cherry tree.

"Tom!"

"H'lo, Ellie." He made no attempt to get up, just took his cigarette from his mouth and looked up at her.

"Tom, where have you been?" She took a step toward him, then thought better of it and set the wicker laundry basket between them.

"Oh, I've been around, here and there. Didja miss me?"

She stared at him. "Of course I didn't miss you. You haven't been here since the night my barn burned down."

"I had business elsewhere."

"*Where* elsewhere?" she demanded.

He didn't answer, just pointed at Cord's shirts on the clothesline. "I see your hired man's still around."

"He most certainly is. He's rebuilding the barn."

"He is, is he? Mighty handy havin' him around, I'd say."

"Tom, did you know about the barn?"

"Yeah. Heard about it in town."

"Then why aren't you helping to rebuild it?"

"Been busy, like I said."

Eleanor eyed him with suspicion. "Someone set that fire on purpose. Did you know that?"

He continued to puff on his cigarette, but his shrug told her that he knew, all right. She began unpinning dry clothes from the line. "Actually, I'm surprised to see you at all, considering that I believe you set that fire."

The sound of hammering carried on the still air, and Tom cocked his head. "New barn's almost finished, I guess."

"Yes, almost. Danny has been helping. He's learning a lot about carpentry."

"Is he, now? Maybe the lad's got smarts, like his father."

Eleanor gritted her teeth. "You should have been teaching him these things, Tom."

"Why should I? It's plain the kid doesn't like me."

She refused to argue with him. He knew very well the farm now belonged to her. And he wasn't getting it back.

"Tom, what are you doing here? What do you want?"

"Well, to start off with, Ellie, I want my wife."

She propped her hands at her waist. "Since you rode in the gate all those weeks ago you have done nothing to earn my regard or my trust. You don't deserve me, Tom. I am no longer your wife."

He rose unsteadily to his feet. "You can't just chuck me out, Ellie. After all, those two kids are *mine*."

Her stomach turned over, but she managed to keep her voice calm. "It takes more than biology to make a father."

He lurched toward her. "Mebbe I want more than bein' a father. I want to sleep in your bed, Ellie. *Our* bed."

She cringed inside. She was afraid to order him off the property, afraid of what he might do if she angered him. Would it be smarter to keep him here, where she could keep an eye on him?

He sent her a sour look, then tipped his head back and puffed a smoke ring into the air.

For a long moment, Eleanor studied the man who lounged before her, every nerve in her body humming with anxiety.

"I want to make something clear, Tom," she said slowly. "You are not welcome in my bed."

Hurriedly she snatched the rest of the washing off the line and stuffed it in the wicker laundry basket. She didn't wait to unhook the rope and wind it back into its metal housing; she just started toward the back door.

Tom stepped into her path. She thrust the laundry basket at him. "Take this around to the front porch and leave it next to the swing." She gave him no chance to refuse, and she had done it on purpose. She wanted Cord to know that Tom was back so he could keep an eye on him.

Without looking back, she went into the house and set the teakettle on the stove. When the water boiled, she brewed a cup of tea, took it into the parlor and sank onto the settee. Through the open front door she now heard the staccato sound of *three* hammers, and she had to smile. Somehow Cord had intimidated the cause of the fire into rebuilding her barn.

Supper that night was unusually quiet. When Cord entered the kitchen he gave her a long, searching look, filled his plate with fried chicken and potato salad and took it out to the front porch. Danny and Molly did not utter a single peep, and they didn't look up even when she dished up the apple crisp.

Tom shoveled in his food hunched over his plate as usual. When Molly accidentally spilled her milk, Tom yelled at her, but he shut right up when Eleanor glared at him. She could not recall a more glum gathering around her kitchen table. It made her want to cry. Or scream. Or both. Her jaw ached from clenching her teeth.

Finally the children bolted out the door to the front porch, and the next minute she heard Cord's low voice and Molly's happy giggle. She guessed they were playing with the kittens, and oh, how she longed to join them!

Tom's voice at her back startled her. "Barn's not finished yet, so I assume I'm sleepin' in the house."

"No," Eleanor said deliberately. "You can sleep outside in the orchard or in town." She began gathering up the supper plates.

He lumbered to his feet. "Hell if I will," he grumbled. He slammed out the back door and Eleanor began washing up the dishes. She dried them and stacked them in the china cabinet and then walked out to the front porch swing.

She was drained, worn-out to the point of numbness. Her brain felt as if it was made of limp string and thick porridge.

Cord motioned for her to sit down, but despite her fatigue she felt too tense to settle in one spot for more than sixty seconds.

"Eleanor, for God's sake, stop pacing and sit down."

"Where is Tom?" she asked.

"Haven't seen him." He hadn't seen him ride out, either, but he figured she didn't need to know that.

She sent the children inside and sank onto the swing beside him, but she didn't say a word. Maybe she didn't have to. It was plain this business with Tom was turning into a bargain no one who wasn't God could win. Something had to stretch or break.

"Eleanor."

"I know," she said, her voice quiet. "When the barn is finished you're going to leave."

"Do you want me to go?"

"No, I don't. You know I don't."

He wanted to pull her into his arms so bad they trembled. "You know I don't want to leave you. Or Molly and Danny. But I can't stay, not with Tom here. Sooner or later I'll end up killing him, and that'd send me straight back to prison for murder."

"I know," she murmured. "I can't see any way to make it work, the three of us in the same square mile of space. But…"

"Yeah," he said softly.

"Oh, Cord, my heart is breaking into little tiny pieces with sharp edges, and every time I take a breath I feel them slicing into me."

"Eleanor, barn or no barn, I won't leave until it's clear that Tom has either pulled himself together or he's left for good. Either way I've got to be sure you and the kids are gonna be safe."

She was quiet for a long time. He couldn't look at her. He knew if he did he'd kiss her, and maybe he wouldn't be able to stop until it was too late. "This is worse than being in a cell behind a forty-foot brick wall."

Tears glistened under her eyelashes.

"You know, my pa said something to me once, the only thing he ever said that made any sense. He sat me down on a hay bale one night and said, 'Don't fall in love, son. It'll ruin your life.'"

"He was right, wasn't he, Cord?"

"No. Hell no. One corner of my life is a bit tattered, but I'm not giving up without a fight."

"You could be happy in California," she said.

"Maybe. Maybe not. It'd take some work, though."

"Don't tell me about it," she said quickly.

Molly tumbled through the screen door, a kitten stuffed into her ruffled pinafore pocket. "You gonna read us another story tonight, Mama?"

Eleanor stared at her daughter and gave a tiny groan.

Cord bent toward the girl. "I'll read your story tonight, Molly. You go find Danny and tell him to get ready for bed."

Molly scampered off to the unfinished barn and in a moment she emerged with Danny at her heels. "Tell us a story, will ya, Cord? 'Bout when you was a boy, like me?"

"I thought I was gonna *read* you a story."

"No!" both children chorused. "Make one up, about you!"

He looked down at the two eager faces, their eyes pleading, and felt his resolve crumble. "All right, here goes. Once upon a time, way down south in Virginia, when I was a boy about your age, Danny, I got a fancy idea in my head about the beehive behind my daddy's barn."

Molly glommed onto his arm. "What kind of idea?"

"I'll tell you what kind in the next chapter, upstairs in your bedroom, okay? When you're under the covers with your faces washed and your pajamas on."

"I don't wear 'jamas," Molly said with a tug on his shirt-sleeve. "I wear a nightie, like Mama. A pink one."

"Well," Cord said, "girls in pink nighties get to hear the story. And boys…" He gave Danny a raised eyebrow. "Maybe boys, too, but they have to have their night duds on."

Both children raced through the front door and up the stairs. Cord watched them, but he didn't move until Eleanor touched his arm. "I want to hear another story, Cord. About what you said to Tom when he came back this afternoon."

"Not much of a story, really. I let him know that I knew the fire was set on purpose and that I'd found the burned-out matches to prove it. He didn't say much after that."

"Cord, do you…do you think Tom could ever turn over a new leaf?"

"I wouldn't count on it, Eleanor. People don't change overnight. It took some time for him to become what he is now, destructive and violent. And," he said, lowering his voice even more, "not being a father to Molly and Danny. I think it will take him a long time to be any different."

When she said nothing he shot a glance at her face and went on. "A lot's gonna depend on what you want. A partner? A husband? Or a boarder."

She wrapped her arms across her midriff. "Right now what I want is none of those. I want my hired man."

He couldn't resist a probing question. "Anything else?"

"Don't tease me, Cord. What else could I possibly want?"

Suddenly a man's voice boomed out of the dark. "Ellie, I wanna talk to you." Tom stomped out of the unfinished barn and started for the porch. "You, too, hired man."

"Eleanor," Cord said under his breath, "go in the house and lock the door."

Without a second's hesitation she stood up and moved through the screen door. A moment later Cord heard the click of the dead bolt, and then Tom tramped up the porch steps.

"Where's Ellie?"

"She's tired. She went up to bed."

Tom glared at the front door. "How come I'm sleepin' in the orchard and the hired man's sleepin' in the house? *My* house?"

"I don't think it *is* your house, Tom."

"Well…I'm still sleepin' outside. How come I can't sleep in the house?"

"I believe Eleanor has made that clear. She doesn't want you inside the house at night."

"Hell and damn, that's not fair! I used to *live* here."

"But you don't live here now," Cord said carefully. "This is Eleanor's house. She can decide anything she wants."

Tom stomped off the porch, then spun around and came back up the steps, propped his hands on his hips and leaned close to Cord. "I bet she's not so unfriendly with her hired man. Maybe *you're* sleepin' in her room, huh?"

"Nope," Cord said calmly. "I sleep in the attic."

"Nah. I don't believe that for one minute."

Cord sat very still, then looked straight into the man's bleary eyes. "You calling me a liar, Tom?"

"Uh, well, not 'xactly. Just wonderin'…"

"Let's call a spade a spade," Cord said evenly. "You're not welcome in Eleanor's house because you don't treat Molly or Daniel like a father should. Eleanor is protecting the children, and herself."

"Protecting herself from *me*? She's my wife! You got that, hired man? *My* wife. I'm her damn husband!"

"Not anymore," Cord said.

"Well," Tom blustered, "I'm the children's father."

"You sure don't act like it. No father treats his kids the way you treat Molly and Daniel."

"Yeah, well." Tom's beefy shoulders drooped. "Mebbe I don't know much about bein' a father, seein' as how the boy was no more'n a baby when I left and the girl…hell, I never even seen the girl before."

"You're gonna have to earn the right to return to this family, Tom. If I were you, I'd hurry it up."

"Well, if that don't beat all," Tom muttered. "Shoulda stayed in Mexico, where they know how to treat a man right."

Cord send him a quick look. "That where you've been all these years since the War?"

"Some." Tom's eyes darted from the porch railing to the barn door and back to the porch. "You…uh…interested in finding gold in California?"

How the devil would Tom know about that? "Maybe."

"Take my advice, go on down to Mexico and find yourself a mine."

"Yeah? And then what?"

Tom snorted. "If you're any kind of a man, you'll figure out how to end up owning it, one way or another. Get yourself a woman, too."

Cord kept his jaw clamped shut. He could guess how Tom Malloy had figured his life out. And in that instant he knew he couldn't leave Eleanor and the children if Tom Malloy was anywhere within five hundred miles of Smoke River.

He stood up. "Guess I'll turn in. Big day tomorrow finishing the barn roof." He waited for Tom to say something, but the stocky man dug his cigarette makings out of his shirt pocket and turned away.

Chapter Thirty-Six

The breaking point came as unexpectedly as a summer thunderstorm, and the consequences were life-changing. The barn was finished, with two additional horse stalls, a bigger tack room, and a new roof made of split cedar shakes. Tom kept disappearing for days at a time with no explanation.

Eleanor grew more disgusted with each passing day. When he turned up at the supper table and gobbled down the fried chicken or the biscuits, she said little. But she watched him. And she listened closely when he spoke to the children. Tom was more angry and short-tempered than ever.

He found fault with everything—Danny's school homework, Molly's fondness for dressing the kittens in her doll clothes, and everything associated with Cord. He made ugly remarks about Cord's shiny bay mare, Sally; the oats Cord purchased for feed; his carefully oiled saddle; even his choice of work shirts and his worn leather vest. "Never saw a man look so raggedy or eat so much free supper in one sitting," Tom growled. "Tells of a mighty poor background."

Not even Eleanor escaped Tom's complaints. "You got all this money from sellin' your apples this season, whyn't you get up a prettier dress than that one you wear day after day? It's all patched and faded. Makes you look old and worn-out, too."

Tight-lipped, she ignored him as much as she could, and then one day she decided she'd had enough. It came at suppertime, after a long, hot day she'd spent laboring over the washboard in the backyard.

"Not beans again!" Tom grumbled. "Can't you come up with anything more appetizing? I'm sick of your corn bread, too!"

Eleanor slapped down the ladle and spun from the stove. "Tom Malloy, if you make one more complaint about anything, anything at all, you will eat elsewhere!"

Molly and Danny glanced at each other, their eyes wide, and both sent Cord apprehensive looks. Cord rolled his eyes to make light of it, but right then and there he resolved that the very next time Tom Malloy opened his mouth to complain he would lay him out flat on the kitchen floor.

Eleanor turned back to the kettle of simmering beans, and Cord knew by the stiffness in her shoulders that she was biting her tongue. Tom lapsed into sullen silence. To Cord's surprise, before he'd even lifted his fork, Danny asked to be excused. Molly did the same.

Something was different tonight. It wasn't just tension he sensed; it was a simmering cauldron of fury about to boil over. He wanted to escape to the front porch with the kids, but he didn't want to leave Eleanor alone in the kitchen with Tom.

Malloy grumbled under his breath while shoveling in beans and stuffing squares of corn bread into his mouth. Eleanor refused to sit down at the table but ate standing up at the sink. Cord sure couldn't blame her.

Finally Tom banged out the front door, still grousing about his supper, and Cord heard his raucous voice yelling at one of the children. Cord's restraint snapped. Deliberately he set his coffee cup back onto the table and stood up.

"That's it. We've all had enough."

Eleanor fled out the back door. Cord quickly gathered up the plates and set them in the pan of hot soapy water in the sink, then strolled as casually as he could to the front door. Some instinct made him check the ammunition in the Colt he now carried with him.

What he saw outside in the half-light of dusk made his blood run cold.

Tom lurched around the corner of the house, dragging Eleanor toward the barn, one meaty hand clamped around her upper arm. Her face looked white and frightened, but her eyes were furious.

Danny jumped off the porch and raced toward her, but when he got within a couple of feet, Tom backhanded him and the boy sprawled into the dirt.

"Malloy!" Cord yelled. "Let her go!"

"Fat chance, hired man. She's *my* wife, not yours!"

Out of the corner of his eye Cord saw Danny get to his feet and start toward him. "Dan," he said, his voice quiet. "Ride for the sheriff."

Danny edged around behind Tom and slipped into the barn. In the next minute Cord's bay mare bolted through the open barn door, sailed over the gate and clattered off down the road. Molly had scrambled under the porch, and Cord prayed she would stay put.

He pulled the revolver from his belt and thumbed the hammer back. "Let her go, Malloy!"

A bullet puffed dust at his feet. "Make me!"

He couldn't fire back; Tom was using Eleanor as a shield. He started forward anyway, and another shot plowed into the ground in front of him. Still, he kept moving forward. If he could get close enough, he could miss Eleanor and hit Malloy. He slipped his finger over the trigger.

At that instant Tom fired again, and a white-hot pain burned into Cord's shoulder. His right arm went slack, and the Colt dangled uselessly from his hand. Eleanor cried out and then suddenly went silent.

Tom's next shot spun Cord's revolver out of his hand and into the dirt. Cord could shoot left-handed, but first he had to pick up his gun. Minutes passed. He didn't know how many, but what he did know was that his shoulder felt like a red-hot coal was grinding into it.

Tom edged toward the barn, moving backward and hauling Eleanor with him. Then he stopped and adjusted his revolver arm.

When he adjusted it again, Cord realized the man was having trouble seeing him in the dark. Good. There was no moon tonight. Tom was just a bulky figure in the shadows; he and Eleanor's white shirtwaist were the only things moving.

He had to get to his revolver, but he knew if he made any sudden move, Tom would put another bullet in him. He couldn't risk losing the use of his other arm; he had to figure out a way to disable Tom without hitting Eleanor, and for that he needed a left hand that worked.

He waited, not moving a muscle. He could hear Eleanor's uneven breathing and Tom's raspy muttering.

Just keep talking, Malloy. Keep on wondering what I'm gonna do, why I'm just standing here like I'm waiting for something.

He had to play for time. He figured Tom had three shots left.

How much time had elapsed, ten minutes? Twenty? How much time did he need? If he could stretch it out, maybe he could get Tom to empty his gun without realizing all his bullets were used up.

He lurched forward and made an obvious, clumsy attempt to kick his Colt closer to his left side.

"Oh, no, you don't, boyo!" Tom powdered the dirt at his feet with another shot aimed to keep him from lunging for his gun. Cord made a show of jumping back, then crouched to circle around the weapon. His shoulder was on fire and he could feel his shirt getting sticky with blood. He bent lower.

And then he got an idea. He groaned and staggered, then clapped his left hand against his bleeding shoulder. *How much time has passed?*

He swayed toward Tom, then began stumbling toward him. He could hear Eleanor sobbing and pleading with the man. Cord took another shaky step closer to his Colt, but on purpose he staggered past it. He figured he could drop and roll and come up with the revolver in his left hand. But he still wouldn't be able to get a clear shot because Eleanor was still in the way.

Unless he could get her to pull free.

He kept moving unsteadily forward. If he could maneuver Tom just a step or two toward him, he could fake a retreat, and that might give him a chance.

How much time has passed?

Cord sucked in a pain-laced breath. "Malloy?"

"Yeah?"

"You a gambling man?"

"Well, sure, but now don't seem like the time."

"Wrong." Cord sidestepped drunkenly. "Now's the perfect time."

"How do you figure that, hired man?"

Cord took another purposely unsteady step. "Just give me a minute, Tom. Gettin' kinda dizzy."

"Take yer time, hired man. I got all night. Well…part of the night."

Don't listen. Don't react. Just keep moving, keep him off balance. Play for time.

He pretended to stumble. "Lemme think a minute, Tom. Had an idea, but…" He lurched to the left, closer to his revolver. "But…hell, I can't remember it now."

"What's your proposition, hired man?"

Cord noted that Eleanor had stopped crying. And talking.

"Okay, Tom, here goes." He clamped his jaw against the pain now streaking through his shoulder and down his arm. "How'd you like to…" He let his voice mumble off into silence.

"Huh? Can't hear you?"

How much time? Lord God, how much time has passed?

"Sorry, Tom. Brain's gettin' a little fuzzy." Another step to the left, and this time when he lurched he made sure to list heavily toward the ground.

"Hurry it up, hired man!"

"Y-yeah," he muttered. "Jus' a minute…"

Tom started to speak and Cord dropped to the ground, rolled to grab his Colt and came up firing. He aimed at Tom's feet, hoping he'd let go of Eleanor, but before he could squeeze the trigger again, Tom danced away, turned sideways and dragged Eleanor with him.

It was now or never. Cord raised his Colt to fire, taking careful aim at the man's belly, but before he could pull the trigger he heard a sharp crack and Tom pitched forward and lay still.

On the other side of the gate, Danny sat on the bay mare, the heavy revolver clutched in both hands.

Chapter Thirty-Seven

Eleanor stumbled to Cord's side. "Are you all right? The way you were acting I thought you were bleeding to death!"

Before he could answer, Danny scrambled off his mount and threw himself at Cord. "I shot him! I shot him, Cord, and I'm not sorry!"

Cord wrapped his good arm around the shaking boy's shoulders and pulled him and Eleanor hard against him. "You did just fine, son. Saved your ma's life. Saved mine, too."

Sheriff Rivera stepped his big roan gelding through the gate, dismounted and bent to roll Tom's body over.

"Good shooting, Dan," the sheriff said. "Guess you saved me having to make an arrest."

Rivera slapped his worn Stetson against one knee. "Guess you might as well know, Miz Malloy. Your husband was wanted for murder down in Mexico. They've been hunting him for months, but just yesterday a poster came across my desk that told us who he was. It wasn't hard to figure out where he'd be."

Eleanor sagged against Cord. "M-murder? Did you say murder?"

"I did, ma'am. Sorry to have to tell you this, but your

husband shot a woman and her young son in a dispute over a mine."

"A mine?"

"A gold mine, yes, ma'am. The dead woman owned it."

Eleanor stared at the sheriff in horror. "Oh, my Lord. My Lord, my Lord!"

"Lucky your boy can shoot, Miz Malloy. Could have been… Well, it's just lucky."

Cord extended his left hand to the sheriff. "Thanks, Hawk."

"You should thank Daniel here. Never saw a kid ride so fast!"

Cord drew in a rough breath. "Eleanor, let's go inside. Maybe you could look at my shoulder."

Eating left-handed provided an endless source of amusement for Molly and Danny. Scrambled eggs dribbled off his fork; his coffee sloshed over the edge of his cup; and he couldn't butter his toast without Molly's help.

But there were advantages. Eleanor fussed and fluttered and kept dropping kisses on top of his head. Danny volunteered to do Cord's share of the dishes. And Molly graciously agreed that he wouldn't have to help her dress the kittens in any doll clothes. Ever.

But the best part was something Cord hadn't expected. After breakfast one morning, he and Eleanor walked out to the front porch to rock on the swing. They didn't say much. Mostly he managed to kiss her using just his left arm, and she managed to kiss him back without jarring his injured shoulder.

The surprise came when Danny and Molly bounded through the screen door.

"Cord?" Molly asked very softly.

"Yeah, honey? What is it?"

She whispered in his ear.

He stared at the girl. "You sure about this, Molly?"

She nodded so hard her blond curls bounced. Over Molly's head Eleanor sent Cord a puzzled look.

"What about you, Dan? You have an opinion?"

"Yes, sir."

"Well? What is it?"

Cord caught Eleanor's suspicious frown. He knew how she hated to be left out of things, but he figured just this once it would be worth it.

Danny caught his lower lip in his teeth. "We, um…we don't want you to go to California. We want you to stay here."

Cord's throat began to feel tight. "What about your mama?"

Danny cleared his throat. "Well, sir, we think whatever she wants won't matter all that much."

Eleanor gave a whoop and clapped her hand over her mouth.

"Okay," Cord said, working to keep a straight face, "what is it that you want that your mama doesn't?"

"We want you to stay and…and…"

Molly poked her finger in her brother's rib cage.

"And be our pa," Danny blurted out.

Cord swallowed hard and exchanged a long look with Eleanor. "Don't you think your mama might have something to say about this?"

"Nah. She won't care."

Cord coughed to hide his chuckle. "What about where your new pa would be sleeping?"

The children exchanged puzzled glances. "Gosh, Cord, can'tcha go on sleeping in the attic?"

"Or maybe you could sleep under the porch with my kitties?" Molly suggested. "You wouldn't have to dress them up or anything."

Cord snaked out his good arm and pulled them both close. "I don't think so," he said seriously.

"Why not?" both children wailed. "Mama likes you, honest she does!"

Convulsed with laughter, Eleanor nodded. Cord cleared his throat again. "You think she likes me enough to…uh… come and sleep with me in my bed?"

Danny sent him an unreadable look. The boy frowned, pursed his lips and finally shook his head. "I think you're gonna have to ask her first."

"Will you be real nice to her?" Molly asked shyly.

"Yes, I will. Real, *real* nice."

"You promise?"

"I promise."

"Then," Molly said in a decisive tone, "you should ask her."

"Go on, Cord!" Danny urged. "Ask her!"

Cord reached to clasp Eleanor's free hand. "What about it, Eleanor? If I agree to be Danny and Molly's pa, do you think I could sleep in your bed?"

She released his hand and leaned over to kiss him. "Yes, absolutely."

"Do you think maybe we should get married before I come to sleep in your bed?"

"Absolutely not."

But they did.

Epilogue

Eleanor looked down the long aisle of the Smoke River Community Church and drew a shaky breath. She had never been so frightened in her whole life.

Imagine being frightened on my wedding day.

She hadn't been frightened when she'd married Tom Malloy all those years ago, and she'd known Tom for years. She'd known Cord barely six months. She closed her eyes.

The organ music swelled into the "Wedding March."

Oh, but I'm not ready!

It was too soon. It was too…permanent, too forever-feeling.

She smoothed one hand over the pale blue dimity dress Verena Forester had created, with a floaty six-gored skirt and lace ruffles at her neck and wrists and so many buttons she couldn't count them all. Tiny ones. Molly wore a dress just like hers only smaller, and Verena had even made a blue wedding dress for Molly's favorite doll. Eleanor fervently hoped it would not end up on one of the kittens.

She risked a glance down the aisle to the altar where Cord waited, his dark hair neatly combed for once, his eyes so blue that even from here they looked like shards of sapphire.

Is he as nervous as I am?

Molly and Daniel stood hand in hand beside Cord, trying

hard to look properly serious but grinning anyway. Cord
was not grinning. He wasn't even smiling, but even from
there his eyes told her things that made her cheeks feel hot
one minute and her hands turn to ice the next.

Heavens, getting married was so difficult! Life was so
unexpected, and it lasted such a long time. What if…what
if… Oh, there were so many what-ifs.

The little church was jammed with well-wishers. Sarah
and Rooney Cloudman and their grandson, Mark, Sheriff Rivera. Even Carl Ness and his wife and twin daughters, Edith and Noralee. Eleanor wondered what color the
mercantile was painted today and suppressed a giggle. It
wouldn't matter; it would be a different color next week.

Reverend Pollock stood before the wooden altar, an open
Bible in his hands. The organ music boomed.

She shifted the bouquet of yellow roses and honeysuckle
into her other hand and wished she could stop trembling.
Rose petals were fluttering onto the polished wooden floor
like little yellow butterflies.

Her palms were damp. Her stomach was doing somer-
saults. Why, *why* was marrying Cord so frightening?

*Because it matters. It matters more than anything,
other than Molly and Danny, because I love him. And that
means… Oh, God, that means I can be hurt. What if he
dies? What if he decides to leave me and go to California
after all? What if he…?*

Suddenly she heard her name. "Eleanor!" Cord's voice.
And then Molly's.

"Hurry up, Mama!"

"Eleanor!" His voice was closer now, and all at once there
he was in front of her. He scooped her up into his arms,
strode down the aisle and set her on her feet at the altar.

He bent toward her. "Let's get married, okay?" he
breathed. "I'm tired of sleeping in the attic."

It was the first time the church congregation had witnessed a wedding ceremony where the bride both wept and laughed all through her marriage vows.

* * * * *

If you enjoyed this story, you won't want
to miss these other great Western stories
from Lynna Banning

BABY ON THE OREGON TRAIL
HER SHERIFF BODYGUARD
PRINTER IN PETTICOATS

YES! Please send me **The Hometown Hearts Collection** in Larger Print. This collection begins with 3 FREE books and 2 FREE gifts in the first shipment. Along with my 3 free books, I'll also get the next 4 books from the Hometown Hearts Collection, in LARGER PRINT, which I may either return and owe nothing, or keep for the low price of $4.99 U.S./ $5.89 CDN each plus $2.99 for shipping and handling per shipment*. If I decide to continue, about once a month for 8 months I'll get 6 or 7 more books, but will only need to pay for 4. That means 2 or 3 books in every shipment will be FREE! If I decide to keep the entire collection, I'll have paid for only 32 books because 19 books are FREE! I understand that accepting the 3 free books and gifts places me under no obligation to buy anything. I can always return a shipment and cancel at any time. My free books and gifts are mine to keep no matter what I decide.

262 HCN 3432 462 HCN 3432

Name	(PLEASE PRINT)

	Apt. #
Address	

City	State/Prov.	Zip/Postal Code

Signature (if under 18, a parent or guardian must sign)

Mail to the **Reader Service:**

IN U.S.A.: P.O. Box 1867, Buffalo, NY. 14240-1867
IN CANADA: P.O. Box 609, Fort Erie, Ontario L2A 5X3

* Terms and prices subject to change without notice. Prices do not include applicable taxes. Sales tax applicable in NY. Canadian residents will be charged applicable taxes. This offer is limited to one order per household. All orders subject to approval. Credit or debit balances in a customer's account(s) may be offset by any other outstanding balance owed by or to the customer. Please allow 4 to 6 weeks for delivery. Offer available while quantities last. Offer not available to Quebec residents.

Your Privacy—The Reader Service is committed to protecting your privacy. Our Privacy Policy is available online at www.ReaderService.com or upon request from the Reader Service.

We make a portion of our mailing list available to reputable third parties that offer products we believe may interest you. If you prefer that we not exchange your name with third parties, or if you wish to clarify or modify your communication preferences, please visit us at www.ReaderService.com/consumerchoice or write to us at Reader Service Preference Service, P.O. Box 9062, Buffalo, NY. 14240-9062. Include your complete name and address.

Get 2 Free Books,
Plus 2 Free Gifts—
just for trying the Reader Service!

HARLEQUIN® Western Romance